MW00939012

# FIRST ENCOUNTER (ASCENSION WARS BOOK 1)

*(2nd Edition)*

by Jasper T. Scott

JasperTscott.com
@JasperTscott

Cover Art by Tom Edwards
TomEdwardsDesign.com

## AUTHOR'S CONTENT
## RATING: PG-13

**Swearing:** Occasional
**Sex:** Mild references
**Violence:** Moderate

**Author's Guarantee:** If you find anything you consider inappropriate for this rating, please e-mail me at JasperTscott@gmail.com and I will either remove the content or change the rating accordingly.

# ACKNOWLEDGMENTS

This book comes to you in its polished state in large part thanks to the hard work of my editing team. A big thanks goes to my editor Aaron Sikes, my proofreader Ian Jedlica, and to each and every one of my advance readers, in particular: B. Allen Thobois, Bob Sirrine, Dara McLain, Dave Topan, Davis Shellabarger, Francis Hinnegan, Gary Matthews, Gaylon Overton, George Goedecke, George P. Dixon, Gordon Sears, Harry Huyler, Howard Cohen, Ian Seccombe, Jackie Gartside, Jim Meinen, Jim Kolter, John Nash, John Parker, Lara Gray, Mary Kastle, Mary Whitehead, Michael Madsen, Paul Burch, Raymond Burt, Rene Young, Richard T. Conkey, Terry Grindstaff, Wade Whitaker, William Lowe, William Dellaway, and William Schmidt. You guys are amazing! You make it so much easier to do what I do.

And as ever, many thanks to the Muse.

To those who dare,
And to those who dream.
To everyone who's stronger than they seem.
—Jasper Scott

*"Believe in me / I know you've waited
for so long / Believe in me / Sometimes
the weak become the strong."*
—STAIND, Believe

# PROLOGUE

**2150 AD**
**—One Week Before Arrival—**

Captain Clayton Cross stood in front of the viewscreens on the bridge of the *UNES Forerunner One*. Three hundred and sixty degrees of uninterrupted visibility. The majority of the ship's control stations and officers were arrayed around the 'front' half of that circle, sitting right behind where he stood.

"Beautiful, isn't it, sir?" Commander Taylor said.

"Quite," Clayton replied, glancing at her. She stood straight as a board beside him with hands clasped behind her back. Commander Taylor was short and trim, dark-skinned, but with light honey-brown eyes. She was his second-in-command and the executive officer of the ship.

Dropping his voice to a hushed whisper, he added, "Any sign of those blips we were tracking?"

Taylor shook her head. Starlight from the viewscreens glanced off her black hair, tucked into a tight bun behind her head. "No, sir."

"I see," he replied, looking back to the fore.

"Maybe they were comets. Or asteroids," Taylor added.

"Then why did they disappear when we got close?"

"I don't know, sir."

He nodded into the gleaming darkness of space. "That's a calculated move, Commander. A conscious decision to hide."

"But how? And if they could do that, why not hide all along?"

"Maybe they had to maneuver first," Clayton suggested.

"Then we're calling this first contact?" Taylor breathed. "Should we inform the Ambassador?"

Clayton regarded her steadily. The United Nations of Earth had been clear when they'd founded the Space Force: space exploration was not a military enterprise, nor should it become one. As such, Ambassador Morgan was the civilian leader in charge of the overall mission.

Clayton looked away from his XO. "Not yet, Commander. He'll just run around like a chicken with no head, spraying doom and gloom everywhere."

"Colorful, sir," Taylor replied, her lips curling under a wrinkled nose.

"We need more info before we tell anyone about this. Keep scanning and let me know what you find."

"Aye, sir."

# TRAPPIST-1

# CHAPTER 1

**—Two Days Before Arrival—**

Clayton sat behind the brushed aluminum desk in his quarters aboard *Forerunner One,* staring at the watch in his hands. It was an older model smart watch. The wallpaper image behind the ticking black hands on the crisp display was Samara's smiling face. Her blue eyes were an even richer and deeper hue than the sky in the background, her blond hair aglow with sunlight.

That was back when they were the young, newly-wedded power couple that everyone else secretly wanted to be: high on life and destined to conquer the world together.

That is, until a car on autopilot cruised through a red light at sixty miles per hour. The car's cameras had been malfunctioning. It hit Samara and three others, killing her and an elderly man instantly. The other two victims had survived, but barely.

Samara had been a practicing resident at the Ronald Reagan Medical Center. She'd had her whole career and life ahead of her. And maybe she still did. It was too soon to say.

He studied the watch again, running his fingertips over the gold-plated bezel around Samara's face. Before she'd died, he and Samara had their neural pathways mapped. He'd made several copies since, one of which was sitting in his hands, saved to the quantum crystal matrix of the watch. He'd bought it for himself and saved Samara's neural map to it before he'd left Earth. Just in case something happened to civilization while he was gone. With Samara's life at stake, he couldn't be too careful.

When Samara had told him about the experimental program at her hospital, he'd thought she was joking. But then he'd seen the results for himself: a browsable, searchable network of all the memories and structures that made a person who they were. Some couples might have balked at that kind of openness, but he and Samara had never kept any secrets from each other. Not big ones, anyway. A week later, they both joined the program and had their neural networks mapped in the name of science. He'd never imagined that they might actually need to use them. But now Samara's mind map was the only hope he had for them to be together again.

Clayton turned the watch over and read the inscription underneath.

*I'm waiting for you.*

It was a reminder to himself. A promise he'd made to Sam, even though she'd already passed on by the time he'd made it. In theory, he had a snapshot of everything that had made Samara who she was. Now he just had to wait for the technology to be developed that could breathe life into that digital effigy.

*One day.*

That was the reason he'd transferred from mission planning to an active duty role on *Forerunner One*. Moving at relativistic speed on their way to Trappist-1 was like hopping in a time machine. At half the speed of light, time was moving 15% slower for him on board *Forerunner One* than it was for everyone else back on Earth. But add to that the fact that he'd spent the past seventy-eight years in cryo, waiting to arrive, and it gave him the best possible chance of living to see the technology that would someday bring Samara back. Seventy-eight years plus 15%. That meant almost ninety years had already passed on Earth. And over one hundred and seventy-nine years would pass before he could possibly return. After all that time, someone had to have found a way to bring Samara back.

They had to.

Clayton pushed those thoughts away and spun his chair around to the viewport behind him, distracting himself with the view. It wasn't a real window. Since there were so many internal rooms, and since radiation shielding wasn't cheap, most of the viewports were actually digital displays tied to real-time holofeeds from the *Forerunner's* external cameras. But that had the added advantage of making the windows all configurable, and they doubled as control interfaces for the ship's systems.

This viewport was already set to show their destination. Dead center of the display was the pale red dot of Trappist-1. Other stars littered the void around it. All of them were blue-shifted by the sheer velocity of *Forerunner One's* approach. The stars didn't look any bluer to him, but his civilian first contact specialist, Dr. Reed, had explained to him that stars emit light across the entire spectrum, so the doppler effect simply shifted visible light into the ultraviolet and x-ray range, and infrared light into the visible spectrum. Go fast enough and you'd actually be able to *see* radar and microwaves with the naked eye. But now that they'd flipped around and were decelerating in advance of their arrival, all of that starlight was gradually shifting back to its usual wavelengths.

Clayton spent a moment mentally tracing imaginary constellations around Trappist-1 using his augmented reality contacts (ARCs). Glowing green lines appeared, guided by his thoughts and his Neuralink implant. He drew a diamond. A lop-sided star. Then an elephant, and then—

He stopped. In the process of removing lines and painting new ones, he'd accidentally drawn a skull.

He waved his hand to wipe the image off the

screen and spun his chair away from the viewport. Strapping his watch back on, he swiped over to the mission timer.

*2d 3h 5m*

In just over two days *Forerunner One* would arrive and make history. By now Forerunners Two and Three had already reached their destinations. They'd been bound for Gliese 667 and Wolf 1061 respectively, both of which were a lot closer than Trappist-1.

A musical chime drew Clayton's eyes up to the door. Connecting to the ship's intercom system, he answered and simultaneously saw an image of the person standing outside: a familiar woman—his first contact specialist—tall and trim with her brown hair tucked into a bun.

"Doctor Reed. Did you need something?" he asked.

She looked up at the camera mounted above his door, her brown eyes wide and bright with excitement. Her head bobbed quickly. "We just had a breakthrough with the Visualizers. We— Dr. Grouse and I—thought you might like to see it for yourself, sir."

A smile tugged at the corners of Clayton's mouth. "You mean you finally got them working?"

"They were always working, sir."

"For us," Clayton corrected.

Reed dismissed that caveat with a shrug and a burgeoning grin. "Well, now they're working for

Charlie, too."

Clayton felt his brow furrowing with genuine surprise. "You got one of them to read a dog's mind?"

"Not just his mind. His *dreams*."

That knocked Clayton back in his chair. He sat blinking in shock, staring at Dr. Reed's grinning face. She was slowly nodding, observing his reaction on her end via the camera mounted on the ceiling inside his quarters.

"So what do dogs dream about?" Clayton asked.

"Uh-uh. No spoilers. You'll have to come down to the lab and see for yourself."

Clayton smiled crookedly and jumped out of his chair. It flew back on a sliding rail, hitting rubber stoppers just before it could reach the viewport. "I'll be right there."

# CHAPTER 2

Clayton left his quarters at a brisk pace, forcing Dr. Reed to run to keep up. After just a few seconds they were both breathing hard. The ship was currently experiencing one point four *G*s as it decelerated, making even light exercise a chore.

Doors to the other crew quarters flashed by on either side. They reached a bank of four elevators at the end of the corridor and stopped. Clayton activated the call button with a thought, and Dr. Reed slumped against the wall, breathing hard, her brow beaded with sweat.

Clayton nodded to her. "You need to schedule more exercise in your downtime."

Reed flashed a wry smile. "What downtime, sir?"

He snorted at that. "Good point."

The elevator on the far right opened, and they strode in. A woman was already standing there. She came to attention and said, "Captain."

He recognized the woman from her gray eyes, jutting chin, and bristly blond hair at the same time as he read the rank and last name over her right breast. His AR contacts made the name tape glow bright blue.

*PO3 Salazar*

"At ease, Petty Officer," he said.

She nodded, and he turned to face the doors with Dr. Reed. Using his ARCs, Clayton selected the Science Lab on level nine.

The elevator slowed to a stop, momentarily adding to the 1.4 Gs already weighing on Clayton's knees. The doors parted quickly, and he led the way around the circular corridor that encircled the elevators. Other passages branched off at right angles like the spokes of a wheel, each of them lined with doors to various laboratories. Clayton took the right-hand passage and walked quickly by the doors and windows to various labs, pausing only once to check on the leafy green rows of vegetables and fruit growing under glowing blue UV lamps.

Then came the labs with biologists and geneticists working in sterile white suits. They were testing and splicing blood samples from the crew, trying to make the human genome more adaptable and resilient to alien environments. Those experiments were still in their infancy, but the hope was that some day colonists would be able to breathe alien atmospheres without the aid of filter masks or oxygen tanks.

Dr. Reed stopped with him to look in on one of those labs. She rapped on the window and shook her head, pointing to a case of blood samples that was in danger of getting elbowed off the counter.

She sighed and they continued down the corridor. "Those samples represent six months of work."

"Have they had any luck?"

"Plenty," Dr. Reed replied. "At this rate, we'll be able to breathe the air on whatever planet we decide to colonize before we even make landfall."

Clayton arched an eyebrow at her. "What about pathogens?"

"We can prevent allergic reactions, but if you mean hostile alien microbes, we'll need to work on vaccines and countermeasures for each strain that we encounter."

They reached the comms lab and Dr. Reed waved the door open and led the way inside. Dr. Grouse was the only other person in the room. He was short and round, chosen for this mission because of his brains and in spite of his physical condition.

Dr. Grouse looked up as they approached, his plump face stretching into a grin. He hefted a malleable electrode helmet with a big, glossy black visor. A goofy grin sprang to his lips that was complemented nicely by his bouncing, curly brown hair and vivid blue eyes. "Captain! You're just in time!"

Clayton's eyes scanned the room. There was a chimp strapped down to a stretcher with a matching helmet on its head and wires trailing to a nearby computer console. The visor on the chimp's helmet was down, and by some miracle, it wasn't fighting its bonds. *Must be sedated,* Clayton decided.

A second stretcher bore a Golden Retriever—Charlie—with another electrode helmet on its head, but no visor. The dog's eyes were closed, its legs kicking spasmodically in its sleep. Clayton noticed drool leaking from the corner of its snout.

He frowned and crossed his arms over his chest, his eyes back on the chimp. What was his name again? "In time for what?" he asked.

Dr. Grouse held out the electrode helmet to him. "Put it on and you'll see."

Clayton hesitated and glanced at Dr. Reed. She nodded. "It's safe, sir, don't worry. I was using it to look inside Charlie's head just a few minutes before I came to see you."

Clayton uncrossed his arms with a sigh, and took the helmet from Dr. Grouse. The other man helped him put it on and shaped it to his head. Electrodes pressed firmly to Clayton's scalp through his razor-short black hair.

"Dr. Reed said you learned how to read a *dog's* thoughts, so what's the chimp doing here?"

"Archimedes is here to join the conversation."

*Archimedes. That's his name.*

"The *conversation?*" Clayton asked.

"You'll see, Captain. You'll see! Are you ready?"

Dr. Grouse's enthusiasm wasn't as infectious as he probably thought it was. If anything, Clayton found it unsettling. He was about to have his brain wired to a dog's and a chimp's via a device that was somehow capable of reading and transmitting mental images directly between all three of them.

"I'm ready..." Clayton said slowly.

Bright images flickered over Dr. Grouse's eyes as he used his ARCs to configure the communicator, and then a prompt appeared on Clayton's own contacts, asking him to authorize a connection between his Neuralink and the communicator. Clayton approved the request, grateful that the technology wasn't so invasive as to somehow project images into his brain without his permission. A glowing green countdown appeared on Clayton's ARCs:

*Ten, nine, eight...*

Dr. Grouse folded the visor down in front of his eyes, blocking out the lab. Clayton frowned, disoriented. He heard a chair rolling on mag wheels. "Here you are, sir," Reed said. "You should be sitting down for this."

He felt around blindly for the chair and then flopped into it with a *whuff* of escaping air from the cushion. The countdown hit zero, and suddenly he was flying through a grassy green field with a bright yellow disk hovering in the air before him. A golden snout with a wet black nose protruded from the lower portion of the screen.

Suddenly, his view jumped up, and the disc was protruding from that snout.

"Come here, boy!" That was Dr. Grouse's voice, followed by the sound of him whistling.

The scene panned around, and Clayton noticed paws galloping in and out of his view as Charlie ran toward his master. Dr. Grouse was stooped down and grinning, clapping for Charlie. "Good boy!" The view shook as he wrestled the Frisbee away and patted Charlie enthusiastically on the head.

Clayton heard Charlie barking for the doctor to throw the Frisbee again. Those sounds came to Clayton's ears through miniature speakers built into the frame of the helmet, rather than through the comm piece in his ear. Again, he appreciated the less invasive approach.

"What is this?" he asked, shaking his head. Even his own dreams weren't this vivid.

"Amazing, right?" Dr. Reed asked, sounding breathless.

"This isn't a dream," Clayton insisted.

"Not exactly, no," Dr. Grouse admitted. "It's a memory that we're triggering during an induced REM cycle."

"So where does the chimp fit in?" Clayton asked.

"Archimedes is a receiver like you. He's watching the same thing," Dr. Grouse explained. "Now look what happens when we make him the transmitter and you and Charlie the receivers."

Clayton's visor went blank for a second. Then it was replaced by a black grid overlaid on a dark room full of gleaming equipment. Clayton recognized the grid squares as the bars of a cage. Then he saw tiny furry hands wrap around those bars and rattle the cage. The chimp began screaming and jumping up and down, shaking Clayton's view.

"This is another memory?"

"Yes," Dr. Grouse confirmed.

Clayton lifted the visor and squinted at him. "How does this help us talk to aliens? You're telling me we'll have to sedate them and tie them down before we can communicate with them?"

Dr. Grouse shook his head quickly. "No. This is just proof that the technology works on non-human subjects. For willing participants, the process is much simpler and more dynamic."

"I'd like to see that."

"Hang on," Dr. Grouse said, and spun away, reaching for something in a nearby wall of lockers and cabinets. He opened one of the cabinets to reveal a fourth communicator helmet. Removing it, he connected it to a snaking bundle of wires and cables on the deck, and then spent a moment configuring the helmet. Clayton watched bright screens flashing over the other man's ARCs. A moment later, Dr. Grouse put the helmet on and pulled the visor down.

"You need to put your visor down," Reed said, nodding to Clayton.

He did as he was told, and saw another access prompt, asking for permission to connect to *Visualizer #1*. He granted access and an image of a soccer ball appeared on his visor, surrounded by blank, black emptiness. Clayton frowned. If this was all that went on in Dr. Grouse's head, he was going to have to assign someone else to this project.

The ball began to roll, and then a potholed road appeared under it, sloping sharply down. Trees, brown grass, bushes, and shrubs appeared on both sides. The ball went skipping down the road, bouncing through potholes on its way to a pebbly beach below. The beach was shaded by tall pine trees creaking in a warm breeze that Clayton was startled to realize he could actually *feel. So much for non-invasive.* The Visualizer was interacting with his neural implant to produce actual sensations.

As the ball disappeared into the trees below, his viewpoint began bouncing down after it with lanky arms and legs swinging into view. Clayton heard indistinct voices. A child's prepubescent voice replied: "Alison kicked it! She should be the one to get it!"

And with that, the scene faded to black.

"Now you try," Dr. Grouse said.

"Try what?" Clayton muttered, shaking his head.

"Picture something," Reed answered. "It can be a memory or you can just use your imagination."

Clayton searched his head for a random image or memory of something. His watch with his wife's smiling face jumped to mind.

"I see a smart watch," Dr. Grouse said. "Your wife's face is the wallpaper."

Startled, Clayton pushed the image away, blanking his mind.

"Now it's gone," Dr. Grouse said.

Clayton sent his thoughts in another direction, picturing something else: the Earth as seen from orbit above the dark side of the planet. Glowing orange lines and splotches of city lights shone clear between scattered wisps of cloud.

"Earth from orbit at night," Dr. Grouse said.

Clayton tried something else. Pure imagination. He imagined flying like a bird low over a rippled blue ocean, the surface gleaming with coppery freckles of reflected light from an alien sun, and a pale green sky soaring up from the horizon.

Dr. Grouse described all of that, too.

"This is incredible," Clayton whispered.

"I thought you might like it," Dr. Reed said.

Clayton reached up and gently pulled the helmet off his head. "But how do we know it will work on an alien species?"

Dr. Grouse removed his own helmet and cocked his head in question. "What do you mean?"

"I mean, this is a *visual* communicator, so

what if they don't have eyes? Or what if their brains work in a way that's completely foreign to us and we can't read the signals?"

Dr. Grouse shrugged. "Then we re-calibrate. Monkeys and dogs don't encode memories exactly the same way that we do, and yet we managed to calibrate the Visualizers for them."

"Hmmm," Clayton replied. "Well then I suppose the only other issue is getting any aliens we meet to cooperate."

"If they're animals, they won't have a choice," Dr. Grouse said. "We'll just sedate them like we did with Charlie and Archimedes."

Clayton frowned at that. Standing up from his chair, he thrust the Visualizer into Dr. Grouse's chest and spent a moment glowering at the other man.

"What?" Dr. Grouse asked.

"What if you accidentally sedate a sentient species?"

"That depends," Dr. Grouse replied. "Are they more advanced than us?"

"Do they need to be?"

"They do if your hypothetical scenario is supposed to be worrisome. Let's put it another way: what if European explorers had this technology back in the day to communicate with the Native Americans? Imagine they captured and chained up one of the natives in order to subject them to a Visualizer. Would the outcome have been any worse than what actually happened?"

"Maybe it would have," Clayton replied.

"Who's to know, but maybe it would have swayed a few people to consider the Native Americans as equals rather than inferior."

Clayton snorted. "That's optimistic considering humanity's history. Have you shown this to Ambassador Morgan yet?"

"More than an hour ago, sir," Dr. Reed replied. "He's already coming up with a protocol to follow before we can use the devices."

"So he thinks it's a good idea to use them?" Clayton asked.

"Of course. Why wouldn't he? If we run into intelligent life, we're going to need some way to communicate."

Clayton glanced between Dr. Reed and Dr. Grouse with an unhappy frown. "Can they be used against us?"

"I can't imagine how," Dr. Grouse said.

"Maybe by reading thoughts and memories that we don't want them to." Clayton turned and nodded to the chimp and the Golden Retriever. Both were still knocked out on their respective stretchers. "We were just reading *their* memories without permission. What if some aliens were to do that to us?"

"That would only work if they knew how to trigger a particular memory, and that still requires a degree of participation. We were only able to induce the memories you saw from Charlie and Archimedes because we recorded them passively days or weeks ago during one of their dreams. After that, we knew exactly what pathways to stimulate so that we could fire up those memories at will."

"That doesn't rule out coercion," Clayton pointed out. "You could be forced to think about something."

Dr. Grouse smiled patiently at him. "Sir, with all due respect, those are unlikely scenarios. How would aliens that don't know how to communicate with us in the first place be able to coerce us into using a technology that they don't even understand? Besides, all of the data exchanges are designed to be logged and monitored by one or more spectators. If we don't like what we see, we can shut the Visualizers down at a moment's notice."

Clayton saw Dr. Reed bobbing her head along with that. "That's why the ambassador is working out a protocol. Don't worry, Captain. We won't use the Visualizers lightly."

"Can you make them more portable?"

Dr. Grouse drew himself up. "Of course. That's the next step. I should have a portable version ready in a matter of hours. I'm planning to work through the night on it."

"Dedicated," Clayton muttered.

"You know me," Dr. Grouse replied.

Clayton jerked his chin to Charlie and Archimedes. "Wake them up."

"Of course," Dr. Grouse replied. He turned

away and went about removing the helmets from each animal and then unstrapping them from the stretchers. Rather than wake the chimp, Dr. Grouse simply carried him to a cage on the other end of the lab. Probably safer that way.

Dr. Reed unstrapped Charlie while he did that. Dr. Grouse returned and the two of them administered an injection in the back of the dog's neck.

Charlie woke up with a start and a drawling bark. He struggled to rise, his tongue lolling from his snout, brown eyes wild and darting.

"What's wrong with him?" Clayton asked.

"I just woke him up with an epi shot," Dr. Grouse replied, struggling to lift the retriever off the stretcher and onto the deck. Paws skittered for a moment before Dr. Grouse let him go. The Retriever ran around the room, barking and jumping up against them.

Clayton managed to get in a few pats on the head before Charlie ran in another circle. The dog's wagging tail bumped a silver tray full of spare electrodes and other components onto the deck, and he scattered them with his paws.

"Hey!" Dr. Grouse objected. "Charlie, calm down!"

And as if he understood, Charlie came to a skidding stop. His tongue vanished into his mouth, and white teeth flashed out in a snarl. He was looking past Clayton to the door. Then he began barking and snarling.

"Whoa, hey there boy," Dr. Grouse said, going down on his haunches beside the dog. "What's the matter, huh?" he asked while stroking Charlie's back.

Charlie barked and growled some more.

Clayton followed the dog's gaze, but he didn't see anything. "What's wrong with him?" he asked, turning back to Dr. Grouse.

"I don't know. He's usually so calm."

Clayton glanced at the door again. He noticed the gleaming observation window beside it. Maybe Charlie had seen someone out in the corridor watching them. Or maybe he was barking at his own reflection in the window. Hard to tell with a dog.

"He's acting like he saw a ghost," Dr. Reed said.

"A ghost that only he can see?" Clayton countered.

"Maybe it's a ghost that only he can *smell*," Dr. Grouse replied, his eyes twinkling with amusement.

Reed laughed, and Clayton frowned. Charlie still hadn't looked away from the door, and his teeth were still bared, but at least he wasn't barking anymore.

Clayton stifled a sigh. "Well, doctors, this has been very interesting. Let me know if you have any further breakthroughs."

"Aye, sir," Dr. Reed replied.

"Sure," Grouse added.

Clayton headed for the door and waved it

open as he approached. He considered going back to his quarters. Technically he was off-duty.

He decided to go to the bridge instead. Maybe Commander Taylor had an update to share about those blips they'd been tracking.

# CHAPTER 3

Dr. Laurisa Reed was still in the comms lab at midnight, trading mental images back and forth with Dr. Grouse. It was a game of associations, a silent conversation. This was the hope for human-alien communication, should it ever occur—that they could at least trade images of their experiences and views in order to hopefully understand one another.

And even if the Visualizers couldn't be configured to read alien brains, their output could still be sent to a holo projector so that aliens would get to see what humanity had to say.

Dr. Grouse sent her an image of a sunflower. She sent a whole field of them back. He sent a little girl skipping through that field. Her mind added the sound of the little girl laughing.

But that laughter died as her thoughts took a sharp right turn into a place filled with fear and despair. A memory of lying in bed at the hospital after her third miscarriage. The look on her then-fiance, Paul's face as they listened to the doctor telling them that they could keep trying, but that their chances were slim. Surrogacy was an option. Paul had stood by her while they'd looked into options. He'd gone through the motions. Her mind wandered to the last time she'd seen him, their fight, her chasing him out into the rain as he ran to his car. The taillights blazing crimson as his wheels spun on the rain-slicked streets to get away.

Her inability to have children had been the beginning of the end for them, and then the engagement had ended just like all of their failed pregnancies.

"Ah... Lori, are you okay?"

She shook herself out of the memories, embarrassed and worried about how much Dr. Grouse had seen through the Visualizers. None of it was news to him, but it was certainly off topic.

"I'm fine. Sorry."

This was the main problem with the technology. Visualizers gave a glimpse into another person's head, but people have filters for a reason. Mental imagery is a shit show of random associations with very little sense to it. A river of consciousness roaring by. With a deliberate effort people can control the flow for a while and keep their thoughts on relevant topics, but the random associations were still there, a powerful current racing underneath, ready to derail any meaningful conversation.

"Let's try something else," Dr. Grouse said.

An image of a rock and a feather falling in vacuum tubes popped into her head. They were both falling at the same rate, an extension of Galileo's contention that objects fall to Earth at the same rate regardless of their mass.

That was a good visual illustration of a higher level concept that any advanced species with a proper understanding of mass and gravity should recognize.

Lori replied with a mental image of herself holding out both hands, giving two thumbs up. "We should add that one to the list of conversation starters."

"Definitely," Dr. Grouse replied.

Their conversation went on for a while, firing back and forth with images of scientific breakthroughs and concepts. Another good conversation starter was a 2D illustration of the universe, starting from a singularity and expanding to a larger and larger size over time. That one image conveyed the Big Bang Theory and the expansion of the universe at the same time. Hopefully any aliens looking at it would understand what they were seeing from the glittering stars and the over-sized spiral galaxies depicted in each progressively larger bubble of the universe. If not, it might turn out to be a head-scratcher.

Lori pulled her helmet off with a sigh and rubbed tired, scratchy eyes. Her vision was blurry from staring at the inside of her visor for so long, and it took a few seconds to clear it.

Dr. Grouse pulled off his helmet and spent a moment vigorously scratching his scalp where electrodes had been pressing the hair against his skin.

Lori checked the clock in the top left of her ARCs. It was after midnight. The ship's clock was set to the same time as Cape Canaveral, where they'd launched from, though by now those clocks would be wildly out of sync.

"We should get some sleep," Lori said.

"You go ahead, I'm going to stay a while and see if I can log some dreams from Charlie and Archimedes."

Lori nodded to him as she rose from her chair and left the gleaming comms lab. She followed the corridor outside past several bio and agro labs to the corridor running around the central column of elevators. She hit the call button with her ARCs and pre-selected the crew deck.

One of the elevators opened with a two-tone chime, and she stepped in, riding it up to the officers' quarters on level twenty-six. She wasn't an officer or even enlisted, but she had a room here because of her importance to the mission—and because Ambassador Morgan had pulled some strings. The corridors were all still and empty as she walked to her room. She spotted a lone officer walking by. He glanced her way and she inclined her head to him. His glowing blue name tape read: Lt. Paulson.

Her ex-fiance, Paul flashed into her mind again, and she looked away with a grimace. She wasn't still hung up on him, but Paul was an unwelcome reminder of why she'd come on this mission in the first place. She didn't have any attachments back home, so why not hop aboard an interstellar colony ship?

Reaching her room, Lori stood in front of the blinking red light of the door scanner. She waved the door open as soon as the light burned green, having recognized her identity.

She stepped in to find the lights already on and turned down to dim, night-cycle yellows. A familiar person was lounging on the small two-seater gray couch opposite her bunk and kitty corner to the room's viewscreen.

"Ambassador Morgan," she began, her brain was too tired to remember that she could call him by his first name when no one else was around. Her stride faltered as she came within a few feet of him. The door slid automatically shut behind her.

Richard rose with an easy smile, the images of whatever he'd been looking at on his ARCs fading from his eyes as he gave her his full attention.

"*Ambassador,* is it?" he asked in a deep voice. Blond eyebrows drifted up, his blue eyes widening underneath. She took a moment to admire his chiseled frame, visible even through his bulky black UNSF uniform. Her eyes tracked back up to his face, taking in the short blond stubble on his jaw, matching hair cut short and combed to one side, and a face so handsome that he could have been starring in movies back home. Or running for president. Lori felt the first stirrings of interest. It was late, but she could use the distraction after all those reminders of her ex-fiance.

Crossing the rest of the way to the couch, she grabbed his hands and pulled him in for a kiss. His lips lingered on hers, and she responded hungrily. Soon they were reaching for each other's magnetic clasps and zippers.

Half an hour later, they lay naked and entwined on her bunk, staring at the stars through the viewscreen at the foot of the bed.

"I waited over an hour for you," Richard said.

"Did you?" she managed to say through the dreamy haze that cloaked her thoughts. Before she could wonder where he was going with that, he told her.

"It wasn't easy sneaking in."

*Not again,* she sighed. "Richard, this is—"

"Don't say *nice,*" he replied.

"Okay, it's horrible. The complete opposite of nice."

"Ha ha," Richard replied dryly. "Just hear me out. Space Force regulations don't forbid relationships between crew members."

"Maybe not, but who says we're in a relationship?" Lori countered. She withdrew a few inches, her naked back pressing against the cold surface of the bulkhead beside her bunk. That cleared her head even more, and she withdrew her arm from his chest to cross it over hers.

Stealing the blankets with her other hand as an extra barrier between them, she sat up and pointed to the door.

"You should go. We need to get some sleep."

Richard propped himself up on one elbow, glanced at the door, then back at her. His eyes were hard, a frown exposing the dimples in his cheeks. "Lori, don't do this."

"Do what?" she asked. "We'll be arriving in just two days. I have a lot of work to get through tomorrow, and I need to get my sleep. So do you."

Richard gave in with a sigh and swung his legs over the side of the bunk. Standing up, he gave her a nice view as he went through the room picking up the discarded pieces of his uniform and putting them back on one at a time.

"Good night," she said, and rolled over to face the bulkhead.

"Night," he replied.

She heard the door swish open, then shut, and settled in for sleep. She could sympathize with Richard wanting more, but relationships weren't her thing. Not anymore. And he'd known that from the start, so he couldn't complain about it now.

# CHAPTER 4

Clayton saw the planet below, a splash of alien colors and misshapen continents. Fluffy white clouds, and an alien sun. He was free-falling toward it. His helmet on, suit pressurized. The sound of his breathing rasping through the suit, came faster and faster to his ears. Short, shallow breaths.

As he fell, friction heated his suit and his skin underneath, at first itching, then burning. His skin began to burn through the suit, and he screamed. He watched in horror as orange flames raced over his body, gobbling up the reflective white fabric like a piece of paper thrown into a fire. His rasping breaths grew shallower and more frantic. Then he screamed as his skin caught ablaze and the flames began to eat him too.

Clayton's eyes shot open, and he stared hard at the ceiling, blinking to clear away the image of his own immolation. It was just a dream. He worked to calm his rapid, rasping breaths. But then he noticed something. He wasn't the one making those sounds. His eyes tracked over to a shadow hunched in front of his desk and the room's viewscreens.

Someone was in his room.

His heart instantly pounding, Clayton tried to sit up, to activate the lights with a verbal command.

But he couldn't. He was paralyzed. He couldn't even scream.

The shadow inched closer to him. It was short, with legs bent at the knee, back arched, and claws reaching. He couldn't see more than a solid black cutout of the creature, it had no features, other than gleaming red pinpricks for eyes. The demon that had haunted him since childhood was back.

*It's just sleep paralysis,* he told himself, working desperately to calm his racing heart. *It's not real.*

The shadowy creature sprang off the deck and landed on top of him, constricting his chest with its weight and making it hard to breathe.

Clayton tried to struggle, but his body was still paralyzed from his REM cycle. *That's all this is,* Clayton insisted. *The lingering effects of sleep.* He just had to wait for it to pass.

The shadowy demon bent low over him, its rasping breaths loud in his ears.

His heart hammered out a painful staccato that echoed in his ears with each beat.

Then he remembered something. His Neuralink implant. His thoughts were still free.

*Lights on!* he screamed inside his head.

The overhead lights blazed on, momentarily blinding him. The shadow on his chest whirled toward the light and reacted with a shrill cry. Clayton saw its silhouette briefly, still a feature-less black shadow, but then it began to glow and shimmer, going from matte black to crystal clear in an instant.

A fading shriek sputtered into a low hiss, and the weight vanished from Clayton's chest.

He sat up and dragged in a deep breath, cast-ing about wildly for the monster that had been there a moment ago. But it was gone.

Sleep paralysis and its accompanying hypna-gogic hallucinations had plagued him for dec-ades. It was always the same shadowy crea-ture that haunted him, always that crouching shadow with the rasping breath.

When he was little, before he'd gone to sleep specialists and learned what sleep paralysis was, he used to think that the shadow was an alien visitor come to abduct him. Eventually he'd learned that all of his symptoms could be ex-plained by a delayed release from REM sleep. Everyone is paralyzed during their REM cycles— the body's way of protecting itself from acting out its dreams. But not everyone is immediately released from paralysis upon waking, and not everyone stops dreaming, either. Waking hallu-cinations and paralysis are the result.

Clayton lay back down with a sigh. *Lights to 25%*, he thought, and they dropped to a soothing golden glow. He lay staring at the ceiling, wondering about the timing. He hadn't experienced an episode of sleep paralysis for years. The last one had been after his wife's funeral. The episodes were triggered by stress.

So what was he stressed about?

Arrival. The mysterious blips on sensors. The possibility of real alien contact.

Half of the reason he'd joined the Space Force was because of episodes like this one. Despite the doctors' reassurances and explanations, he'd still suspected for a long time that his hallucinations were alien visitations.

Now he knew better.

Or did he?

Raising his voice, he said, "Call the Bridge."

Hidden speakers began trilling, then a click as someone answered—

"Captain, is something wrong?" He recognized the voice of Lieutenant Ashley Devon, OOD of the ship's night watch. Devon was a red-haired, freckle-faced beauty with a reputation for being a ball-buster, which was exactly why he trusted her with the bridge when both he and Commander Taylor were off-duty.

"You tell me, Devon. Anything on sensors?" he asked.

"Not a blip, sir."

He let out a shaky sigh. "Carry on, then."

"Aye, sir..."

"Cross out." The call ended with another

click, and he rolled over to stare at the spot beside his desk where he'd seen the demon after waking.

Nothing there now.

He put it down to nerves. He'd visit Doctor Stevens in the morning and get his stress levels checked. Clayton was the captain of an interstellar colony ship. He couldn't afford to be jumping at shadows—literally—the day before arrival.

# CHAPTER 5

**—One Day Before Arrival—**

Clayton stared at the dim red star dead center of the forward viewscreens. Scarcely larger than the tip of his pinkie finger at this range, that sun was an ultra-cool red dwarf with no less than seven rocky planets in a tight orbit.

"Trappist-1," Clayton breathed.

"The ice cube of stars," Commander Taylor commented from where she stood beside him.

"And the holy grail of habitable star systems, with three rocky planets in its Goldilocks zone," Clayton replied.

He turned from the viewscreens to address the rest of the crew.

"Flight ops—"

Lieutenant Celia Asher looked up from her station. "Sir?" Her short, white-blond hair glowed silver in the light of her screens. Ice-blue eyes gleamed like sapphires.

"Launch probes to all seven planets, but concentrate our primary efforts on planets C, D, and E."

"Aye, sir," Celia replied.

"Nav, set course for Trappist-1E."

Clayton looked to Lieutenant Craig "Delta" Sanders, the gray-haired former Marine at the nav station. He was also the ship's chief of security. The man nodded without looking up, eyes level on his screens. "Setting course, sir."

"Placing your bet already?" Commander Taylor asked quietly.

Clayton turned to see her regarding him with eyebrows raised. "It's approximately Earth-sized and receives only slightly less solar radiation than Earth. Without any additional data to go on, it's the most likely candidate for a colony. We'll adjust course if the probes reveal otherwise. We still have a day before we reach orbit."

"Actually, sir—"

Clayton turned to see Delta studying him from the Nav.

"Yes?" he replied.

"That estimate was for how long it would take us to reach a safe orbit around the system's sun. Trappist E is currently between us and the system's star. We're looking at an ETA of twelve hours and seven minutes.

Clayton checked the clock in the top left of his ARCs. 10:15. "So we'll be arriving at twenty-two hundred?"

"Aye."

"Even better." Clayton clapped his hands for attention. "All right people, start running through your checklists. Looks like we'll be making history ahead of schedule!"

A cheer from the crew answered that news, and he traded grins with Commander Taylor.

\* \* \*

### Twelve Hours Later...

Video data from probe flyovers had revealed plenty of alien flora and fauna. They'd all watched in awe as the holofeeds had come in: towering trees with fan-like leaves, buzzing swarms of insects that schooled like fish. Giant, winged creatures skimming the treetops and scooping them up like whales...

The day side of Trappist-1E lay directly in front of them. Clayton admired that cloud streaked blue-green marble. Scans hadn't picked up any oceans, but the surface was pocked blue with lakes and striated with rivers. Ragged black mountains capped with snow ringed the lakes. Clayton suspected the mountains were the rims of old impact craters.

Mottled blue and green jungles colored the dry land in the valleys, but those vibrant colors faded gradually to windswept yellows, whites, and browns that filled bone-dry craters near the dark side of the planet.

"It's tidally locked," Commander Taylor said from where she stood beside him. "That means strong winds and a volatile climate around the day-night terminator. We should land as close to the middle of the day side as possible to avoid those concerns. Sunlight will be the strongest there, and the climate should be relatively stable."

"Agreed," Clayton replied. "Hopefully the mountains around the craters will buffer any winds that reach us in the valleys."

"Aye," Taylor said.

The probe data had borne out Clayton's bet. Trappist-1E was the only planet in the entire star system with liquid surface water and an oxygen-rich atmosphere. It was also very close to the size of Earth, with a comfortable 0.7 $Gs$ of surface gravity. The air was breathable, but not long-term because it was too thin. Unassisted breathing on the surface would be like trying to breathe at the top of Mount Everest. Even if they cleared it as safe to breathe, they would need to supplement with $O_2$ tanks. Atmospheric pressure was a comfortable 0.8 atm at the bottoms of the craters, so pressure suits weren't strictly necessary, but they'd use them anyway to protect against alien micro organisms and allergens.

Clayton tore his eyes away from the viewscreens to address the crew. "Lieutenant Davies —"

The man looked up from the comms station, his green eyes wide and blinking, his shaved head gleaming in the dim light.

"Alert the ground team, and summon Lieutenant Devon and her section to the bridge for the handover of the watch. We're going down to the surface."

"Aye, sir," Davies replied.

"*We*, sir?" Commander Taylor asked.

He turned to her. "Yes. You and I are both going down with team Alpha."

Taylor's brow furrowed. "I must have missed you on the team roster."

"You didn't. I added myself at the last minute."

"I see. Permission to speak frankly, Captain?"

"Granted."

"I think you should stay with the ship."

He arched an eyebrow at her, waiting for her to explain.

A muscle jerked in Taylor's cheek and one of her dimples appeared. "We don't know what kind of threats we may encounter. It could be dangerous. We can't afford to lose you."

"We can't afford to lose anyone, Commander, and I won't ask my crew to take risks that I wouldn't take myself. Besides, you can't possibly believe that I'd be willing to take a backseat on this. That would be like asking Neil Armstrong to stay in the moon lander—and *he* didn't have to travel for seventy-eight years to get there."

Taylor cracked a wry smile at that. "Fair enough, sir. Did you clear it with the ambassador?"

Clayton smirked and placed a finger to his

lips. "It'll be our little secret. Why do you think I was a *last-minute* addition?"

Taylor's eyes glittered with amusement. "Understood, sir."

Clayton had disagreed from the start with the UNE's decision to set up both civilian and military chains of command aboard the *Forerunners*. Now that he was almost a century away from Earth, he'd be damned if he was going to let some politician piss all over his command. Clayton would decide how best to safeguard his ship and its crew, and right now that meant getting his own boots on the ground to identify and analyze each and every potential threat and hazard for himself. If Ambassador Morgan didn't like that, too bad. Clayton couldn't disobey an order that he'd never technically been given.

# CHAPTER 6

Clayton placed a palm against the inner pane of the window beside him—

And withdrew it sharply as the glass scalded him. "Damn," he muttered. The glass had been super-heated from atmospheric entry.

The shuttle bucked and shivered; cargo straps slapped the sides of the crates they held. Their handles rattled. Clouds swept past the viewports on both sides. Dead ahead, through the cockpit canopy, blue-green jungles peeked through the cottony haze below. Rain drops freckled the glass, streaking quickly away.

Commander Taylor sat in the pilot's seat, shaking her head at Clayton.

He grinned back at her like a kid. "What?"

"Can't take you anywhere, sir."

A muffled *boom* shivered through the hull, stealing away his reply before he could utter it.

"What was that?" he asked to no one in particular.

"Thunderstorm, sir," Taylor replied, pointing to a tower of black clouds to starboard.

A forking flash of lighting came through Clayton's window, confirming her analysis. Black clouds towered over the rim of the crater that they'd chosen for their landing site.

"Looks like some bad weather coming," Delta commented from the back. "We need to set this bucket down before crosswinds hit us."

"I know how to fly, Lieutenant," Taylor replied.

"Just saying, ma'am."

Delta had been a Scimitar Pilot with the Space Marines until his knees got too old for high-G, so he was something of an expert on the topic of flying.

"Hopefully we have some time to explore before the storm hits," Ambassador Morgan added from the row of seats directly behind theirs.

Clayton frowned and tossed a glance over his shoulder at the other man. As it turned out, he'd read the situation all wrong. Ambassador Morgan didn't care if *he* joined the ground team, but Morgan wanted to join them, too—along with both of the mission's first contact specialists, Doctors Reed and Grouse.

After seeing all of the alien creatures revealed by the probes' flyovers, Morgan had apparently decided that the chances of first contact with an intelligent alien species were high enough that he needed to be there.

Alpha Team now had seven members. Clayton and Commander Taylor up front. Ambassador Morgan and Dr. Reed in the second row. Delta and Dr. Grouse in the second to last row, and Doctor Stevens in the back. Stevens was the chief medical officer of *Forerunner One*. He was a first lieutenant, but everyone just called him Doctor Stevens or "Doc" for short.

The clouds sweeping across the cockpit canopy abruptly parted, and gasps went up from passengers. Even Clayton's breath caught in his throat.

"It's beautiful," Doctor Stevens said in an awed whisper.

"Copy *that...*" Taylor added.

Towering trees rose to varying heights with massive blue-green leaves interlocking to form several different flat surfaces high above the ground. *Islands in the sky,* Clayton thought. He wouldn't be surprised if they could actually walk on them. The various levels of tree canopies sparkled with crimson freckles of light— the system's star reflecting off puddles from a recent rain. The sky was a pale green where it wasn't already black with the building thunderstorm, and dead ahead, the lake they were headed for was a dark teal, sunlight shimmering on the surface like a field of rubies.

Clayton sucked in a shaky breath and smiled. *This* was why he'd joined *Forerunner One*. He couldn't even begin to imagine all the astounding things they'd discover once they set foot on the ground.

* * *

Lori Reed pressed a white-gloved hand to her

helmet visor, shading her eyes. She stared up at the trunks of monolithic trees bordering the beach they'd landed on. Her breathing quickened as her eyes darted from the treetops to the multiple *levels* of tree canopies, to the ghostly fairyland of faintly glowing vegetation on the forest floor. Her breath echoed inside her helmet, loud against the backdrop of alien hoots and chirps conveyed by her suit's external audio pickups and the helmet's internal speakers. The forest itself was humming like high-voltage power lines, and howling eerily with the wind gusting across the lake behind them.

"How high are those trees?" Richard asked.

Lori turned to see the ambassador gazing up at the trees and backpedaling quickly to get some distance so he could glimpse the treetops. Spiky stalks of blue-green grass crunched underfoot and rasped past the fabric of his suit as he went.

The rest of the team stood close by, contemplating the forest. The military officers distinguished themselves by carrying rifles that dangled from shoulder straps, and stun pistols holstered at their hips. Lori and Dr. Grouse saved all of their energy to carry the Visualizers and holo projectors in their packs, as well as a variety of other scanners. Doctor Stevens had the sample jars and vials in his pack, while the soldiers carried survival gear and spare ammo in theirs.

If there were any intelligent aliens down here,

Lori hoped the soldiers would have the good sense to hold their fire.

"Let's head in," Captain Cross said, turning to regard them with one hand on the grip of his stocky, short-barreled white and gray rifle. Lori didn't know much about firearms, but Richard had told her while the soldiers were all arming themselves in the hangar that those rifles were called *coil guns*. They apparently shot hypervelocity rounds that could pierce armored targets and punch fist-sized holes through living ones.

The others nodded their agreement, and Captain Cross led the way into the forest. Commander Taylor and the former Marine, Delta, followed close behind.

They each had enough oxygen for two hours. A timer on the bright green heads-up-display projected on the inside of Lori's helmet showed that she had an hour and fifty-one minutes left. Still plenty of time to explore before they headed back.

Shadows descended over them as they passed beneath the tree canopies. The deeper they went, the darker it got, but faintly glowing growths on the tree trunks and the forest floor emitted a ghostly white light. The level of illumination was similar to that of a full moon on Earth. For Lori, it was enough to see by, but the officers quickly snapped on the ring lights around their helmet visors. Lori and Richard belatedly followed suit with their own helmet lamps.

Small creatures with too many legs skittered away from the beam shining out of Lori's helmet. Other creatures took flight, absorbing and re-emitting the light cast by their helmets in a shimmering rainbow of colors.

"Look at that!" Dr. Grouse said, pointing to one of them. "What *is* it?"

"Rainbow bug," Delta grunted.

"Good a name as any," Captain Cross replied.

Lori slowed to watch one of them as it flew away, bobbing upward on four, perfectly circular wings at the ends of long straight black stalks. The creature's translucent body pulsed blue, then violet, then green, then yellow, then red.... The bugs flew in lazy spirals, somehow looking both graceful and clumsy at the same time.

The landing party walked on for another ten minutes, marveling at the sheer number of creeping and crawling creatures, most of which began glowing as soon as the party's helmet lamps hit them. Each creature was stranger and more exotic than the last.

The group had to stop periodically for Doctor Stevens to take samples of the flora. He even captured one of the glowing rainbow bugs in a jar, which he spirited away into his pack before the captain could say anything about it. All of the sample containers were perfectly sealed to prevent contamination of the shuttle when they returned, which meant that poor bug would die in the name of science. Lori tried not to let that bother her, but it did.

"Everybody freeze!" Captain Cross's voice stopped Lori cold before she even realized what he'd said.

She noticed something up ahead, frozen under the captain's helmet lights and clinging to a tree trunk about twenty feet up. This was a much larger creature than any of the others they'd encountered so far. It had brown skin, the color of the tree, and *ten* long, lanky legs with what looked like two elbows each. Loose folds of skin hung under some of those legs, stretched taut in other places. *It's limbs are webbed,* Lori thought. The creature looked to be hairless, but it had sharp quills running down its back, and a bony, triangular face with a sharp black beak and two dark eyes that seemed to blaze with curiosity. Or perhaps they were blazing with something deadlier than that.

Before any of them could react, the creature's eyes flared to twice their size, and it's beak parted in a feral cry. A glowing collar of skin fanned out from its neck. It gave a rattling hiss that reminded her of a rattle snake, and then everything was washed out by a blinding flash of light. They stumbled around, trying to clear their vision. Lori recovered in time to see a dark shadow leaping away from the tree, the webbed folds of skin under its legs pulling taut and catching the air like a parachute. The creature screamed as it swooped down on them, and the soldiers' weapons snapped up, taking aim.

"No!" Lori cried.

# CHAPTER 7

"Hold your fire!" Clayton cried even as he reached for his sidearm and took aim.

He flicked off the safety and left his coil gun to swing free at the end of the strap as he tracked the ten-legged brown monkey-creature gliding down on them.

He aimed for center mass and squeezed the trigger. A long silver projectile exploded from the barrel heading straight for the flying monkey. The projectile broke apart and spread out like a net just before reaching the target. Multiple sharp metal rods embedded themselves into the alien, all connected by hair-thin wires to the central rod. Forks of bright blue electricity coursed over the creature, lighting it up like a Christmas tree. It shrieked and shivered, limbs spasming and curling in around its body. As soon as it did that, it fell like a stone and hit hard in the ankle-deep cushion of vegetation on the forest floor.

Silence rang, and the creature didn't stir.

"Good shot, sir!" Delta crowed as he strode toward the target with his coil gun raised. "Target neutralized," he confirmed a moment later. "Life signs are good. I think. Looks like I'm getting... *two* heart beats. Or... three? I'm not qualified for this. Doc!"

Doctor Stevens hurried over, shaking his head. "No animal could possibly have three hearts. They'd wind up pumping blood in opposite directions!"

Clayton and the others crowded around, and his own heads-up display revealed the same thing that Delta had just reported. Three distinct pulses, starting in the head, then the chest, and finally a third one in the stomach. They fired in a tandem rhythm, one after another, but the periodic pulses of electricity from the stun round were visibly interrupting that rhythm. With each shock, the creature tensed up and let out a whistling cry that sounded too weak and pitiful to be menacing.

Clayton frowned, wondering how to deal with the situation. If they removed the stun rods, the creature could recover and attack them, and then they might be forced to answer with lethal force.

"Let it go! Now!" Dr. Reed cried, dropping to her haunches beside the creature. "You're going to kill it!"

"She's right, sir," Commander Taylor said.

Clayton could see the commander's expression pinched in sympathy behind her mask. Somehow that flying monkey had gone from hostile alien to three-legged puppy in a span of seconds, and he was the one who had crippled it.

"Sir?" Delta looked to him for confirmation.

Clayton gave in with a sigh and a nod. "Do it. Everyone else, back up and give the man some space."

Delta waited a beat while they withdrew, then bent down and yanked the stun rods out in one smooth motion. He leapt back, his rifle snapping up to his shoulder to cover the creature as he moved away.

The creature struggled to rise, almost collapsing twice in the process. Finally it regained its footing, but it held two of its ten legs up at crooked angles. Clayton winced, realizing that it must have broken those limbs in the fall. The creature was still making that whistling sound. The sound of alien pain. It shook itself out like a dog, and then its eight good legs scuttled as it turned on the spot to face them with wide, angry black eyes.

Clayton waited, his breath rasping and loud inside his helmet. This thing was either going to bolt or charge. Fight or flight.

It chose option three and threw its head back to release a deafening cry. Echoes of that sound bounced back from the trees at different pitches and volumes. Clayton searched the canopy for the source. Dozens of glowing collars flared out, peppering the darkness with bright flashes of light and ominous rattling sounds.

Then, all at once, those glowing creatures

began drifting down from the trees, angling in swiftly from all sides.

"Captain! What are your orders?" Delta asked, his voice rising in alarm as he swept his coil gun back and forth.

There had to be at least fifty of those monkeys descending on them. Clayton hadn't landed on Trappist-1E to initiate a mass slaughter of the first complex lifeforms that they encountered. For all they knew, these creatures could even be intelligent.

"Fall back!" Clayton cried.

"You heard the Captain! Double time! Move, move, move! Back to the shuttle!"

Alpha Team hesitated for the briefest second, and then broke and ran, their collective boots hammering the forest floor in a stampede. The ring lamps from their helmets bobbed and weaved as they went, throwing dancing beams of light and shadow through the forest. Rainbow bugs spiraled around them, reflecting the light from their lamps in ever-changing hues. Clayton brought up the rear with Commander Taylor and Lieutenant Delta. He glanced back periodically to check for signs of pursuit—of which there were plenty. Dozens of those monkeys were soaring down, overtaking them on both sides, their glowing neck rings making them easy targets in the gloomy forest.

"They're trying to outflank us, sir!" Delta said. "Permission to rattle their feathers with live ammo?"

Clayton shook his head and spared a breath to say, "Denied. Just keep running! We don't know if they're hostile yet."

"They're acting pretty hostile, sir!" Delta replied.

"He's right," Taylor added. "We need to scare them off. Or at least thin their numbers."

"Fine, but no live rounds! Stun only. Aim for the ones closest to the ground. We don't want the fall to kill or hurt them."

"Copy that," Delta said, already drawing his stun pistol and taking aim. Taylor did the same, and Clayton reluctantly drew his own sidearm again. Each weapon was packed with a clip of ten stun rounds.

Glinting silver darts flashed out to all sides as they ran, but aiming and running were mutually exclusive, and most of those shots missed. The ones that hit had much the same effect as the last time. Outstretched limbs curled inward and those creatures fell with a crash.

"You could still be killing them with those stun rounds!" Dr. Reed pointed out from the front of the group where she ran behind Ambassador Morgan. He was leading the charge back to the shuttle.

They reached the edge of the trees and burst into the field of spiky blue-green grass where they'd landed. A sequence of alien cries followed them out, and thunder rolled overhead. The storm was directly above them now. Fat drops of rain splatted noisily on their pressure suits.

The dark sky swirled with rain. Ten-legged monsters chased them out on both sides, corralling them back to their shuttle.

Maybe they really were intelligent.

They reached the shuttle without incident, and ran up the short landing ramp to the airlock. Clayton triggered it open remotely and they piled in just as they reached the top of the ramp. He shut the outer door on a cacophony of shrill cries, and Commander Taylor used the control panel to activate the decontamination cycle.

Flashing red lights warned of the danger if they didn't keep their helmets and gloves on. A computerized female voice added an extra warning: "Decontamination commencing..."

Doctor Stevens unslung his pack, zipped it open, and began removing the sample jars, placing them in a decon bin to one side of the airlock.

A fine mist began hissing out to all sides, fogging the visors of their helmets, and blurring their view of one another. That went on for ten seconds before the flashing red lights stopped and began pulsing out blue light as well as several other invisible and more dangerous wavelengths. Their suits would protect them from that brief exposure, but any alien microbes should be annihilated by the combination of sprays and radiation pulses.

Finally, the lights stopped pulsing, and the mist cleared. A green light snapped on above the inner airlock door and a pleasant chime sounded as it slid open.

"Decontamination sequence complete," the voice from before said.

Not even bothering to exit the airlock first, Clayton reached up and unsnapped the seals around his neck and then pulled his helmet off, sucking in a deep breath. The air was sharp and bitter with decon chemicals.

Several others took their helmets off, too. Delta pushed through the airlock and started down the rows of seats in the cabin. He leaned over to the nearest window and peered out.

"No sign of the bastards," he muttered.

Clayton nodded and followed Dr. Reed, Morgan, and Taylor out. Doctor Stevens hung back to retrieve his sample jars from the decon bin.

They crowded the aisle of the shuttle, each picking a window to stare out. Rain streaked the glass, pelting the hull with tinny reports.

Morgan breathed a sigh. "I guess we'll have to wait for the storm to pass before we go back out."

"Go back out?" Clayton echoed. He shook his head. "We're going back up to the Forerunner."

"*What?*" Morgan cried, his blue eyes hard and blond eyebrows dropping dark shadows over them. "This is what we came here for. We need to make contact with those creatures! I hope you're not suggesting that we go hide in our ship."

"If you'd let me finish, I was about to suggest that we go up and analyze Doctor Stevens' samples. Then we can send down the HEROs. In fact, we probably should have led with that as our first option. We wouldn't have had to run out of that forest if we were remote-piloting HEROs instead of running around in meat suits." Clayton plucked at the fabric of his Space Force uniform.

"You can't make first contact with a robot!" Morgan objected. "UNE protocols are clear on that. Besides, where is your spirit of adventure?"

"I burned it off running from alien predators."

Dr. Reed's gaze skipped between them, as if she wasn't sure whose side to take. Then she abruptly frowned and began looking around in alarm.

"Is there something wrong, Dr. Reed?" Clayton asked.

"Where is David?" she asked in a low voice. "Where is Dr. Grouse?" she asked again, her voice jumping up an octave with alarm.

Clayton spun in a quick circle, taking a head count. Dr. Grouse was missing. He stared hard at the airlock along with Taylor and Delta.

"No one noticed that he was missing?" Clayton asked, reprimanding himself with that statement as much as anyone else.

"I volunteer to go out and look for him, sir," Delta said.

"Negative. We're going out together—Commander Taylor update the Forerunner. Tell them to send down the HEROs. We're going to grid search this entire area all night if we have to."

"Copy that," Taylor said, already striding for the cockpit.

"Delta, on me," Clayton said as he headed for the airlock. He dropped his helmet back on and snapped the seals into place.

But just as he was about to cycle the airlock, he heard something.

A heavy *thunk* on the outer door. "Did you hear that, Lieutenant?"

"Affirmative," Delta said and jammed the stock of his coil gun into his shoulder to aim it at the doors.

But no more sounds followed.

"Could just be the storm blowing something into the hull," he said.

And then the sound came again. *Thunk... thunk thunk... thunk...*

Ambassador Morgan walked past them and placed his naked ear to the outer airlock door.

The sound came again. *Thunk... thunk thunk... thunk...*

"They're knocking on the door!" Morgan cried.

# CHAPTER 8

Silence hung frozen in the air as they all considered what to do next. Clayton was torn. They had to look for Dr. Grouse, but they couldn't leave with a horde of angry aliens outside waiting for them. Tactically, it was suicide.

Dr. Reed was the first to break the silence. "What if we misinterpreted their behavior? They're not all banging on the sides of the shuttle like some angry mob. They're knocking like a civilized species."

"Could be a trick," Delta pointed out.

"That degree of cunning requires a high level of intelligence," Ambassador Morgan added, stepping into the airlock and drawing himself up. "That means this is officially first contact with an intelligent species."

Clayton arched an eyebrow at him. "We don't know that yet. Even a monkey can knock on a door. Besides, that doesn't change the rules of engagement. They can be hostile and intelligent at the same time. Rising to the bait would simply initiate the hostilities. They might be calling us out to answer for what we did to their friends—or family—stunning them. As far as they're concerned, we attacked first. Now it's their turn."

"I disagree," Morgan replied. "As Lori—" He caught himself. "As Dr. Reed pointed out, they would be banging on the sides of the shuttle like actual monkeys if their intentions were hostile."

Clayton shared a dubious look with Commander Taylor. She rolled her eyes. Clayton nodded to the ambassador. "They're aliens. We can't pretend to know how they would act in any given situation. As much as I want to get out and rescue Dr. Grouse, we can't risk more personnel. We'll have to wait for the HEROs to get here. It's the only way to deescalate at this point."

"Because landing an army here won't be escalating conflict," Dr. Reed muttered.

"They can attack the HEROs all day long if they want. They won't even make a dent in the armor."

"I'm sorry, Clayton," Ambassador Morgan said, shaking his head. "But I'm pulling rank here. We don't have that kind of time to waste. They could kill Dr. Grouse while we're waiting, and this might be our only chance to save him."

"And how do you propose we do that? We can't exactly tell these aliens that we mean them no harm."

"We can," Dr. Reed replied. "We'll use the Visualizers to explain ourselves. Then maybe we can get them to wear one and calibrate it so we can have a conversation."

"Too risky," Clayton said again.

"This whole venture is risky," Dr. Reed replied. "We all knew what we were getting into when we signed up."

Delta caught Clayton's eye and gave his head a slight shake.

"Fine, but I'm going out, too," Clayton said.

"No, you're not," Morgan replied.

"Excuse me?" Clayton could feel his blood pressure rising, his face growing hot with it.

"You were the one who opened fire. In fact, all of you shot at them," Morgan said, his eyes skipping between the soldiers. "None of you can come out with us."

Clayton blew out a stale breath. "This is a bad idea."

"Your objections have been noted," Morgan said. "Ready, Dr. Reed?"

She nodded. "Whenever you are."

"Everyone else out of the airlock," Clayton said.

"Sir, you can't be serious!" Delta began. "This is suicide."

"The ambassador has left us no choice. The chain of command is clear. Civilians are in charge when it comes to first contact."

Morgan smiled patiently as they withdrew from the airlock. "Thank you, Captain. We'll be in touch soon."

Clayton glared coldly back. "Not if you're dead."

Morgan looked away, and Dr. Reed shouldered her pack with the Visualizer in it. Clayton keyed the inner doors shut and watched through the small windows in the top of those doors as Reed and Morgan went through decon once more. This time those sprays and radiation pulses were to protect the alien environment from *their* microorganisms. The last thing they needed was to come in peace and wind up killing all the aliens with the equivalent of small pox. The old world meets the new all over again. Clayton opened a sealed compartment in his suit and retrieved his ear piece. He at least needed to stay in comms contact with Dr. Reed and Ambassador Morgan while they were out there.

The flashing lights and misting sprays stopped. A light burned green above the outer airlock doors, and then they parted to reveal a horde of alien monkeys. One of them was right outside the doors. It reared up on four legs to an impressive height, and its other six limbs folded in against its torso like arms.

Clayton tensed up, waiting for it to pounce inside the airlock.

But instead, the alien cocked its brown head and blinked big black eyes at Dr. Reed and Morgan. It backed up a few steps, making room for them to get out.

Dr. Reed slowly unslung her pack, and the creature at the top of the ramp grew agitated. Its neck collar flared out, glowing brightly and rattling in warning. All six of its arms spread wide from its body.

Morgan stepped between them with his hands raised in surrender. He probably thought that was a good idea, but he was unintentionally mimicking the creature's aggressive stance.

"Morgan! Put down your hands!" Clayton screamed over the comms.

# CHAPTER 9

Lori watched Richard step in front of her and raise his hands. The alien's neck collar began rattling louder and more ominously. Lori almost screamed for him to put his hands back down, but screaming would be an equally bad idea right now.

Captain Cross did it for her, his voice booming over the speakers inside their helmets. "Morgan, you idiot! Put down your hands!"

Richard dropped his hands in a hurry, and the alien standing on the ramp slowly lowered its hands, too. All six of them.

Lori removed the Visualizer from her pack. There was just one problem that she and Richard had yet to resolve with the prototypes: they couldn't wear a suit helmet and a Visualizer helmet at the same time. Lori glanced at the readings on her HUD. The air out here was breathable. She'd get light-headed from low oxygen in the thinner air, but she could take it for a while.

Lori unsnapped the seals at her neck. Captain Cross's voice crackled to life almost instantly. "Don't you dare, Lori!"

They hadn't thought this through. She should

have been wearing an O2 mask. Lori pulled off her helmet with a hiss of escaping air from the higher pressure inside her suit. Her ears popped and she sucked in an unfiltered breath of the alien air. It was cold and smelled like cinnamon. A gentle breeze gusted in, and she caught a whiff of something else—the alien in front of her gave off a gamy scent. Lori's head was already swimming from the lack of oxygen. She hurriedly put on the Visualizer helmet, and set the holo projector in front of her.

She raised the visor of the helmet so she could still see, then blanked her mind and focused on transmitting an image of Dr. Grouse.

Dr. Grouse's face appeared, projected above the device. The alien reacted with a sudden hiss and took a quick step back.

Lori tried again. This time, she pictured him wandering around the forest, stumbling in the dark.

The alien cocked its head at her, big eyes blinking, black beak opening and closing restlessly. At least it hadn't tried to attack them yet.

*So far so good,* Lori thought. She tried another image. She showed them Trappist-1E from orbit: a cloud-swept blue and green marble striated with rivers and pocked with lakes. The mountain ridges formed bald black rings around the vegetated areas.

The creature in front of Lori reacted by retracting its glowing neck ring and sinking down to all ten of its limbs. It bowed its head and let out a low growl. The aliens behind it mimicked that posture and the growl—all fifty of them.

Lori frowned at that. They'd gone from hostile to obeisant. What had triggered that reaction? She stared at their planet hovering above the projector. If they had recognized that image, then that meant they'd been up to orbit before. But they weren't even wearing clothes and had no visible weapons or technology of any kind. This species, however intelligent they might be, wasn't space-faring. So who had taken them up to space? And why?

An uneasy chill coursed through her. Black spots danced before her eyes, and a foggy haze filled her head from breathing the thin air. She blinked, and suddenly she was lying flat on the boarding ramp, staring up at Richard's helmet, his expression pinched with worry behind his visor.

"Lori! Lori!" Richard said over the comms. He was slapping her cheek gently to rouse her.

"I'm here." She rose to a sitting position and shook her head to clear it. The aliens were still bowing to them, as if waiting for a command from her.

"Why are they acting like that?" she asked aloud. "They were angry a moment ago."

"Does it matter?" Richard replied. "Try to get one of them to wear a helmet. We need to make this a two-way conversation."

Lori nodded quickly and withdrew a malleable electrode helmet from her bag. She passed it to Richard, not trusting herself to get up and carry it to the creature in front of them. Besides, she'd compromised her suit's integrity. The less contact she had the better. She didn't want to make these aliens sick, or vice versa.

Richard took the helmet to the creature on the landing ramp and said, "Greetings. I am Richard Morgan of the United Nations of Earth."

The creature glanced up to see him standing there, but quickly dropped its head again.

Richard stepped into reach and tried lowering the helmet over its head, expanding the malleable frame to fit.

"Ambassador, I hope you know what you're doing," Captain Cross said.

"So do I," he whispered back.

The creature reacted with a growl, but didn't resist as Richard shaped the helmet to its triangular head. He didn't lower the screen over its eyes. It wouldn't have fit over the creature's beak, anyway.

He hurried back to Lori's side, and she busied herself by mentally issuing commands to the holo-projector. She linked it to both helmets and divided the projection into two—the left side for the alien's messages, right for hers.

The left side was hazy and flickering with indistinct images. The helmet still had to be calibrated. Lori took a deep breath, feeling faint again. Under ideal circumstances she would have had hours to calibrate the device, but right now she had only a few seconds. Using her side of the holo projector to pull up a calibration interface, she began hunting for visual signals in the mess of activity going on inside the alien's head.

Every time she picked out a halfway discernible image on the alien's side of the projector, she tagged and prioritized those neural pathways. The images became progressively clearer, gradually snapping into blurry focus. It was an image of Alpha Team walking through the forest, seen from above, the beams of their helmet lamps sweeping back and forth.

The alien looked up, saw the imagery, and its eyes flared wide. A hiss escaped from its beak and its collar flared out briefly before flattening once more.

Lori tried showing them the image of their world from orbit again. This time she added an image of the *Forerunner,* as seen from their shuttle flying down to Trappist-1E.

A reciprocal image flickered to life on the alien's side. It was peering down on its own world from orbit, standing in front of a broad window on a matte gray surface. But something was different. The planet had all the right colors —blue-green with white streaks of cloud, but it lacked the black rings of mountains. The impact craters were missing.

Maybe this was a different planet. Either way

she was right. They had been up to space. But *were* they space-faring? Had she been wrong about that? She tried picturing one of these ten-legged aliens in a spacesuit that looked vaguely like a Space Force uniform.

The alien's side of the Visualizer blanked, then returned. It showed the same scene from orbit, but this time bright, glowing orange balls were flashing down and vanishing against the planet below. Moments later they bloomed into dazzling flashes of light and angry black clouds of debris rolled across the surface of the world.

The craters. Was this the meteor storm that had scarred their world?

Then the scene shifted to one side, and black teardrop-shaped vessels flashed into view. Bright blue thrusters glowed behind them, and more glowing orange balls were raining down from them.

The scene clicked in Lori's brain. Spaceships. Weapons. This was an orbital attack.

She gasped.

"Holy shit..." Commander Taylor muttered over the comms. Lori glanced back to see her and Captain Cross pressing their faces to the windows in the outer doors of the shuttle's airlock. They had their helmets on, ready to come out with guns blazing at a moment's notice. Lori waved them away and summoned another mental image.

She showed the planet without the black

rings of the mountain ranges, just as the alien had shown her. Then she showed the same scene that it had, with those fiery orange missiles raining down, followed by an orbital view of the planet as it was now: with the rims of blast craters dividing the jungles.

The alien replied by repeating the same before and after images of the planet. This time the imagery was accompanied by a soft whistling sound. Pain? Sadness?

It was confirmation enough for her.

"What does it mean?" Richard asked.

Lori was too light-headed to reply. The black spots dancing before her eyes converged into a solid sheet of black, and time dragged into an endless moment.

She woke up lying on her back inside the airlock with an oxygen mask on and Doctor Stevens crouching over her with an empty syringe. He was still wearing his helmet. She was now a potential source of contamination. Quarantine measures were in effect.

"What..." Lori rocked her head from side to side. "What happened?" she asked, her voice muffled by the oxygen mask. She pushed up onto elbows and twisted to look at the outer doors. Doctor Stevens was the only one in the airlock with her. The inner doors were also shut. "Where is everyone?"

"They left," Stevens replied. "To go look for Dr. Grouse."

"I have to join them! They'll need my help to communicate with—"

Stevens pushed her back down gently and shook his head. "You need to rest. Let the Captain handle it."

"But what if they start shooting again?"

"The aliens are more docile now. You seem to have earned their respect."

Lori thought back over the exchange. They'd 'talked' about a cataclysmic attack on this planet, but it must have happened a long time ago, since the jungles had all grown back to fill in the blast craters.

That alien had told her about the last first contact event in their history. This was the second such event. And to them, both meetings were somehow linked. That realization struck her like a lightning bolt. "I didn't earn their respect. They're *afraid* of us. They might even think we are the ones who attacked them all those years ago."

Doctor Stevens frowned behind his helmet, and the lines of his craggy face multiplied. "Even if that's true, a healthy dose of fear will help keep us safe. It might not be a bad thing."

Lori rocked her head again. "You think that's okay? Claiming responsibility for attempted genocide against their people?"

"Maybe you're wrong," Stevens said. "Maybe you misunderstood. Visualizers are hardly a precise form of communications."

"Maybe," Lori admitted. "Or maybe I'm right. Regardless, you realize what this means, don't you?"

Doctor Stevens' expression grew grave behind his helmet. "Yes. It means that there may be two intelligent species on this planet besides ourselves."

Lori nodded. "We've met the natives, but we have yet to meet the genocidal invaders."

"Let's hope that we never do."

# CHAPTER 10

"Commander, activate Dr. Grouse's emergency locator beacon and share the results with us please," Clayton said as soon as they left the airlock. The aliens were still there, crouching in the blue-green grass with their heads bowed, but there were fewer of them than before. They parted quickly to make way for Clayton and his crew as they descended the boarding ramp. Delta and Commander Taylor kept wary aim on them with their coil guns. Clayton had a firm grip on his own weapon, just in case.

"I've got a signal," Commander Taylor said. "It's weak... flickering. Roughly three klicks from here."

"Three klicks," Clayton muttered, staring at the red dot of Dr. Grouse's locator beacon on the miniature map in the top left of his HUD. Three kilometers over rough terrain. Average walking speed was around five klicks per hour. He checked his air. One hour and five minutes. They'd have to move fast to get there and back.

"Air supply check," Clayton ordered as he strode for the forest.

Everyone reported in one after another saying they had just over an hour of air left. It was enough, but barely.

"He's just sitting there," Ambassador Morgan said. "Why isn't he moving?"

"Could be wounded," Delta said.

"Should we go back for Doc?" Commander Taylor asked.

"No," Clayton replied. "He needs to watch Dr. Reed for any adverse reactions after breathing the air down here. Besides, we all have first aid training."

They plunged into the trees and darkness enveloped them once more. They snapped their ring lights on. Delta and Commander Taylor began scanning the treetops. Leaves from the first canopy formed a hazy ceiling about a hundred meters up.

"You think the other monkeys got the memo?" Delta asked.

"The memo?" the ambassador asked.

"That we're the good guys."

"Are we?" Commander Taylor countered.

They left that question hanging. *Time will tell,* Clayton thought. Founding a human colony on this world was bound to lead to friction with the natives. The Native Americans had been friendly enough to European settlers until they'd begun colonizing in earnest.

The eerie glow of phosphorescent vegetation on the forest floor competed with the beams of their head lamps as they tracked toward the blinking red dot of Dr. Grouse's locator. Massive trees swept by them, bigger than any redwood back home. These trees had to be ancient. So how long ago had that invasion taken place? And how did these alien monkeys still remember it?

"We need a name for them," Ambassador Morgan said suddenly.

Silence answered him.

Clayton decided to bite. "I assume you have a suggestion."

"What about Trappans? Or Trappians?"

"I like monkeys," Delta said. "Call it what it is."

"They have ten legs and they evolved on another planet," the ambassador objected. "And they have beaks like birds, and quills like porcupines. They are hardly analogous to monkeys from Earth."

"Po-tay-to, po-tah-to."

"How about we call *you* a monkey?" Morgan replied.

Delta glared at him, and Morgan shut up. Commander Taylor and Clayton traded grim smiles.

Rainbow bugs began spiraling around them, making the forest seem wondrous and beautiful rather than sinister or dangerous.

They walked on, the minutes passing slowly. Every now and then they caught a gleam of alien eyes watching them from the trees, but this time nothing leaped down on them, and no glowing neck collars flared out to blind them. A low rattling sound followed them through the forest, however. To Clayton that said it all. *We'll let you walk around in our forest, but we don't have to like it.*

As they drew near to the red dot blinking on Clayton's HUD, he turned and nodded to the others. "Eyes and ears everyone. We're coming up on Dr. Grouse's location now."

"He still hasn't moved..." Commander Taylor pointed out. "It's been almost thirty minutes. I hate to say it but..."

"Then don't, Commander," Clayton replied. "No one is dying today."

"Unless they're already dead," Ambassador Morgan muttered.

Clayton chose not to repeat himself. They'd see soon enough.

"Fifteen meters..." he said.

A pair of massive trees were flanking Dr. Grouse's location, but there was no sign of him lying in the rotting carpet of fallen leaves or the faintly glowing underbrush.

"Where is he?" Commander Taylor asked.

"Doctor Grouse!" Clayton called out, trying him on an open comms channel as they covered the last few steps to his location.

Static was the only reply.

He activated his helmet's external speakers and tried again. "Doctor Grouse! Say something if you can hear me!"

Still no answer.

They reached the exact spot of the locator beacon, but they still couldn't see him. Everyone cast about, searching the forest floor with their head lamps.

"He has to be here..." Taylor said. She got down on her haunches and began clearing away spongy masses of rotting vegetation at their feet. Clayton watched intently, expecting to see a hand or foot sticking out... or maybe a broken helmet with dead, staring eyes.

But there was no sign of Dr. Grouse anywhere. Taylor straightened with an irritated sigh, shaking her hands and flinging away stringy gobs of muck and rotting leaves.

"I don't get it," Ambassador Morgan said. "His locator is broadcasting from here."

"He has to be around here somewhere," Taylor insisted.

"Maybe it's just the tracker," Delta added in a low voice. "Something chewed him up and spat out his implant."

Clayton was just about to reply when he saw something of interest. A nearby tree had a giant cleft in the trunk, a shadowy hollow where something—or someone—could be hiding.

Being more optimistic, Clayton thought maybe Dr. Grouse had dragged himself in there to hide from his attackers. He walked wordlessly over to the tree and shone his light into the gap in the trunk. Shadows parted and...

Nothing. It was just a cavernous hole in a tree.

Delta and Commander Taylor came up behind him, adding the beams of their lights to his.

Clayton stepped inside and began feeling around through the mess of leaves and roots on the floor of the arboreal cave. It was big enough in here to fit a small house. He moved around in circles, feeling through the ground cover for what they all knew they were really looking for: a body.

Clayton's hand grazed something. A chill raced down his spine as he felt what he thought was a hand.

He pulled on it, expecting to uncover the body that the Trappans had buried here. Instead, his arm pulled taut against a handle. Something groaned, and the floor lifted up, leaves and all.

Taylor gasped, and Delta jumped back, his rifle snapping up.

"What in the..." Clayton heaved, putting his back into it. A metal hatch covered in dirt and leaves folded away to reveal a long sloping path snaking down into darkness.

"Shit," Delta muttered.

"I'm getting a stronger signal from Dr. Grouse," Taylor said. "He's definitely down there somewhere."

"I thought we were right on top of the signal?" Ambassador Morgan asked.

"We were, but we were tracking in 2D," Taylor explained. "We didn't think to check vertical displacement. He's sixty meters down.

Clayton grimaced. "That's the height of a small skyscraper. So much for the Trappans being peaceful."

"Or primitive," Delta said. "You'd need heavy machinery to dig a tunnel that deep. They probably hit bedrock after the first ten meters or so."

"Not likely," Commander Taylor said. "The trees here are massive, so the soil must run very deep. Let's not make too many assumptions yet."

"We have just over thirty minutes of air left," Clayton said. "How far do you think we're talking to get to the locator beacon?"

"Hard to say. If the slope stays constant, maybe one meter down for every five meters forward... about three hundred meters from here."

"That won't take more than a few minutes," Clayton decided.

"If we run the whole way back, we'll make it," Taylor added.

"And if we don't?" Morgan asked. "We'll have to take off our helmets and breathe the air."

"Then we'll share the same fate as your girlfriend," Clayton replied.

Morgan bristled at the outing of his supposed-to-be secret affair. What he and Dr. Reed didn't know was that it had never been a secret. Spaceships are far too small for secrets to last long.

"The real problem isn't possible contamination; it's passing out from a lack of oxygen," Taylor said. "Taking off our helmets will only buy us another ten minutes."

"Then I guess we'd better hurry," Clayton said. Gripping his coil gun in both hands, he started down into the tunnel. "Alphas, on me."

"I got your back, sir," Delta replied.

# CHAPTER 11

Booted feet echoed down the trail behind Clayton, thumping with quasi-hollow reports in the root-filled ground. Those roots were everywhere, jutting like hairs from the walls of the tunnel, but the walls were otherwise smooth and hard, as if they'd been paved with concrete, or carved out of solid rock.

Darkness was thick and heavy at the end of the tunnel. Light from their headlamps vanished into empty space as the path snaked down endlessly before them. Watching the map on his HUD, Clayton realized they were winding down in lazy circles, a corkscrew spiral into the bowels of Trappist-1E.

Delta was close behind him, his breathing loud over the comms. "I don't like this, sir. We have no idea what we're walking into, and I'm pretty sure this is the only way in or out."

"We can't leave Dr. Grouse down here, Lieutenant," Clayton replied, shaking his head.

"Yes, sir..." Delta sighed.

"What if he's already dead?" Ambassador Morgan asked from the back of the group.

"His life signs are steady," Commander Taylor

replied. "That means he's alive."

The trail wound around another circle, still no end in sight. Clayton glanced at the map. The beacon was just nine meters away. They rounded another corner and he half expected to find Dr. Grouse lying on the trail, half-eaten, barely alive...

Instead, their headlamps flashed off a reflective surface. A metal door. Clayton stopped, his rifle's stock pressed hard into his shoulder as he sighted down the barrel, waiting for that door to burst open.

"Still think they're primitives?" Delta asked.

Clayton checked the range to the beacon: five meters. Then he checked his remaining air: twenty-nine minutes. They needed to get in and out fast if they were going to make it back to the shuttle without taking off their helmets.

"No sign of a door handle," Taylor said.

Delta replied, "Maybe it opens automatically. Keyed to a remote or biometrics."

"Doesn't matter," Clayton said. "Let's make a hole."

"On it, sir." Delta stepped past Clayton and dropped to his haunches to examine the barrier.

"Back it up," Clayton ordered as he matched action to words. The others shuffled away with him until they'd ducked around the nearest bend in the tunnel.

Delta laid a remote-detonating charge in front of the door and hurried to join them. "Fire in the hole!" he yelled.

A muffled boom rumbled through the tunnel, and a blast of air whipped by them. "On me," Clayton said before taking his coil gun in a two-handed grip and stalking back around the corner.

The tunnel was bathed in smoke, but Clayton could see that the chamber on the other side of the door was brightly-lit. His gut told him this was a mistake, but it was too late to back out now. He inched forward, hands sweating inside his gloves as he crept toward the ragged, glowing metal frame where the door had been a moment ago.

"Activate infrared overlays," Clayton whispered.

Acknowledging clicks answered over the comms.

Clayton scanned for heat signatures through the smoke as he neared the broken door. Of course, the Trappans could be cold-blooded, but it was the best he could do.

Stepping through the hole, Clayton emerged in a gleaming metal chamber with high, echoing ceilings that stretched into darkness above them. The floor was made of something like polished concrete, and they were surrounded by strangely-colored holograms and oddly crafted control consoles. Those displays and consoles crawled high up the curving walls. He wondered how anything could access the upper levels, but a metal rail running in front of the displays made him think of a tram. Equipment beeped steadily from the distant recesses of the chamber. Rows of what looked like cubicles lay at the far end. They had open ceilings, but were surrounded by four walls, and each of them had a glass door.

"What is this place?" Ambassador Morgan asked over the comms.

"It looks like a lab of some kind," Commander Taylor ventured.

Clayton nodded along with that, but one look at the nearest *chair* told him that it wasn't designed for the ten-legged Trappans. Metal rails ran in front of the ground level consoles, too.

*It's a perch,* Clayton realized. He peered up into the shadowy recesses of the ceiling once more. The high ceilings were another clue. "I think an avian species built this," Clayton said, searching the shadows with his infrared overlay for signs of life.

Not a blip.

"Not the Trappans, then," Ambassador Morgan replied.

"No," Clayton confirmed, bringing his gaze back down. Dr. Grouse's beacon was coming from the cubicles at the back. He swallowed hard, his skin crawling with terror. "Whoever they are, they're not here now. Let's get Dr. Grouse and RTB." Clayton stalked toward the tracking signal.

"RTB?" Ambassador Morgan asked.

"Return to base," Commander Taylor supplied.

They reached the first of several cubicles and Clayton peered in through the glass door. A big metal bed with a Trappan strapped to it filled the room. All ten of its legs were draped over the sides, and the creature's head was encased in a gleaming helmet with wires trailing to a nearby console. Equipment beeped steadily around the creature, and a bundle of tubes trailed from its chest.

"Found him!" Commander Taylor crowed.

Clayton whirled around to find her standing at the final door on the right. Clayton counted doors to ten cubicles as he ran to join her. Half of them were filled with Trappans, the other half empty.

"We need to get this door open," Taylor said while struggling with a horizontal metal loop for a handle. It was located down near the floor, just two feet off the ground—a clue that the aliens who'd built this place must be relatively short.

"Shit," Delta said as he crowded in and peered through the glass door.

Dr. Grouse was lying on a metal bed that was ten sizes too big for him, strapped down, and apparently unconscious. His helmet was off, cast away to one side, but he had a breathing mask on, and another helmet covered his scalp. Whoever or whatever had put him in here must have understood his body's needs for higher concentrations of oxygen than the local air could provide.

Just like the Trappan in the first room, wires trailed from Dr. Grouse's helmet to a nearby console, and he also had three fat tubes snaking out of his chest. One was blood red, another black, and another clear.

"Just break the door," Clayton said.

Taylor was still trying to force it open. "Yes, sir." She straightened and flipped her coil gun around, hammering the glass with the butt of the weapon.

Not a crack.

"Damn it, it's strong!" Commander Taylor said.

"Delta, you give it a try—no offense, Commander."

She stepped back. "None taken, sir."

Delta could bench four hundred pounds in Earth gravity. Down here at point seven $G$s, he could probably lift a small car. He stepped up and hammered the door just as Commander Taylor had done.

Same result. He tried twice more without effect and then stepped back, breathing hard and rolling out his shoulders. "No can do, sir. We'll have to blast it open."

"If we do that, we risk injuring Dr. Grouse." Clayton glanced up to the top of the wall. One of them could probably reach the rim with a boost.

"We'll climb over." He bent to one knee and cupped his hands. "Commander, you're up!"

She stepped into his hands and he launched her up to the top of the wall. She grabbed it and pulled herself over. A moment later, she hit the deck on the other side of the door and waved through the glass. She spent a moment examining that door from the other side, then bent down. Something *thunked* and the door slid aside. Clayton hurried through.

"It was locked from the inside," Commander Taylor said, pointing to a simple mechanical bolt on the inside.

No key or automatic mechanism would open that. It meant that whoever was running this place usually came in from the air. The doors were probably just there to drag the subjects in and out.

Clayton glanced up again into the deepening shadows of the ceiling, half-expecting to see eyes peering down.

He didn't see any, but that didn't mean they weren't being watched. He nodded toward Dr. Grouse and crossed the cubicle to reach his side. "Commander, help me disconnect him." The tubes snaking from Dr. Grouse's chest could be dangerous to remove. Damn it if Taylor hadn't been right about going back for Doctor Stevens. He went to try the helmet first, grabbing it in both hands and easing it off. It slid off easily, revealing trickles of dried blood around Dr.

Grouse's ears. He set the helmet down on the floor and breathed out a shaky sigh.

Taylor was using her multi-tool to cut Dr. Grouse's suit away around the bundle of tubes protruding from his chest. A rubbery sucker was attached to the end of that bundle of tubes, and it was connected directly to Dr. Grouse's sternum. Had they drilled holes through his chest?

Clayton grimaced.

"There's no easy way to do this," Commander Taylor concluded.

Clayton nodded quickly. His air was down to twenty minutes. Even at a flat sprint they weren't going to make it back in time. Hopefully by now the HEROs had landed and they could call for them to come with spare O2 packs. "Give me an action plan, Commander."

"We cut the lines and tie them off. Let Doc deal with extracting the catheter."

"Big ass catheter," Delta said.

"Do it, Commander," Clayton replied.

Taylor folded out the serrated knife on her multi-tool and grabbed the bundle of tubes about a foot away from Dr. Grouse's chest. She bent them to put a kink in the lines and a piece of equipment began screaming somewhere in the room. An alarm had just sounded.

"Better hurry!" Delta said.

Taylor sliced all three tubes with a quick flick of the wrist. Blood and other unknown fluids spurted all over her suit. The lines still connected to the machines sprinkled all of them, twisting and snaking through the room under the pressure of the fluids pumping through them. Delta grabbed those tubes and tied them off just as Taylor did the same with the ends still attached to Dr. Grouse's chest.

That alarm continued shrieking.

Clayton kept his eyes on the shadowy ceiling, tracking back and forth with his coil gun.

"He's still unconscious," the ambassador said.

Clayton almost didn't hear what he said. He could have sworn he'd just seen something moving around up there.

"Get him up!" Clayton snapped.

"What about his air supply?" Taylor replied, looking at the black mask over his mouth and nose.

"Put his helmet back on. Hopefully he has some air left."

"Yes, sir," she replied, and went to collect his helmet.

Another wraith-like shimmer disturbed the hazy darkness above. A flash of dim red light followed.

*Eyes?* Clayton's heart hammered hard in his chest, his breathing fast and ragged. His gaze snapped down for a split-second, just in time to see Delta slinging Dr. Grouse over his back and shoulders.

"Move out," Clayton said, already stepping through the door. His eyes flicked between the ceiling and the jagged hole that they'd blown in the subterranean entrance to this place. Clayton was beginning to suspect there was a ground level access somewhere in the darkened hollows of the ceiling.

Just before they reached the exit, Clayton heard a loud *whooshing* sound, and his eyes snapped up to see a black shape plummeting down. Translucent wings spread wide just before it landed in front of them. It stood only waist-high, but its wingspan had to be at least twelve feet.

Guns snapped up with a clattering sound.

"Hold your fire!" Ambassador Morgan said, stepping forward with his hands raised. He really hadn't learned about that.

The ambassador and alien stood facing off with each other for a silent, breathless moment.

Clayton studied the creature as it folded its wings away against its back. Two short legs with vicious talons were planted on the ground, and two slender arms were curled up against the creature's chest. Sharp red eyes glared at them out of a bony head with streamlined features and hairless, translucent skin that revealed a fish scale pattern of black veins running through it. Four short tentacles rose from the back of its head that rotated independently in a new direction each time one of them made a sound. Ears of some kind. The creature wore a black mask with a grille over what was probably its mouth

JASPER T. SCOTT

and nose, and a matte black suit with a vague fish scale pattern covered its torso. The suit was cut away at the feet, arms, and wings.

"We left the Visualizer with Reed at the shuttle," Taylor whispered over the comms.

Clayton risked glancing back down to the cubicles. Dr. Grouse had a pack with a Visualizer in it when he'd gone missing. Where was it now?

"Greetings in the name of the United Nations of Earth," Ambassador Morgan tried, as if this thing would understand him.

The creature chattered something in a sing-song voice. Silence followed.

Clayton glanced at his air supply. Fourteen minutes and twelve seconds. "We need to get out of here, Ambassador..."

The winged creature chattered something else and ghostly-white membranes nictated over red eyes, turning them a rheumy color.

Clayton took a step toward it and pointed to Dr. Grouse. "We need to get him out of here. He'll die if we don't get him oxygen soon." Clayton hoped the creature would at least understand his tone if not his words.

Another sing-song reply. Clayton advanced another step, and it stepped away from him.

Was it afraid of him?

"Captain, look out!" Commander Taylor cried. Hands seized his shoulders and pulled him roughly aside.

A bright green flash of light dazzled Clayton

eyes, and a puff of red mist exploded from Commander Taylor's back.

Clayton's heart froze and his coil gun snapped up. The creature's wings flared out and *whooshed* as it leapt off the floor.

Both Clayton and Delta tracked it and opened fire as Taylor sank to her knees.

The coil guns erupted with bright white muzzle flashes as hypervelocity rounds leapt out and punched hard into the alien soaring over their heads.

The creature cried out and black blood gushed over them as it careened to the deck. It landed with a *thud* and lay still. Clayton stared at it for a breathless second, and then Taylor flopped onto her face.

"Keera!" he cried, her last name no longer good enough to convey the depth of his concern.

# CHAPTER 12

Clayton landed on his knees beside Taylor and rolled her over. Her helmet was splashed with blood from the inside. Her chest was a blackened scorch mark where the alien had shot her.

Delta crowded in with a gasp and a muttered curse. "No life signs, sir."

Morgan crouched into view as Clayton unsnapped the seals of Taylor's helmet with shaking hands. "Is she..."

Clayton removed the helmet to reveal what they all already knew. Blank, staring eyes greeted them. Clayton stood up, casting about with his weapon for targets. His whole body shivered with adrenaline and rage.

"We need to go, sir," Delta said as he crouched down to pick up Dr. Grouse's unconscious form. "There could be more of them up there. Or on their way down."

"I agree," the ambassador put in.

Clayton warred with himself briefly over what to do with the body. He wanted to take Taylor back with them, but he needed his hands free for his rifle. "Morgan! Pick her up."

"Me? H-how?"

"Over your shoulders. Hurry up."

The ambassador bent down and slung Commander Taylor's body over his shoulders. He straightened with a grunt of effort and shaking legs.

"Good." Clayton grabbed his weapon in both hands and turned for the exit. "Everyone on me."

They pounded back up the winding trail, headlamps bobbing and flashing over the root-invaded walls.

Before they'd even made it halfway up, Morgan collapsed and cried out, "Wait! I can't... I need a break..."

Clayton glared at him. No one else could afford to carry Taylor, and stopping every half a klick for Morgan to recover was just going to get them all killed. "We'll have to leave her," he gritted out. "Keep moving!"

A few minutes later, they burst out into the gloomy forest, and Clayton got on the comms to Doctor Stevens as they ran.

"Sir?" he answered.

"Are the HEROs there yet?"

"Yes, sir. I've ordered them to fan out and protect the landing site."

"I need you to send four of them to my location with fresh O2."

"Copy that. Just four? You were unable to recover Dr. Grouse?"

Clayton's breath caught in his throat. "We did,

but Commander Taylor didn't make it."

Silence was loud on the other end of the comms. "Understood, sir," Stevens said in a low voice. "HEROs on their way."

"Good. Cross out," Clayton said.

Trees flashed by in a blur. Glimmering rainbow bugs danced. They jumped over fallen branches and logs, not daring to slow down.

Ten minutes passed and Clayton's remaining air became four zeros, flashing red at the bottom of his HUD.

"I'm out!" Delta gasped. "Have to get this bucket off!"

"One minute left," the ambassador added.

Clayton stopped and turned to see Delta stumble and stagger before laying Dr. Grouse out on the forest floor and pulling off his helmet. He sucked in deep, desperate breaths of the alien air.

Clayton's head swam, dark spots crowding in, a warning that he was just seconds away from being forced to do the same. He was just about to contact Stevens and ask where their air was when a wave of four green dots came racing in on Clayton's HUD map. Cracking branches and thundering feet heralded the HEROs approach even before Clayton saw his headlamp flashing off their metal armor.

*Just in time.* The HEROs arrived and handed over the spare O2 packs. Everyone shouldered off their gear bags and hit the releases for their air packs so the HEROs could replace them. Delta put his helmet back on, and one of the HEROs bent down to replace Dr. Grouse's O2 pack.

Doctor Stevens' voice crackled out of that HERO as it straightened and slowly shook its metal head. "How long has he been unconscious?"

"Unknown, Doc," Clayton replied.

"We need to get him to sickbay on the *Forerunner.*"

Clayton nodded. "Let's move!" He left his empty oxygen pack on the forest floor and waited for Doctor Stevens to pick up Dr. Grouse. Delta aborted a half-hearted attempt to pick the man up himself, and then they were off again, their boots drawing steady thunder from the forest floor.

The clearing appeared, still bright in the light of the planet's unending day. Their shuttle gleamed with the crimson hues of Trappist-1. Another smaller craft with a mirror-smooth black hull sat beside the shuttle—an HAT, or HERO Assault Transport.

The comms crackled with a new voice before they were even halfway from the tree line to the shuttle.

"Captain, *Forerunner* actual here—" Lieutenant Devon broke off, her voice hitching strangely as she spoke.

"*Forerunner,* we're on our way back to you. Get sickbay ready."

"Copy. Better make it quick, sir. We have multiple contacts inbound, hot. Range four hundred and sixty million klicks."

*Contacts.* That word echoed raggedly through Clayton's head as he ran for the airlock of the shuttle.

"What do you mean, *contacts?*" Delta replied, asking before anyone else could.

"Sensors classify them as metallic, low density. They're accelerating toward us."

"ETA?" Clayton asked as his boots touched the bottom of the shuttle's landing ramp. The airlock hissed open to reveal Dr. Reed and Doctor Stevens both standing inside, waving them in. Reed was wearing her helmet again.

A garbled reply came back from Devon as they piled in with the HEROs. Doctor Stevens took a moment to examine Dr. Grouse in person, his hands hesitating over the bundle of tubes protruding from his chest.

"What happened to him?" Stevens asked.

Clayton just shook his head, his attention on the conversation with Devon.

"Say again, *Forerunner*, you're breaking up," Clayton said as Delta shut the outer doors and initiated the decon cycle.

Red lights flashed and decon sprays misted the air.

"Contacts are twenty-two hours out. Repeat, ETA less than *one* Earth day."

Clayton blinked in shock. One day to cover four hundred and sixty million kilometers?

"How fast are they going? And why am I only hearing about this now, Lieutenant?"

"Current velocity is just over ten kilometers per second. Acceleration is one hundred and five meters per second squared, and you're only hearing about this now because sensors didn't pick anything up until now."

Clayton mulled over those details in silence as decon sprays misted his faceplate and ran in glistening rivulets off his suit.

The timing was too much of a coincidence. Those ships had shown up within half an hour of them killing that bird-creature and rescuing Dr. Grouse. Now they'd appeared, seemingly out of nowhere, and were accelerating toward the *Forerunner* at over ten Gs. No living creature that they knew of could survive that kind of acceleration for long.

"Captain, please advise! Should we launch fighters?"

The decontamination sequence ended, and a green light snapped on above the inner doors. They slid open to reveal the interior cabin space and cockpit of the shuttle. "I read you, *Forerunner*. No launches yet. Set an outbound course—one G of acceleration, and wait for us to get there."

"Copy. Outbound, where? Earth?"

"No, not Earth. Just get us away from this planet. We'll set more precise coordinates after I arrive."

"Understood, sir."

"Cross out."

* * *

Lori lay pinned against the outer airlock doors between Delta and Dr. Grouse. The shuttle's thrusters thrummed and roared behind them, the vibrations rattling through Lori's bones.

They'd all been exposed to the air on Trappist-1E, so they were sharing a rudimentary quarantine away from the others inside the airlock. They were all wearing their suits, but Dr. Grouse's suit wasn't fully pressurized thanks to the alien catheter sticking out of his chest.

Stevens needed access to proper scanning equipment and a surgical room to be able to remove it safely. They'd reach the *Forerunner* soon enough. At that point they'd all have to go through rigorous tests to make sure they hadn't been infected by alien microorganisms.

The news from Lieutenant Devon and the *Forerunner* was shocking, but it made perfect sense after Delta had explained to Lori where and how they'd found Dr. Grouse. He'd been the subject of God knows what kinds of tests and experiments.

But he'd only been missing for a little over an hour. Lori hoped that meant they'd rescued him in time—but in time for what?

None of them knew what had been done to him, and this new alien species was clearly both advanced and intelligent. It was staggering to think that they'd made contact with two different sentient species in a matter of just a few hours. Lori couldn't help but think that the second species had something to do with the visions she'd seen from the Trappans. *Birdmen,* Delta had called them. As good a name as any. What Lori wouldn't have given to have met them first, to have had the chance to establish communications with a Visualizer. But Dr. Grouse had already had that chance, and look where it had gotten him.

The deafening roar of the shuttle's thrusters quieted and the acceleration eased. They must have reached orbit. Now the forces pinning them to the airlock doors felt only slightly stronger than regular Earth gravity. Lori let out a shuddering breath and felt a sharp pain from her ribs.

Someone shoved Lori hard in her shoulder. It was Delta. He was pointing to Dr. Grouse. "Look! He's coming to!"

Lori rolled her head to look. Delta was right. Dr. Grouse's hand was twitching. Then his arm. And then his whole body began jumping and skipping against the airlock doors like a fish flopping on the ground.

"He's having a seizure!" Lori pushed off the airlock and straddled him, struggling to remove his helmet. He was foaming at the mouth behind his faceplate. Lori yanked off the helmet with

Dr. Grouse thrashing around under her. His blue eyes were so wide that they were practically leaping out of his head.

Lori heard Delta on the comms. "Doc, we need you in the airlock now!"

"I'm on my way. Hang on!"

Lori struggled to hold Dr. Grouse's head still, to stop him from bashing his skull repeatedly on the outer doors. His eyes rolled around like marbles, his jaws alternately clamping and gaping. She could feel his breathing getting faster and shallower.

"He can't breathe!" she said. And then he stopped thrashing and his chest heaved out one final sigh. "No!" Lori screamed.

Reaching up, she unsnapped the seals of her helmet and threw it off.

"Doctor Reed what are you doing!" Delta said. "He's contaminated!"

"We're *all* contaminated!" she replied as she began administering chest compressions. She paused, hesitating only briefly before pinching his nose shut and giving Dr. Grouse the kiss of life. The inner airlock doors slid open, and Doctor Steven's voice trickled in. "Almost there. Good job Lori. Keep his blood pumping and air in those lungs."

She just nodded. Sweat-matted brown hair fell in front of her eyes.

What felt like only a few seconds later, hands were pulling her away, and Doctor Stevens jammed a big needle into Dr. Grouse's chest beside the trunk of severed tubes still protruding from him.

Dr. Grouse's body jumped. He sucked in a ragged breath and sat up with a scream. He began pawing wide-eyed at the tubes sticking out of his chest.

"Dr. Grouse! No!" Stevens cried, trying to pull his hands away. "Reed, help me!"

She grabbed one arm and pulled it away while Stevens held the other. Dr. Grouse's chest was heaving hard, his eyes wide and terrified, his lips blue and skin waxy and ashen. He looked like death, but he was alive.

"David! Hey! It's okay! You're okay," Lori soothed. He looked to her with those wide, staring eyes and some of the fight went out of him. "You just passed out again," she explained. A small twisting of the truth.

He didn't seem to have heard her. His eyes were out of focus, staring straight through her.

"They know."

"They? What do they know, David?" Lori asked.

He blinked and his eyes finally focused on her. He swallowed visibly and tried again, this time in a rasping voice, "They know where Earth is."

# CHAPTER 13

Clayton left the shuttle airlock at a flat sprint, darting past Doctor Stevens and his three new patients on their way to sickbay. The ship was under one *G* of linear thrust, so moving around felt perfectly natural. Clayton briefly noted on his way out that they had wrangled Dr. Grouse into a new pressure suit, one without the hole around the catheter in his chest. That should keep him from contaminating the air aboard the *Forerunner* while they moved him down to sickbay.

Clayton was also aware of Dr. Grouse's revelation about his avian captors. Apparently, the aliens had used their version of a Visualizer on him, and they'd picked his brain until he had literally bled from his ears.

The ambassador hung back with Dr. Reed, leaving Clayton to run up to the bridge alone. He made contact with Lieutenant Devon before he arrived, asking for an update.

The news wasn't good.

She told him that the inbound alien ships had changed course to match the *Forerunner's* outbound trajectory.

Clayton reached the bridge and used his ARCs to open the doors. Heavy metal slabs rumbled open, and he strode through.

A Marine standing guard inside the doors came to attention and called out, "Captain on deck!"

The rest of the crew rose to their feet.

"At ease!" He strode quickly down the aisle between control stations to reach the forward viewscreens. Lieutenant Devon was waiting for him, her red hair a frizzy mess leaking out of a tangled bun.

"Sir," she said, inclining her head to him as he came to stand beside her. They turned in unison to face the viewscreens.

"Show them to me," he ordered.

The stars on the viewscreens panned swiftly away, scrolling sideways until they came to rest on a cluster of small red target boxes. "Computer, enhance targets to maximum magnification."

Those boxes blew up, zooming in until actual ships and discernible shapes appeared. They were black soul-sucking shadows that barely stood out from the darkness of space, six of them, long and streamlined, as if wind resistance were somehow a factor. Those ships all looked to be the same type. They were flying in a close formation with one in the lead and the others fanning out and trailing behind it with increasing distance. It took Clayton a moment to recognize that formation as a V. *Of course it is,* he thought. But then he checked that thought: these creatures weren't from Earth, so the idea that they might naturally flock together in a V-formation was likely flawed.

"How big are they?" he asked.

"Six hundred and ten meters."

"Six hundred!" Clayton echoed.

The *Forerunner* was only four hundred meters long, and it was the largest class of spaceship that the UNE had ever built.

Clayton blew out a breath. The odds were six against one, and just one of those ships could probably wipe them out in seconds. He was starting to question the wisdom of evacuating to orbit. Maybe they should have all gone down to the surface and run into the forests to hide.

"We need to attempt to establish contact. They need to know that we're not hostile."

"We already tried to hail them, sir," Devon said, shaking her head.

"Then we try again!"

Clayton rounded on the comms officer. An ensign he barely recognized. Reynolds. He had a round face and bright green eyes. Short black hair. Clayton was less familiar with the men and women from Devon's team than he was with his own bridge crew, but there was no point switching them out now.

"Ensign, hail them on every frequency you can think of. Don't stop until you get some kind of response."

"Yes, sir! What's the message, sir?"

The message. There was no way to communicate. No common language. Not even common encryptions. For all he knew trying to hail them with modulated beams of electromagnetic radiation could be interpreted as some type of attack. He grimaced and shook his head. "Never mind. No comms."

"Yes, sir..."

He turned back to the viewscreens.

"What are we going to do, sir?" Devon asked.

"We're going to pray that those aren't warships, Lieutenant, and while we're praying, we're going to arm every missile, rail gun, and laser that we've got and aim them aft at those ships. We're also going to have our fighter pilots standing by and ready to scramble to their Scimitars."

"Yes, sir," Devon replied in a whisper of a voice. She turned and nodded to the officer at the flight ops station. "You heard the captain! Get our pilots suited up and ready to go!"

"Yes, ma'am!"

Clayton stared hard at those streamlined shadows, all six of them somehow racing ahead at ten Gs. If they had live crews on board, how were they able to survive that?

Clayton cleared his head to focus on a strategy. Some plan to dissuade their pursuers or at least a way to give them hell if they couldn't be dissuaded.

The problem was, he had absolutely no idea what kind of threat those ships presented. Were they armed? And if so, with what?

His mind flashed back to the laser weapon that the creature from the lab had used to kill Commander Taylor. It was a bad sign that these aliens had developed such lethal handheld lasers. The ones they mounted on their spaceships would undoubtedly be a lot more powerful. For all Clayton knew, the *Forerunner* might already be inside of the their effective weapons envelope.

* * *

Lori lay strapped to a gurney in sickbay, peering over the tips of her boots at Dr. Grouse and Delta; they were strapped down, too, but the straps were for their safety—in case the ship needed to make any sudden maneuvers.

The idea of a firefight in space was absurd. Just a day ago even first contact with an intelligent alien race would have been a milestone. Now they were talking about a military engagement with one.

Lori couldn't help thinking that it was some kind of misunderstanding. There had to be a way to communicate to these beings that they meant them no harm—that their intentions were peaceful.

Dr. Grouse cried out, and Doctor Stevens barked an order at his assistant. "Get me suction, damn it! Yes! Now more gauze! Pack it in! There..."

The erratic beeping of Dr. Grouse's heart rate monitor set the tone for Lori's own heartbeat. A gloved hand reached into hers and squeezed. It was Richard, smiling down on her through two separate layers of helmets and pressure suits. She wished they could peel those layers away so that he could hold her for real. This was probably the end—death had come for them aboard six, six hundred-meter long starships. Add one more six to that, and it could have been the Devil himself who had come for them.

"There, he's stable," Doctor Stevens declared. Tools clattered to a mag-locked cart, and the doctor came striding over. "You're next," he said, smiling tightly at Lori. "Ready?"

"Next for *what?*" she asked, her eyes on Dr. Grouse's bandage-wrapped chest.

"No, no, just routine testing," Stevens assured. He tried a broader smile to put her at ease.

Lori nodded, but didn't smile back.

The next two hours were filled with tests and scans of every type imaginable for both her and Delta. Stevens eventually left them alone and went to an adjacent lab to check the results. He returned after what felt like an eternity to give them the news.

"You're both clear to leave," he said. "No sign of any alien organisms in your blood, saliva, feces, or urine."

"Great," Lori said. Her eyes strayed once more to her colleague on the gurney opposite hers. "And what about Dr. Grouse?"

Doctor Stevens' expression became cagey behind his helmet. He glanced at Dr. Grouse, lying sedated on his gurney, his chest now stuffed with gauze and wrapped in bandages.

"I'd like to keep him here for further testing."

"That wasn't an answer," Lori pointed out.

"It wasn't meant to be," Stevens replied. "We don't know enough yet about what was done to him."

"Are there alien organisms in his blood?"

Stevens shook his head, but said nothing.

"Come on," Richard said, already unclipping the restraints that pinned her to the gurney. He helped her up, and she swung her legs over the side and dropped to the deck. Across from her, Delta did the same on his own.

"Thanks, Doc," he said, and brushed by them on his way out.

"Remember to wait for the decon cycle before you leave! Don't take off your suit before you've done that," Stevens called after him.

"I'm not an idiot, Doc!" Delta called back.

Stevens looked back to Lori. "There is one other thing."

Fear sent acid boiling up into the back of her throat. "Yes?"

Stevens looked to Richard, then back to her, and put on a grim smile. "This may or may not be good news, but..."

"But?" Lori prompted. "Just get to the point, Stevens."

"You're pregnant."

Lori's world tipped on its end and slid off into absurdity. A giggle escaped her lips, and she shook her head. "You're joking, right?"

"I'm afraid not."

Richard looked to her with a furrowed brow, as if this were her fault.

"But that's impossible!" Lori said. "I have an implant!"

"Implants can malfunction just like any other contraceptive. No birth control is perfect, Dr. Reed."

Richard grabbed Lori's hand again. "This is good news," he said.

"Is it?" Lori challenged. "We're talking about bringing a new life into... into what? Vacuum?" She threw up her hands. "We're all going to be dead soon, so this is neither good nor bad news. It's just another death to tally."

"We don't know that yet," Stevens said quietly.

"He's right," Richard added.

Lori shook her head in frustration. Her throat had constricted with a painful knot, and her eyes were burning with the threat of tears. She turned to leave, stalking after Delta.

This was everything that she had ever wanted, but it was all wrong! She couldn't be happy about an accidental pregnancy soon to be aborted by either her own defective uterus, or by aliens attacking the ship.

"They might not be hostile!" Richard called after her. "They might just want to talk to us!"

But Lori wasn't listening. She couldn't bear to hold onto empty hope. Something very bad was about to happen. If anyone needed any proof of that, they need look no further than Dr. Grouse and Commander Taylor.

*We're all going to die,* Lori thought as she entered the quarantine airlock and initiated the decontamination cycle. Crimson light pulsed all around her, making the decon sprays look like blood.

# CHAPTER 14

**Twenty Hours Later...**

The air on the bridge could have been cut with a knife. It was thick and sour with sweat and fear. Clayton considered himself cool under pressure, but this standoff was even beginning to wear on him. His Scimitar pilots were all sitting in their cockpits, by now their legs probably cramping to the point of paralysis. The gunnery chief on the bridge looked like he could have been wrung out like a wet cloth.

"Lieutenant Devon, any change?" Clayton asked, his eyes fixed on the six black bullet-shaped vessels chasing them away from the pale red star that was Trappist-1. He sat at his control station in the center of the bridge, leaning on the armrests with both elbows, his hands steepled with thumbs out and propping up his chin.

"No change, sir," Devon said from the XO's chair beside him. "Range is holding steady."

He nodded, but gave no reply. The alien ships had closed to just one million klicks without launching a single fighter or firing even so much as a warning shot, and then they'd matched accelerations with the *Forerunner.* Clayton had given his crew strict orders not to launch or fire anything either. He knew they were outgunned. They would be vaporized in seconds if they started a pissing contest. This was like an un-armed hiker running into a grizzly bear in the wild. No sudden moves. Back away slowly.

Clayton let out a breath and rolled his head and shoulders. His neck cracked loudly as he did so. Six hours. The alien ships had been in range of the *Forerunner's* lasers for *six* hours. Surely that meant that the *Forerunner* had been within range of their adversary's guns for a lot longer. The effective range of a laser was a simple function of its power level and the sophistication of its focusing tech. The *Forerunner* could shoot a dust mote at five hundred million klicks and vaporize it, but that wouldn't do anything to an armored target.

"What do they want?" he asked of no one in particular. "They're not closing on us anymore. Not firing their guns. Not trying to contact us in any way..."

Lieutenant Devon glanced at him, her green eyes gleaming in the low light of the bridge and its viewscreens.

"Something on your mind, Lieutenant?"

"Yes, sir. What if they're following us?"

He frowned. "They are. I think you mean *why* are they following us?"

She nodded and supplied the answer. "To get

to Earth."

He grimaced. It had occurred to him, too, but he hadn't wanted to say it aloud. "Let's say that's true. Do you think they're going to follow us for the next seventy-eight years while we fly home?"

"Maybe. Maybe they have cryo pods like us. Or maybe they're immortal and time means nothing to them."

A muscle in Clayton's jaw twitched. "Anything is possible." This was why they hadn't set a course for Earth yet. They couldn't afford to reveal anything else about its location. It was bad enough that Dr. Grouse claimed the aliens had somehow stolen its location from his brain.

"Captain, we are coming up on the heliopause," the officer of the helm announced. "ETA four minutes and seven seconds."

Clayton nodded. "Carry on, Ensign. Alert me once we've crossed it."

"Aye, sir."

Trappist-1 was an ultra-cool red dwarf eleven times smaller than the Sun. Its solar wind was pathetically weak. Even though they'd only traveled about forty million klicks from the star, they were already about to cross the outermost boundary of the solar system, marking their return to interstellar space.

The seconds ticked away with silence gathering like a storm inside of Clayton. His chest felt tight. His head hot. He pulled up a map from his control station, a colorful hologram that hovered in the air before his eyes. He watched a green-shaded 3D icon of the Forerunner inching steadily closer to a sky blue line that circled the system's sun.

They darted across that line, and a subtle vibration shivered through the ship as they crossed the heliopause.

Then something else happened. An alarm squawked.

"Sir! The enemy ships are changing course!" the ensign at the sensors station reported.

"Ready all weapons!" Clayton barked. "Flight ops, tell our pilots to—"

"They're not accelerating, sir," the sensors operator interrupted. "They're peeling away. Look—"

Clayton minimized his map as a more detailed version of it appeared on the forward viewscreens. Six black, bullet-shaped vessels were turning and burning toward Trappist-1, their aft ends glowing bright blue.

"Their acceleration is increasing," Devon said. "Two Gs... four... five... holding steady at five Gs. They're beating a hasty retreat, sir."

Sighs and muttered curses filled the air. People stretched at their stations. Relief flowed out from the crew like a wave. The pressure in Clayton's chest released, and he slumped in his chair. The standoff was over. Even better yet, it looked like these aliens weren't planning to follow the *Forerunner* back to Earth. So why had they wanted to learn its location from Dr. Grouse?

Maybe he was mistaken. Or maybe they were simply curious where humans came from.

Clayton released his safety harness and stood up on creaking knees. "Lieutenant Devon, set condition yellow throughout the ship."

"Yes, sir," she replied. A bright yellow light pulsed through the bridge and an automated voice declared the reduced alert level over the intercom. "Going somewhere?" Devon asked.

"Sick bay. You have the conn, Lieutenant. Alert me the instant anything changes up here."

"Understood, sir. Shall I assume you're going to speak with Doctor Grouse?"

Clayton inclined his head at that. "We need answers."

"With all due respect, sir, what if we already have those answers?"

"Explain."

She unbuckled and rose from her chair. "They escorted us out of their territory. No shots were fired. We killed one of theirs and they killed one of ours. Maybe that puts us even in their books. They're not hostile *per se*, but they're definitely territorial. The message seems pretty clear: *Trappist-1 belongs to us*. Stay away."

Clayton smiled grimly at her assessment. "I agree, but then why all the interest in where we come from?"

"Intel."

He arched an eyebrow at her. "Intel for what? You don't gather intel on your friends. Certainly not by strapping them down and squeezing it out of their brains. So if we're not their friends, then what are we?"

"Just because they know where we come from doesn't mean they want to go there, sir."

"It doesn't mean that they don't, either."

"So why did they break off pursuit?" Devon asked.

Clayton snorted. "They might be waiting for reinforcements. It's been over ninety years since we last saw Earth. By now our orbital defense fleet has probably doubled or tripled in size."

"What could they possibly want from us?" Devon asked, shaking her head.

"That's what I'm going to ask Dr. Grouse."

# CHAPTER 15

Dr. Grouse was awake and sitting up when Clayton walked in wearing a helmet and an O2 pack. The man's skin was waxy and gray, his eyes half-lidded, and his hair had fallen out in giant clumps, leaving bald patches of flaking scalp. Even his arms and beard were bald in places.

Clayton stood off to one side, watching with Doctor Stevens as a corpsman in a pressure suit held a bucket for Dr. Grouse to puke his guts into.

"He's been throwing up for the past six hours straight," Doctor Stevens explained over a private comms channel. The doctor's voice was loud inside Clayton helmet, but it wouldn't carry to Dr. Grouse's ears. "That's why he looks so bad. Well, that, and the virus that's causing it."

"Virus?" Clayton asked. "You mean he's infected with something?"

"Yes, sir. I've never seen anything like it. It spreads so fast you can literally watch it multiply, and it's having a strange, morphological effect on Dr. Grouse's DNA."

"What does that mean?"

"It's making random genetic changes all over the place. Most of the cells it changes simply die,

123

but others are thriving."

"So Dr. Grouse was subjected to some kind of genetic experiment? How is that possible? We were only separated from him for an hour! You're telling me those birds created a designer virus tailored to humans in less than sixty minutes?"

"I don't think this virus was designed for us, sir. I believe it was adapted for us," Stevens said.

"A smart virus?"

"Or at least a configurable one. Regardless, if it continues to progress at this rate, Dr. Grouse will be dead in a matter of hours."

"There's nothing you can do?"

Stevens shook his head. "We could put him in cryo and wait to get home in the hope that specialists on Earth can find a cure. Their tech will be far ahead of ours by the time we arrive. One hundred and eighty years ahead to be exact. That could be enough to save him."

Clayton grimaced and absently rubbed his smart watch through the sleeve of his suit. Hopefully a hundred and eighty years would be enough to save his wife, too.

"Let's do it, but first I need to speak with him."

"Of course, sir."

Clayton led the way to Dr. Grouse's bedside. The man stopped dry-heaving into his bucket and lay back against the gurney with a groan.

"Hi, Captain."

"It's good to see you awake, Dr. Grouse."

"Is it?"

"You're alive."

"I'd rather be dead."

Clayton noticed that Dr. Grouse's eyes were pink and striated with broken blood vessels. There were four lumps on his head, bulging from matching bald spots, as if horns were growing there, but those lumps were at the back of his head. The scalp over them was flaking and red. Clayton pointed to one of the growths. "What is that?" he asked over the comms.

Doctor Stevens shook his head and leaned in closer to examine one of them. "A tumor, perhaps?"

"You haven't done a biopsy?"

"They weren't there fifteen minutes ago."

Fifteen minutes. This virus, whatever it was, was moving incredibly fast. Clayton switched back to external speakers. "Dr. Grouse, I need to ask you a few questions."

"Sure," he rasped, his eyes closing in a wince. His Adam's apple bobbed slowly up and down in his throat.

"What did they do to you?"

"I already told Lori."

"You said to her that they wanted to know where Earth was. What made you think that?"

"You watch holovids, Captain?"

He frowned. "Of course..."

"Imagine watching one in your head. It's playing on a loop, over and over again, flashing in front of your eyes at ten times speed. Everything you know about Earth flashes through your mind's eye in an instant. And then it happens again, and again, and—" Dr. Grouse cut himself off, his stomach heaving visibly as his whole body spasmed, making him buck off the gurney. His cheeks bulged and his mouth parted, but nothing came out. He subsided with a whimper and a ragged cry: "Just kill me!"

Clayton shook his head. "We're going to get you back to Earth and get you the help you need. You're going into cryo before this gets any worse."

Dr. Grouse's head lolled from side to side on the cushioned gurney. "Then hurry up..." he whispered. "I can't..."

"Dr. Grouse, we will. I promise, but this is important: what did the aliens who took you want?"

"There was just one. A flying thing with a mask..."

"We killed him."

"Good," Dr. Grouse croaked.

"What did he want?"

"I told you! Earth."

"And? That's it? Did he tell you anything about them?"

Dr. Grouse rocked his head from side to side again.

"Nothing, not even a vague impression?"

Clayton insisted. "Anything that could help us to characterize their motives would be helpful."

Dr. Grouse's eyelids fluttered, and his heart monitor began beeping erratically. Thin lines of black blood trickled from his eyes. Doctor Stevens leapt into action.

"Get the crash cart!" he barked at the corpsman who'd been holding the bucket for Dr. Grouse.

And then the monitor flat-lined, and Clayton backed away, watching as Doctor Stevens injected something straight into Dr. Grouse's heart. At the same time, the corpsman ripped Dr. Grouse's gown open to expose his bare chest and hurriedly placed patches on either side of his torso.

Clayton's eyes bulged at the sight of Dr. Grouse's hairless chest—not just because he was bald where before he'd been hairy enough to rival a gorilla, but because the skin and bones had become translucent. Dr. Grouse's arteries and his heart were clearly visible inside of his chest.

"Clear!" Stevens yelled, and then shocked Dr. Grouse. His body skipped with that jolt. Stevens waited a beat, then shouted, "Clear!" again. He shocked Grouse twice more to no effect.

A chill coursed down Clayton's spine. Whatever this was, they couldn't let it escape quarantine.

But then a soft, wretched beep escaped from

the heart monitor, followed by another, and then a quick succession of them as Dr. Grouse's pulse raced back up to speed.

Clayton could actually *see* Dr. Grouse's heart fluttering inside of his chest. The man's eyes flew wide, looking more bloodshot than ever, and a gut-wrenching scream tore from his lips. He grabbed Doctor Stevens and pulled him down close, wrapping both hands around Stevens' throat and baring his teeth in a manic, blood-spattered snarl.

Clayton blinked in shock.

"Sedate him!" Doctor Stevens cried.

The corpsman fumbled for a nearby syringe and struggled with shaking hands to fill it from a vial of clear fluid. Clayton ran back over to the gurney and pried at Dr. Grouse's hands—

But he was wickedly strong for a dying man.

Stevens' face was turning purple inside his helmet, and he was slapping Dr. Grouse's thigh repeatedly, as if trying to tap out of a fight.

"Dr. Grouse, let him go!" Clayton screamed.

A watery hiccup escaped Dr. Grouse's lips. Was that a laugh? He coughed up a giant clot of black blood that splattered Clayton's faceplate.

And then suddenly Dr. Grouse's arms went slack and fell away from Doctor Stevens' throat. He collapsed to the deck, choking and coughing, gasping for air.

"What the hell was that?" Clayton demanded, wiping the blood from his faceplate on his sleeve and staring through a smeary crimson haze at Dr. Grouse's now-placid features.

The corpsman stepped away with an empty syringe.

"I don't..." Stevens trailed off with another cough.

Clayton's comms crackled. "Captain, Devon here. I have an urgent update for you. Are you secure?"

Clayton walked away from the gurney and mentally killed his shared comms channel with Doctor Stevens. "I am now," he said. "What's going on, Devon?"

"The ships that were chasing us, sir. They just vanished."

"Vanished? What do you mean they vanished? They passed out of scanning range already?"

"No, sir. They were still well within range, only a few million klicks away. One minute they were there, burning away at five Gs, and the next they were gone."

Clayton's guts clenched and churned. A cold weight settled inside of him, and he felt the blood draining from his face. He remembered the blips that he and Commander Taylor had been secretly tracking on their approach to Trappist-1. The same thing had happened then, too: there one minute, gone the next.

"They must have jumped out," he said, his voice barely a whisper.

"Jumped out, sir?" Lieutenant Devon asked.

"FTL, Lieutenant. They have faster-than-light drives. That, or cloaking tech. Or both." He let that sink in for a second before stating the obvious. "They don't need to follow us to Earth, Devon. They already know where it is, so why wait ninety years for us to lead the way when they can beat us there by decades? For all we know, they could reach Earth inside a month."

Silence and static answered that pronouncement. Clayton stumbled over to the nearest bulkhead and leaned heavily against it. There was nothing either of them could say. All he could think about was those images that the Trappans had shown them. The before and after pictures of their world—how it had looked before the fire and brimstone had rained down from orbit... and how it now looked after: pocked with craters from the attack.

What would the before and after pictures of Earth look like? Clayton sank to the deck, staring at his hands through the smeary crimson veil of Dr. Grouse's blood.

"Let's not assume the worst, sir," Lieutenant Devon whispered. "We don't know that it's FTL. It could be cloaking as you say."

"Then for all we know they could have turned back around to follow us again. That's not any better, Lieutenant."

*We were fools to come here,* he thought. Fools to aspire to meeting other civilizations. Humanity's greatest hubris was to reach for the stars and now it would be their downfall. History had taught them better than this. *But we never learn.*

"What are your orders, sir?"

Clayton just shook his head. *Orders?* The word rattled around in his brain. His instincts took over, supplying the answer from the deepest, most animal recesses of his mind. They had just two options. Fight or flight. Go home and fight, or run away and hide on some other world. If the latter, they would just have to hope and pray that these bird-creatures never found them. And that was no way to live.

"We go home, Lieutenant. We go home and we warn Earth before it's too late."

"Yes, sir, plotting course for—"

"No. Plot a course for Proxima. We'll go there first and send a message ahead. Just in case we *are* being followed."

"Understood, sir."

Clayton eased up onto wooden legs. "One more thing, Lieutenant."

"Sir?"

"Not a word of this gets out. We don't want to incite a panic."

"Yes, sir."

# CHAPTER 16

As soon as Clayton entered the cryo chamber, Ambassador Morgan came striding over. He grabbed Clayton's arm and pulled him aside.

"Captain, you and I both know what could be out there," he whispered. "You need to add me to the crew rotations."

Clayton glared at Ambassador Morgan's hand where it held to his arm. The ambassador seemed to realize that he'd gone too far and removed it.

"You're still a civilian on this ship, Ambassador," Clayton explained. "Only the crew will be rotating in and out of cryo."

"I represent the UNE. I need to be the first to handle any additional interactions with the *Avari*."

Clayton frowned at the name. The ambassador had taken it upon himself to name them. It was better than Birdmen, but not by much. *At least it's less sexist,* he thought.

"We'll wake you if we encounter anything," Clayton replied.

"How do I know that's true?" Morgan countered, his eyes cinching down to slits.

He was right to be suspicious. Clayton had no intention of waking him. They held each other's gaze for a few seconds. Clayton was tempted to leave it at that, but he gave in with a sigh and a nod. He would have to answer to UNE command when he got home. Keeping Morgan out of the loop wasn't worth it. Besides, what was the worst that Morgan could do if they woke him up a few times a year?

Clayton turned to look around for Lieutenant Devon, scanning the myriad heads and faces of colonists and crew crowding the cryo chamber. He spotted her fire-red hair clear across on the other side of the deck. Mentally activating his comms, he contacted her. "Devon. I have the Ambassador here saying he wants to be on the active duty roster. Slot him into the same rotations as me." That meant they'd both be awake once every six months for one week at a time.

"Are you sure, sir?"

"Not much choice. He *is* in charge, after all," Clayton added that with a dry twist of his lips.

Morgan smiled thinly and said, "Add Dr. Reed to the rotation as well. She's the first contact specialist."

"Dr. Reed?" Clayton asked, feeling his brow scrunch up like an accordion. "She's pregnant!"

"Exactly."

"She'll wind up giving birth before we get home. We can't put babies in cryo."

The ambassador nodded. "But you *can* put

toddlers in. When she's ready to give birth, we'll stay awake for the next two years and then all three of us will go back into cryo together."

Clayton was getting ready to put his foot down when Morgan added, "I'm not asking, Captain. I wouldn't want to have to put *insubordination* in my report to the UNE when we get home."

"Devon... add Dr. Reed to the same rotation schedule," Clayton said.

"Copy, sir," Devon replied.

"Captain Cross out." He ended the call and nodded to the ambassador. "Satisfied?"

"Yes." Morgan smiled. "Your cooperation has been noted."

Clayton watched as he turned and walked away, melting back into the crowds of colonists and crew busy lining up for cryo.

Two weeks per year for seventy-eight years. Clayton did the math in his head. That meant he was going to have put up with Morgan for almost three years. At least it was only for a week at a time.

And Dr. Reed... she would reach full term after just eighteen years of rotations—assuming she carried the baby to term. They wouldn't even be a quarter of the way back to Earth by the time she gave birth.

Clayton shook his head to clear it and pushed through the waiting crowds to reach Doctor Stevens. The doc was busy directing corpsmen as they guided the crew into their cryo pods. Blue lights illuminated the tubes from within. Covers swung shut and loud hissing sounds escaped as the occupants were placed in cryonic suspension.

Clayton bumped into Dr. Reed before he could reach Stevens.

"Captain," she said. "Did Richard—I mean Ambassador Morgan have a chance to speak with you?"

"Yes." Clayton flattened his mouth and shook his head.

She looked crestfallen. Her hands fell self-consciously to her abdomen. "Please. I have to have her before we get back."

"Her?" Clayton asked. "Isn't it too soon to tell what sex the baby is?"

Dr. Reed's lips quirked into a tentative smile. "Well, I *think* it's a she, but I guess we'll see."

"If you have her on board, you'll be stuck on The Wheel with her for two whole years."

Dr. Reed nodded. "I know."

The Wheel was exactly what it sounded like: a giant, spinning wheel with spokes to connect it to the middle of the ship. It was usually empty, but for long voyages where the crew would be awake for extended periods, The Wheel could be spun up to simulate Earth's gravity. It was the only way for Dr. Reed and Morgan to safely raise their child on the ship until it was old enough to rotate in and out of cryo.

"Are you sure about this?" Clayton asked.

"Positive."

"Then I guess we'll see each other in six months."

"Six months?"

"I had Devon add you and Ambassador Morgan to my rotations. We're going to be seeing a lot more of each other before that baby is born—and after, I suppose."

Dr. Reed smiled and nodded, rubbing her flat stomach. "Thank you, sir. You have no idea how much this means to me—to us."

Clayton smiled tightly and nodded back, his gaze already straying to Doctor Stevens.

"It's not for sure yet, because, well... you know, we don't actually know the sex, but I was thinking about calling her Keera. In honor of Commander Taylor."

A knot rose into Clayton's throat with the reminder of his late XO. She was lying dead and rotting in that underground lab back on Trappist-1E. He fought back tears, and spoke in a gravelly whisper, "She would be honored."

Dr. Reed smiled. "If it's a boy, we're thinking Keeran."

"He or she, that kid is going to have some big boots to fill."

"She'll have time to grow into them," Dr. Reed replied.

Clayton was struggling to hold it together. If he had to deal with this for even a second longer, he was going to lose it. He cleared his throat and said, "Excuse me."

Walking on to the front of the nearest line of people waiting to enter cryo, he found Doctor Stevens and said, "How are we doing, Doc?"

Corpsmen walked around the circumference of the chamber, checking readout screens and settings on their control tablets before triggering pods shut. The pods sealed with a steaming hiss of flash-freezing cryo fluids and condensing moisture that curled out along the deck like smoke.

Doctor Stevens turned away from supervising the process. "Everything is going very well. At this rate, we'll have everyone in cryo within the hour."

The corpsmen shut the last of the pods on the deck, and then Doctor Stevens said, "Next section, please!"

The cryo pods shifted from forty-five degrees to vertical with a collective groan of machinery, followed by a loud *clunk* of locking bolts. Then those pods sank down to the deck below and the ones from the level above came sliding down. The cryo pods were built into rotating belts that circulated between the outer and inner hulls so that they could be filled or emptied one ring at a time on this level. Glass covers popped open—all except for one, which remained shut and illuminated, indicating that it was already occupied.

Clayton pointed to it. "Is that Dr. Grouse's pod?"

"Yes," Doctor Stevens confirmed.

They'd placed him in cryo yesterday, before any more of him could mutate and die.

"Did you need something, Captain?" Doctor Stevens asked, his bushy gray eyebrows drifting up.

Clayton watched corpsmen waving to the next people in line. They injected sedatives and guided colonists and crew stumbling into their pods, their eyes already heavy with sleep.

Sleep sounded good right about now. Clayton hadn't been getting much of it lately. There were too many ghosts inside his head, and his sleep paralysis was getting worse.

"Yes..." Clayton trailed off, dragging his eyes away from the pods. "I'd like to jump the queue."

Stevens' rugged features screwed up in confusion. "You want me to put you in next?"

"Yes."

"May I ask why?"

Clayton drew in a shaky breath. He was the captain; he was supposed to set an example. How could he explain that all of this waiting around was just too much, that he couldn't stand to be awake for another second because now he had two people haunting him: the wife he'd lost, and the work wife who'd stood by his side through Samara's funeral, his subsequent depression, and everything in-between. Keera Taylor was *dead*, and he didn't even have the delusional dream of someday bringing her back from a mind map. Clayton glanced at his smart watch and Samara's smiling face appeared. Everything that she had ever been was condensed down to a single picture and a string of ones and zeros etched into a crystal matrix. The sheer absurdity of that fully struck him for the first time.

"Sir?" Stevens prompted.

He jerked his head up with a crumbling smile. "Yes, I'd like to go next."

"Of course..." Stevens snapped his fingers to a nearby corpsman. That man paused just before he could inject someone else with a sedative. "Over here, Sellis; Captain Cross is next."

The corpsman nodded and walked over with a bemused frown. "This way, please, sir."

Clayton let Sellis lead him to an empty pod. "Ready?"

"When you are, Corpsman. Need me to roll up my sleeve?"

"No, sir. It self-sterilizes." Sellis said, and then stabbed him with the needle.

The pain was like a bee sting, but it lasted for only a second before a spreading warmth overtook it. That feeling cascaded down to his knees making them feel weak. A blissful sigh escaped Clayton's lips as the corpsman led him into the nearest pod.

"See you next rotation, sir," Stevens said, crowding into view and tossing a quick salute.

Clayton tried to return it, but failed to raise his arm. His eyes sank shut and the sound of his pod groaning shut came distantly to his ears, followed by a loud *hiss* that snuffed out all the light and warmth left in his being.

# THE LONG
# JOURNEY HOME

# CHAPTER 17

**Ten Years Later...**

*—2160 AD—*
*35.42 Light Years from Earth*

"Y̲ou've been having contractions?" Dr. Stevens scratched the grizzled shadow of stubble growing along his jaw. He squinted at Lori in the bright lights of sickbay. She'd woken him up in the middle of his sleep cycle, and it showed.

"Yes—" Lori nodded quickly, and broke off in a wince and a gasp as another contraction hit. She braced herself on the edge of the examination table, gritting her teeth and gripping the table with whitening knuckles. The contraction ended just as quickly as it began, leaving her body so drained that she almost fell off the table. Richard steadied her.

"That's not all. I think my water broke. When I woke up, the bed was wet."

Stevens' face paled, but he quickly covered his reaction. Lori knew what he was thinking. She was only twenty-four weeks. It was far too soon for her to have the baby. He gave a tight smile. "There are other possibilities, but let's take a look, shall we? Lie down, please."

Both he and Richard helped support her as she lay back against the table.

"What if it is labor?" Lori asked as Stevens left her side. Richard stayed close, smiling and holding her hand. She clutched her massive belly with her other hand—felt a swift kick, and rubbed her hand back and forth reassuringly.

At twenty-four weeks the fetus was already huge—approximately eight pounds according to the ultrasounds. So far there was no explanation for it, but fear was a constant companion in this pregnancy. If she actually carried to term, she'd probably explode. Stevens had already explained to her that they'd have to perform an emergency C-section if she got much bigger, so at this point, a premature birth wouldn't be all bad—except that they didn't know how far along the fetus really was. Were her lungs developed yet?

Stevens returned a few seconds later, dragging over a mag-wheeled supply cart and a stool. "Let's take a look and see what's going on."

Lori nodded, her eyes sliding shut as she took a deep breath to steady her nerves.

"Would you mind if I removed your underwear, or would you prefer to do it?"

Lori reached under her nightgown and began sliding her underwear off. She only got it down a few inches before she had to stop as another contraction hit and stole her breath away.

"Let me do that," Richard said quickly, and hurriedly pulled off her panties.

This time a guttural cry escaped Lori's lips and prickles of sweat beaded her brow and back.

Dr. Stevens removed a speculum from the cart and lubricated it. "Try to relax," he said.

"You relax," Lori muttered. She winced as the instrument went in, and then Stevens flicked on his headlamp and leaned down for a look.

He froze.

"What is it?" Lori asked, her voice soft and ragged as she peered over her pregnant belly at him.

Stevens looked up with a tight smile. "You're already dilated nine centimeters. You're about to give birth, Lori."

That news hit her like a bucket of cold water. "But I'm only twenty-four weeks!"

"Maybe so, but your baby is ready now."

"How do you know she's ready?" Lori screamed as another contraction hit.

"It'll be okay, Miss Reed. I promise. We have all the facilities here to care for your child whether she's fully developed or not, and all of our ultrasounds suggest that she's been developing more rapidly than expected. Regardless, right now all you need to focus on is getting her out. Are you ready to push?"

The contraction ended and Lori sobbed, "It's too hard..." Her head lolled suddenly to one side, the pain making her feel faint.

"Hey, stay with me, Lori." Richard squeezed her hand hard, and pushed her head back. "You can do this. I'm right here, okay?"

Somehow Lori found the strength to nod. She heard Dr. Stevens on his comms to one of his staff. She tried to listen to what he was saying, but another contraction came and stole all of her attention with sparking flashes of white-hot agony. An animal cry tore from her lips, and spittle flew from her lips as she propped herself up onto her elbows and crushed Richard's hand in hers. Her legs went reflexively up to her chest.

"I can see the head!" Stevens said. "Keep pushing!"

Lori let go with a gasp and slumped back against the table. "I can't..."

"Yes, you can!" Richard insisted. "Keera is counting on you."

The next contraction came and she pushed again with another scream. It felt like she was turning herself inside out. This time the pain went on and on. She couldn't see, couldn't think, couldn't hear—

"You did it!" Stevens said.

Lori gasped as all of her muscles turned to jelly on the table. Her eyes slid shut with exhaustion as an intense feeling of relief and fulfillment spread through her.

"What... what is *that?*" Richard asked, his voice pitching high with alarm.

Lori's eyes flew open once more, and she propped herself up to see Stevens standing frozen with a ghostly white baby in his arms. Her scalp and body were whorled and striated with black veins, and her head was misshapen with four rounded lumps rising out of it.

Stevens just stood there staring at the child. It wasn't moving. Lori's thoughts spun away with horror, and her whole body tensed right up again. But somehow, her baby's appearance wasn't what had struck fear into her. It was the fact that Keera wasn't moving.

"Stevens!" she cried. "Do something!"

# CHAPTER 18

Dr. Stevens clamped and cut the umbilical cord, and then ran over to an infant-sized gurney with a bright heating lamp shining down. The light of the lamp made Keera look even paler than she had a moment ago, and the black veins snapped into sharper focus, forming strange patterns beneath her skin.

A thick knot of fear broke loose inside of her, making room for something else: revulsion.

"What..." Richard trailed off, backing away quickly and shaking his head. His expression was twisted up with disgust. "What *is* she?"

Doctor Stevens positioned Keera's head to open her airways and began clearing her mouth and nose with a suction bulb while vigorously rubbing and drying her with a downy white blanket.

"Is she breathing?" Lori asked.

But Stevens gave no reply; he simply went through the motions as if on autopilot.

The door to the examination room swished open and a corpsman with spiky blond hair and bright blue eyes rushed in wearing scrubs.

Dr. Stevens looked up briefly. "Get over here,

Sellis!"

The corpsman hurried over, and then jumped back a step at the sight of Keera.

"What the hell?" he cried. "What is *that?*"

"I said give me a hand, damn it!" Stevens snapped.

Sellis crept back in, and Lori watched as both of them hunched over her little girl, their hands and elbows flying as they worked with their backs turned to her, blocking sight of Keera.

*Enough!* Lori decided. She wasn't going to just lie here and wait. Gathering her strength, she pushed off the examination table, ignoring the sharp stabs of pain that the movements provoked from her loose belly and shredded pelvic muscles.

Her gaze flicked to Richard. He was hugging his shoulders and slowly shaking his head as he cowered in the far corner of the room, right beside the exit.

A flash of loathing shot through Lori. *Coward! I'm coming Keera,* she thought. *Mommy's coming...*

And then she heard it, the most beautiful sound in the world—

Keera began to cry. It was a pitiful, whistling and whooping sound that made her fear Keera's lungs weren't properly developed despite her healthy birth weight. Lori pitched off the examination table and her bare feet hit the cold deck with an agonizing jolt. Her knees buckled instantly, but her hand shot out and grabbed Stevens' cart of instruments for support.

"Get the incubator!" Stevens snapped at his assistant as he wrapped Keera up in the blanket. Sellis darted for the exit while Stevens turned and carried Keera over.

Lori scrambled back up onto the examination table to receive her child. Dr. Stevens' expression was grave as he approached, his eyes hard as he stared into Keera's face. Even now that she was breathing, she was just as pale as before. Fish scale patterns of black veins struck a fierce contrast to her glossy white skin. Between Keera's jutting cheek bones and chin, her sharply sloping forehead and deeply sunken eyes, her face looked frighteningly aquiline. Her nose was just as bony and sharp as everything else, and her mouth protruded slightly with thin black lips that were parted slightly to reveal an equally black tongue.

Lori finally realized what she was looking at. She hadn't seen the Avari firsthand, but she'd heard Richard and Captain Cross describe them. Now she understood why Richard was cringing in the corner. He *knew.* He'd recognized Keera instantly.

"Open your robe," Stevens instructed. "You need to hold her to your chest. Skin to skin."

"H-how is this possible?" Lori stuttered as she fumbled with the buttons of her night gown. She hadn't had any contact with the Avari. Not like Dr. Grouse, whom they'd infected with some kind of—

Her thoughts broke off there. Dr. Grouse had stopped breathing in the airlock, and she'd administered CPR and mouth-to-mouth to bring him back.

"I don't know how," Stevens replied.

"But you cleared me!" she cried. "I wasn't infected!"

"I obviously missed something." He nodded to her. "You should hold your daughter."

Stevens held Keera out and Lori accepted the infant from him, placing its bony face against her bare chest.

She sucked in a sharp breath as Keera's cheek touched her. "She's hot!"

A muscle in Stevens' jaw twitched and he nodded. "That might be normal for her spec—"

"You can say it. Her *species,*" Lori said.

Keera was nosing around, searching for something. Her whistling cries quieted, and her eyelids fluttered a few times. Then her eyes cracked open to slits and locked on Lori's—those eyes were a piercing *red*. A tiny hand popped out of the blanket and found her breast; then Keera's mouth seized on her nipple and she began sucking hard.

Lori gasped—then smiled as a feeling of warmth and contentment like nothing she'd ever known before spread through her. Sheer bliss overcame any revulsion that she'd felt up till now. Whatever Keera was, she was *her* little girl, and that was all that mattered.

The door swished open and Corpsman Sellis appeared, dragging an incubator behind him. Richard let out a muffled cry and then darted out the door, fleeing the examination room.

"I don't think we'll be needing that," Dr. Stevens said as he glanced back at Sellis. A tight smile touched his lips as he watched Keera feed. "It looks like twenty-four weeks is full term for an Avari baby."

# CHAPTER 19

Clayton stood in sickbay, watching real-time security footage from the corpsman's station. He stared hard at the holoscreen, a chill coursing down his spine as he watched Dr. Reed breastfeeding her baby. Dr. Stevens and Ambassador Morgan were crowded around the screen with him, and Corpsman Sellis was in the room with her, standing by the door and watching with wary eyes.

"Have you taken any DNA samples yet?" Clayton asked.

"Yes..." Dr. Stevens said.

"And?"

"Her DNA *is* human, but it's like nothing we've sequenced before."

"How so?"

Doctor Stevens scratched his cheek and shook his head. "The child has forty-eight chromosomes. There's an extra set."

Clayton arched an eyebrow at that. "Alien down syndrome?"

"Perhaps," Stevens replied.

"Am I the father?" Ambassador Morgan asked. Clayton glanced at him. Morgan's eyes were fixed on the screen, his voice soft and trembling.

"Yes," Doctor Stevens replied.

The ambassador rounded on him. "Then how did this happen?!"

Stevens just shook his head. "We don't know. Dr. Reed believes she may have become contaminated when she resuscitated Dr. Grouse."

Clayton's gaze skipped from Stevens to Morgan and back again. "So this is the final evolution of the virus that was killing Dr. Grouse?"

Stevens nodded. "Maybe. Or maybe the virus doesn't kill everyone that it infects. It might even be less dangerous to a developing fetus than to an adult."

"So what you're saying is that this child is some kind of human-alien hybrid," Clayton concluded.

Ambassador Morgan looked like he was about to be sick. "But Lori isn't infected?" he asked.

"No, she's not..." Dr. Stevens replied. "At least not in the way that Dr. Grouse was."

"Is the child contagious?" Clayton asked. "Should we be observing quarantine protocols again?"

Stevens sighed. "If it is contagious, then Lori should have been infected. Regardless, we've all been exposed by this point. Myself, Corpsman Sellis, the ambassador..." Stevens' eyes found Clayton. "And now you, sir."

Clayton glared at the ambassador. If Morgan had stopped to think before he'd fled sickbay to go running through the ship like a headless chicken, he would have realized that he could be contaminating everyone on board in the process.

But maybe not. Maybe whatever this was it could only be spread through fluids. Maybe they still had a chance to contain it.

"All the same, Doctor, we'd better observe quarantine from here on out. I'll have Lieutenant Devon seal us all in sickbay until we're cleared."

Ambassador Morgan's eyes flew wide. "You can't do that! What if we're not infected yet?"

"We'll stay in separate rooms to isolate us from Dr. Reed and her child. Thanks to you, it's the best that we can do to keep everyone else safe."

Dr. Stevens nodded along with that.

"And if we're not infected?" Morgan asked. His eyes snapped back to the holoscreen. "What will you do with the child?"

"*The child?*" Clayton asked. "Don't you mean your daughter?"

Morgan slowly shook his head. "That *thing* isn't my daughter."

Clayton sighed. "Well, before we go deciding her fate, first we need to understand what kind of threat she represents, if any."

"Agreed," Doctor Stevens said.

"Excuse me, gentlemen." Clayton turned away, activating his comms. "Call Lieutenant

Devon," he said.

The comms trilled briefly in his ear, and then Devon's voice answered: "Sir?"

"Seal the sickbay, Lieutenant. Don't let any of us out until we've been cleared for release."

"Cleared by who, sir?"

"Wake up Doctor Torres. From here on, she's in charge of quarantine."

"Yes, sir... is everything all right down there?"

Clayton glanced back at the holoscreen. Both the baby and her mother were asleep, and Corpsman Sellis was cautiously arranging the blankets to cover them.

"I hope so, Lieutenant."

# CHAPTER 20

**Two Days Later...**

"Y̲ou're clear, Captain."

Clayton squinted into the light that Dr. Torres was shining into his eyes. "Are you sure?"

Torres put her penlight away with a frown. He stared through the transparent visor of her pressure suit, searching her hazel eyes.

"Positive, sir," Torres replied. "All of your tests have come back clean."

"What about the others?"

"Same."

"And the infant?"

"She's not contagious..."

"But?"

Torres cracked a fading smile. "But, she's fiercely resistant to contact with anyone besides her mother. I've never seen anything quite like it."

"What do you mean?"

"Well, she's just a few days old. Normally newborns are helpless and docile. Keera is aggressive and distrustful."

"Maybe her species *is* more aggressive."

"Maybe," Torres agreed.

"And you're sure she's not contagious?"

"Not at all, sir."

"Thank you, Doctor." Clayton rose from the bed on creaking knees and headed for the locker with his uniform in it. He was wearing a hospital gown, open at the back.

The door chime sounded.

"Come in," Clayton said, glancing back to see Ambassador Morgan and Dr. Stevens walking in, both already wearing their uniforms.

He nodded to them as they approached. "Ambassador. Doctor."

"Captain," Stevens replied.

Clayton shrugged out of his gown, heedless of their presence. Modesty has no place on a starship.

"You can't release them," Morgan said.

"No? And why not?" Clayton asked as he got dressed in the mirror on the locker door. He pulled on his uniform—black with gold stripes and the four gold bars of a UNSF captain glittering above each shoulder. After zipping up and buttoning the collar, he clipped the UNSF emblem to the right side of his chest, a five-pointed silver star with a laurel wreath around it. The symbol of victory. Finally, he bent to put on his mag boots.

"Because it's not human, Captain! We don't know what it could do. It could kill us all in our sleep!"

Clayton turned from the mirror to regard Morgan with a frown. *This xenophobe is who the Union chose to make first contact?* "Ambassador, we don't judge people by their genes, human or otherwise. We'll take sensible precautions, but if everything works out the way I'm hoping, Keera will be given all of the same rights as any other citizen of the Union when we return to Earth."

"You can't possibly believe that," Ambassador Morgan replied. "She'll be whisked away to a Union black site the minute we reach Sol. She'll spend her life in captivity, poked and prodded and studied until the day she dies!"

Clayton snorted. "As her father, you don't sound very concerned about that, Ambassador."

"I'm a realist, Captain. Even if she were allowed to live freely, she'd be persecuted relentlessly just because of the way she looks. And if people knew what she is..." Morgan trailed off shaking his head. "It wouldn't be long before someone killed her."

Clayton scowled. "Yes, we humans are lovely creatures aren't we?"

"He's right, Captain," Torres put in softly, her voice rippling out of the speaker grille in her helmet.

"Maybe, but we're not going to add to those attitudes of prejudice and persecution. You are to clear both Dr. Reed and her daughter to return to their quarters effective immediately."

"Belay that!" Morgan snapped. "Do *not* release them, Torres."

"This is my ship, Ambassador," Clayton replied.

"And I could have you court-martialed when we return, *Captain*."

Torres' eyes darted uncertainly between the two of them.

Clayton nodded to her. "Release them."

"Yes, sir," Torres replied.

"You're going to regret this," Morgan intoned.

"That's my prerogative, Ambassador. Let me worry about my regrets and save your energy to worry about your own."

* * *

Clayton stood in the cargo transfer airlock outside the entrance of one of the elevators leading to The Wheel. Since the ship was still under active acceleration, that elevator would actually function more like a tram, moving horizontally away from the direction of thrust and gravity.

In front of him stood Dr. Reed with her daughter, Keera, bundled in her arms. Ambassador Morgan was here, too, to see them off, but he looked intensely uncomfortable.

Dr. Reed had insisted he come say goodbye to them, but Morgan had been hesitant. Ever since they'd all been quarantined together in sickbay, Morgan had kept his distance from both Dr. Reed and Keera. He couldn't accept that the hybrid was his daughter. Clayton wasn't sure if he blamed the man, but as a rule, it was generally best to assume that whatever Richard Morgan did, one should do the opposite.

"I guess this is goodbye, Captain," Dr. Reed said. She was gently bouncing Keera in her arms, and the infant's piercing red eyes were sinking steadily closer to shut.

Clayton nodded.

Delta stood beside him for added security, but so far there'd been no signs from Keera to warrant any kind of concern. She was just a baby —with alien DNA—but a baby nonetheless.

"We'll see you in six months," Clayton replied. The skeleton crews would take over from here on out: just two officers to watch the bridge for one week at a time between the more comprehensive bi-annual rotations in which routine maintenance, cleaning, and repairs were conducted. The thrusters would be offline for the two-man rotations, so there would be no gravity beyond The Wheel, which meant that Dr. Reed and Keera would have to stay there until six months from now when Clayton and the rest of his section came out of cryo.

Dr. Reed nodded and flashed a wan smile before walking down the line to stop in front of Morgan.

"Richard," she said. Tension crowded the air between them and neither one said anything for several seconds.

"Lori, look, I'm sorry. I really am. I just..." His eyes were on Keera. "I can't."

"Yes, you can." Dr. Reed reached out and grabbed his hand. She dragged it up and placed it on top of Keera's head.

Morgan leaned away, looking like he might chew his own arm off just to get away.

Keera's eyes cracked open and she regarded him with a flinty look. Then she stirred and wriggled around inside of the blanket that Dr. Reed had her bundled in.

Clayton watched with a bemused frown.

"Let me go, Lori," Morgan said.

"Just wait. She's doing something."

Richard shook his head vigorously, but then two pale, fish-scale patterned hands and arms popped out of the blankets.

A whistling cry escaped Keera's black lips, and then she reached for the ambassador with both arms.

Morgan hesitated, and the baby sucked in her bottom lip. Her eyes grew wide and teary, and she began sniffling. *If she weren't so damn ugly it would be cute,* Clayton thought. But then he chided himself for thinking that way. He couldn't allow himself to judge by appearances. That would make him no better than Morgan.

"She wants you to hold her!" Dr. Reed said, and pushed Keera out from her chest.

Morgan didn't immediately recoil or respond. He seemed to be frozen with indecision.

Then he snapped out of it, and took Keera from her mother. The infant wrapped both of her arms around his neck and nuzzled her head into the hollow between his head and shoulder. Keera's cries instantly quieted, and her eyes began sliding shut once more.

"She knows that you're her father," Dr. Reed said quietly.

"I..." Morgan trailed off, looking and sounding confused. "She's..."

"Amazing, right?"

He nodded slowly, his face and jaw slack.

"This is one hell of a freak show you invited me to, Cap," Delta muttered.

Clayton glanced at him and back without comment, not wanting to ruin the moment by saying the wrong thing. He backed up a few steps, and then nodded sideways for Delta to follow. "Let's give them some space," he whispered.

"You still want to go into cryo and leave me to raise her on my own?" Reed asked, her eyes searching Morgan's.

The ambassador said nothing to that. He just quietly stroked the infant's back and leaned his head against hers. The suddenness of Morgan's change of attitude did set off an alarm bell in Clayton's head, but maybe it was just a natural biological response to holding one's offspring for the first time. He'd heard second-hand accounts of parents speaking about transformational moments like these before. Usually they occurred right after a baby was born... *But isn't that also when babies typically have first contact with their parents?*

*First contact.* Clayton smiled wryly at the choice of words.

"You can't leave us," Dr. Reed said, stepping in to wrap her arms around them both. "Don't let appearances fool you. She's ours, more human than anything else."

Morgan heaved a sigh. "Okay."

Dr. Reed withdrew to an arm's length, her eyes bright and sparkling with joy. "You mean it?"

Morgan still didn't look a hundred percent convinced, but he gave in with a nod. "I do."

A grin sprang to Reed's lips, and she crushed Morgan and their daughter into another hug. "You won't regret it. I promise."

Morgan said nothing to that, but it was a miracle he'd come this far. Maybe he'd been on the fence to begin with. Days had passed since the quarantine, and the entire crew had been given a chance to see that Keera wasn't dangerous. She was antisocial, however, and just as Doctor Torres had first pointed out, she'd fiercely rejected contact with anyone besides her mother.

Now she'd expanded that sphere to include her father. Was that progress, or would Keera's world remain that small forever? It was too soon to tell, and isolating them on The Wheel probably wasn't going to help matters.

"Are you three ready to go?" Clayton asked.

"Almost," Morgan replied, half-turning to him with a tight smile. "I need to go pack up a few things from my quarters."

"We'll be waiting for you," Dr. Reed said. Morgan passed Keera back to her—almost reluctantly. The infant squirmed and whimpered as she traded bosoms, but Dr. Reed adjusted the blanket to cover her and block out the light, and then Keera nuzzled in close and fell back to sleep with a sigh.

Clayton watched Morgan and Reed pull apart like glue—contact stretching and thinning until at last their fingertips slipped through each other's hands. "I'll be there soon," Morgan replied, and then he turned and hurried out of the cargo transfer airlock.

Clayton nodded to Dr. Reed's luggage—three large crates on a mag-wheeled dolly. "We'll help you with that."

"Thank you, Captain."

Delta grabbed the handle of the dolly before Clayton could, and began pushing it toward the elevator doors. Clayton mentally opened the elevator and selected The Wheel for a destination. There was only one other possible stop besides that, at the mid-point airlock along the spoke, but it was only ever used for external maintenance and repairs.

Once they had the dolly inside the elevator, Clayton nodded to Dr. Reed and said, "I wish you three all the best."

"Thank you, Captain."

"If you need anything, and I mean anything, don't hesitate to call the bridge. And if the officers in charge need to, they can wake me at a moment's notice. Understood?"

"Yes. And I appreciate it. I know you've been one of Keera's strongest advocates since the day she was born."

"I've always been a bigger believer in nurture than nature. Genes are just physical instructions. As far as I'm concerned, the difference between Keera and us is no bigger than the difference between two different breeds of dogs."

Reed's lips quirked into a wry smile. "Are you calling my daughter a bitch, Captain?"

He snorted and held up both hands in apology. "Sorry, bad analogy."

"Yes, it was." But Reed's eyes were sparkling with amusement.

Clayton backed the rest of the way out of the elevator with Delta matching his every step. He tossed a crooked salute from his brow. "See you in six months, Doctor Reed."

"Call me Lori. I think friends should call each other by their first names."

"Lori it is," Clayton replied. His gaze dropped a few degrees. "See you soon, Keera. I can't wait to see you crawling around and driving your parents crazy."

Lori laughed at that, and Clayton triggered

the door shut with his ARCs. A few seconds later he and Delta watched through the window in the top of the door as the elevator shot away, racing down the spoke like a train car in a tunnel.

Delta shook his head. "I don't like this, sir. Something is seriously wrong with that kid."

Clayton arched an eyebrow at him. "Something besides the way she looks? You have anything to go on besides a hunch, Lieutenant? If so, you'd better start talking."

Delta pursed his lips into a thoughtful pout. "Nothing that specific, sir."

"Then I don't want to hear it. That kid is going to have enough problems with people judging and discriminating against her without us adding to it. Let's try to set the bar a little higher, shall we?"

"Yes, sir."

Clayton turned and headed for the exit of the cargo transfer airlock. His mind was already switching gears, running through the remainder of his final checklist. In just eighteen hours he'd be handing over the bridge to the first in a long line of two-person crews whose job it would be to watch over the ship for the next six months. He still had a lot of reports to read and inspections to perform before that happened. Not to mention he had to get some sleep. At this point he probably wouldn't get more than a few hours. Everything needed to be running perfectly before he went back into cryo.

The cargo doors rumbled open, and Clayton started down the circular corridor that ran around this particular deck: one of seven storage decks on the ship. Curving rectangular viewscreens ran around the outer circumference of the corridor, giving them a stunning view of the myriad stars shining all around them. Those screens gave the illusion that space was just on the other side of a thin barrier, but in reality the cryo pod rings and a whole other layer of hull still separated them from the void.

As they walked, Clayton felt Delta's eyes on him. "Something else on your mind, Lieutenant?"

"We should at least lock them in."

Clayton looked to his chief of security with a frown. "Lock them in?"

"Yes, sir."

"Like prisoners."

"The Wheel is hardly a prison, sir. And they're confined to it, anyway. What would be the difference?"

Clayton resisted the smile tugging at the corners of his lips, but he couldn't hold it, and it quickly blossomed into a grin. "Are you afraid of a baby, Delta?"

The former Marine's eyes narrowed slightly at that, but he said nothing.

"If she were contagious, then we'd all be infected by now," Clayton added. "Dr. Grouse started showing symptoms almost immediately, so we know the incubation period is short."

"Yeah, maybe," Delta replied.

"So if she's not contagious, what else is there to worry about? Keera can't even crawl, let alone walk. She has no teeth, no *claws...*" Clayton broke off laughing.

"Not yet, sir, but in six months she'll have some."

"Barely. And we'll have plenty of warning from her parents if she starts showing signs that she might be a threat. Even then, I'd liken it to a puppy who might bite or scratch you if you're not too careful. I'm pretty sure we can handle that." Clayton shook his head. "Let's not let our imaginations run away with us, Lieutenant."

"Yes, sir."

\* \* \*

Clayton woke up in darkness, feeling like he couldn't breathe. There was a dark shadow at the foot of his bed, approaching steadily.

He tried to scream, but his mouth wouldn't move. He tried to sit up, but his muscles were not responding.

*Not again. Lights on!* he thought.

A blaze of white light flooded the room, and the approaching shadow shimmered and vanished with the light. Gradually, control of his muscles returned and he sat up, looking around his quarters for any lingering signs of the hallucination.

Clayton flopped back down with a sigh. "Lights to twenty percent," he said, and they diminished to a soft golden hue.

His bouts of sleep paralysis were getting so frequent now that they'd become routine. Dragging his hand up from the covers, Clayton checked his watch. It glowed to life and Samara's smiling face greeted him. Four AM. The perfect witching hour. *Maybe that's what this is; some kind of curse.* Going back into cryo would be a relief. No more interrupted nights.

Clayton lay blinking up at the ceiling, his heart rate slowing as his eyes once again grew heavy with sleep. Not long now and he'd be enjoying six months of uninterrupted slumber. Not that cryo actually functioned like sleep, but it was a comforting thought to drift off with all the same.

# CHAPTER 21

### Six Months Later...

Lori cooed in her daughter's ear to no effect. "Shhhh, it's okay. It's okay." Keera was wailing incessantly.

"What is it *now?*" Richard growled, rising from the bed and stomping over like an angry giant. Keera had been having these crying fits for weeks now, but this was by far the worst.

Lori shook her head, bouncing Keera in her arms as she paced the deck in front of the windows in their quarters. Unlike most of the other windows in the ship, these were real. Seeing the stars usually calmed Keera, but tonight she was inconsolable.

"Maybe she's sick." Lori grunted as she hefted Keera up to a better position, draping her over one shoulder rather than cradling her like a baby. Keera was only six months old, but she weighed forty-five pounds now, and she measured one point two meters tall. She was already walking and talking in full sentences. Her development was completely off the charts for any normal human growth curve—more comparable to that of a six-year-old girl, not a six-month-old baby.

"Keera, what's wrong, honey?" Lori tried for the umpteenth time.

"Bad. Bad. Very bad! Pain!"

"You're in pain? Where does it hurt?"

"No! Not hurt me. Pain!"

"Talk to me, sweetie. What's wrong."

"Pain!" Keera cried again.

"Did she have a nightmare?" Richard asked as she paced back his way.

Lori shook her head. "No. She says she couldn't sleep."

"She's been awake all night?"

Lori shrugged helplessly.

"Did you try feeding her?"

She stopped pacing to glare at him. "Of course I tried!" She'd tried, despite the fact that her breasts were swollen, shriveled lumps covered in scabs and bite marks. Keeping infection at bay was a daily struggle. Keera still didn't want to accept formula as a substitute for breast milk, and at her size she needed a lot of breast milk. Fortunately, she'd begun eating solid foods after just one month, and she received most of her calories that way.

Keera's cries went on and on, shrill and keening.

"So what's wrong!?" Richard demanded.

"She might be sick," Lori suggested again while rubbing Keera's bony back. Her vertebrae

stuck out sharply, forming an unusually prominent ridge running down her spine.

Richard walked around behind Lori to put his
angry face in Keera's. "What is wrong with you?!"

Keera cried all the louder with that rebuke,
and Lori whirled away from him, her eyes flashing. "Why don't you go sleep in one of the other
rooms? I'll stay up with her."

Richard crossed his arms over his chest, revealing a collection of thin, long white scars on
his forearms. Lori had all of the same marks and
more, but they went up and down her chest, too.
When Keera's claws had started coming in, it had
taken a while for her to learn to be *careful* with
them. If it weren't for accelerated healing sprays
and the cache of antibiotics that they had on
board, they might have died from infection by
now.

Lori turned Keera in circles, bouncing her,
rubbing her back, and whispering reassurances
in her ear.

"Maybe it's time we admitted that we can't
handle her anymore," Richard said.

"What are you suggesting?" Lori asked, her
eyes narrowing on his.

"We could go into cryo with her. I don't think
it would be dangerous anymore."

"No." Lori shook her head vigorously. If Keera
went into cryo now, she wouldn't be awoken
until they reached Earth. None of them would.
And then who knew what would happen next.

Keera would probably be taken to a government facility, maybe separated from them forever.

Suddenly Keera's cries quieted, replaced by a sniffling sound. A moment later it was followed by her small, husky voice: "Mommy, I wanna stay here with you."

"It's okay, honey, I'm not going to leave. Daddy is going to go to one of the other rooms so he can sleep. I'm going to stay with you, okay?"

"Promise?" Keera leaned away from Lori's shoulder. Her sunken red eyes looked brighter than usual from all the tears, and her pale face was flushed a dark gray. All four of Keera's cranial stems turned toward Lori, the ear canals flaring into small funnel shapes, indicating that her whole attention was fixed on her mother. Unlike a human, Keera didn't have ears in the sides of her head. She had them on top—four ears attached to short, flexible appendages. With them she could hear frequencies of sound far outside of the normal human range of hearing.

"I promise," Lori said.

Keera nodded and subsided against her shoulder once more. Whatever had been wrong, at least now she'd stopped crying. Maybe now she would finally fall asleep.

Richard held Lori's gaze with a heavy frown, his brow dropping a dark shadow over his eyes.

"What?" Lori hissed.

"We're going to talk seriously about this when the captain wakes up."

"We already talked about it," Lori replied.

"Not with him."

"You will not speak to him."

"You can't stop me. He needs to know what's been going on. How she's developing. When he sees her and hears about everything, it won't be up to you or me anymore. He's going to put her in cryo whether you like it or not."

Keera glared at her father, and a low, mewling hiss escaped her lips.

"Look at the way she's looking at me! Like she wants to kill me! And I'm her father."

"Then maybe you should start acting like it!"

Richard threw up his hands. "I give up. We'll talk in the morning."

Richard stalked toward the exit and waved the door open as he approached. It opened with a whisper and then slid shut behind him with a muffled *thump.*

"Is it true?" Keera asked.

"Is what true, sweetheart?"

"That they gonna put me in *cwhyo.*"

"*Cryo,* sweetie. I won't let them. Not yet, anyway. It's too soon. We still have time."

"What is *cwhyo?*"

Lori carried her daughter over to the bed and set her down on the edge. She took a moment to arch her aching back and stretch out her burning arms. Keera was getting harder and harder to carry.

"Cryo is where they freeze you," she explained.

Keera gave an involuntary shiver. "They make you cold?" She grabbed the blankets and drew them up around her shoulders.

Lori helped wrap her up. She shook her head, smiling reassuringly. "Yes, sweetie, but you don't feel it. They put you to sleep first."

"For how long?"

"Well… that depends. Sometimes just for a few months. Sometimes years."

"But they wanna fweeze me for a long time."

"Maybe. But I'll be right there with you."

Keera's expression darkened and she shook her head. She absently flexed her hands in her lap, raking claws over the blankets. A tearing sound reached Lori's ears, and rips appeared in the fabric.

"Don't do that, honey."

"Sawy." She stopped.

"You mean *sorry*."

"Yes, sawy."

Lori smiled at Keera's persistent lisp. She was still working on pronunciation. Sometimes she got it right, and other times she defaulted to old bad habits. Somehow Richard missed all of this. He only saw what his eyes showed him: sharp claws and teeth, a frightening face and demonic eyes. He didn't see the very human personality emerging underneath, or how sweet and vulnerable Keera could be. As far as Lori was concerned, she was just like any other human child, only her appearance and physiology set her apart.

"What if we make *them* sleep instead? Then I can stay awake with you."

Lori hesitated. "What do you mean, honey? They're already asleep."

"We could make it so that they don't wake up." Keera was staring sightlessly at the door by which her father had left.

Goosebumps appeared on Lori's bare arms, and she rubbed them away. "They're going to wake up automatically, whether we like it or not."

"But you can stop them. Make them stay asleep."

"No, I can't. I'd have to go to the bridge to deactivate the auto-wake cycle, and even if I did that, there are two officers on the bridge right now who are taking turns watching it. One of them would stop me if I tried anything like that."

"Then they are the problem," Keera said.

"No, darling. No one is a problem."

Keera tore her eyes away from the door. "But the captain will make me sleep if he wakes up."

Lori offered another reassuring smile and slowly shook her head. "I'll talk to him. He agreed to let us raise you here until you're two years old. You still have another year and seven months to go."

"Daddy doesn't want to wait." Another hiss

escaped Keera's lips, and she bared her long, pointed teeth, making it clear what she thought about that. Her hands flexed into talons again and the blankets bunched up in her lap.

Lori placed her hand over Keera's. "He's just scared."

"Of what?"

Lori hesitated. She'd painted herself into a corner. How to tell your child that her father is afraid of her? She couldn't tell Keera that. "He's afraid of things he doesn't understand."

"Things like me," Keera said. Her hands relaxed and her gaze drifted out of focus, staring into her wrinkly white palms.

Keera was getting harder and harder to fool. She was incredibly perceptive—more so than most adults.

"It's not your fault," Lori said.

"I know you love me," Keera replied, and leaned her head against Lori's shoulder. The implication was that she didn't think her father loved her. Lori winced and swallowed past a painful knot in her throat. *Damn you, Richard.*

She wrapped an arm around Keera's shoulders, and they sat staring out the windows at the dizzying swirl of the stars. The jutting gray spear of the *Forerunner's* central column seemed to be looping endlessly around them, but in reality, of course, *they* were the ones who were spinning.

"Lights off," Lori said, and darkness enveloped them. They sat there quietly with the minutes trickling by, their faces agleam with starlight as they stared into the swirling void.

Growing dizzy, Lori looked away. There was a setting to activate the windows as viewscreens and show a rock-steady view from an external camera in the stationary center of the ship. But ever since Keera was a baby, she had preferred it this way. The movement soothed her.

As Lori's body and mind grew heavy with sleep, she thought to ask Keera one more time —maybe now she had enough distance from her emotions to make sense out of them. "What were you crying about before, sweetheart?"

Several seconds passed before Keera replied. And when she did, her voice was a ragged whisper. "I saw blood everywhere, and... they were screaming."

Another chill prickled Lori's skin. "Who was screaming?"

Keera shook her head. "I don't know. A man and a woman."

*Us?* she almost blurted out, but that would be giving in to Richard's paranoia. Keera had just said that she didn't know who they were.

"How did you see them? Was it a dream?"

"No. I wasn't asleep. I saw them up here." Keera tapped the side of her head with one wickedly curling black claw.

"In your head... you mean you imagined it?"

Keera nodded.

Maybe she did need to ask. "Was it your father

and me you saw?"

Keera shook her head quickly, her red eyes flashing with alarm.

"But it was a man and a woman. Did you recognize them?"

Another shake.

Lori frowned. Keera had never met anyone besides her parents. Not in the last six months, anyway, and Lori doubted that Keera had formed any lasting memories as a newborn.

But they had watched enough holovids to feed her imagination.

"Were they people you saw in a movie?"

Keera shrugged. "Maybe."

"You mentioned blood. Did something happen to them?"

Keera's eyes filled with tears and her lower lip began to tremble. "Yes."

"What's wrong?"

"Nothing!" Keera whirled away and scooted down to the end of the bed. She wiped her tears away furiously.

Lori got up and went to sit beside her again. "It's okay. You can tell me anything. I'll always love you. No matter what. Whatever it is, it's not real. It's just your imagination."

"No."

"No, what?"

"You can't love me! I'm bad. I'm very bad."

"No, you're not, Keera! You haven't done anything wrong." Lori wrapped her in a hug, but

Keera resisted, trying to wriggle free.

"Let me go!"

"No."

"I killed them!" she screamed.

Lori recoiled from the force of her words as much as from what Keera had said. Her reaction lasted only a second, but the damage was already done. Keera smiled bitterly, her cheeks streaked with tears. "You see? You don't love me."

"Honey, it wasn't real. You haven't even left this deck. There isn't anyone here for you to have hurt, and even if there were, I don't believe that you would hurt anyone."

Keera's expression blanked, becoming suddenly very serious. She reached out with a trembling hand and ran her fingers lightly over the scars on Lori's arm.

"That's different. Those were accidents."

"Not accidents. It is what I am—" Keera broke off, her expression twisting up in self-loathing. "—a killer." She began sobbing in earnest now. Her bony, coat hangar shoulders rocked violently and air whistled in and out of her sharp, narrow nose.

Lori pulled her into a hug and kissed the top of her head. "You're not a killer, Keera," she whispered. "Killers don't cry because they are killers. They don't feel bad about what they do. You haven't done anything, but you can't even stand the thought that you might. That's not how killers act."

"You don't understand," Keera said in a muffled voice.

"What do you mean?" Lori whispered. "Talk to me."

"Sometimes I want to hurt Daddy."

Lori felt her blood run cold. Rather than give in to it, she held fast to what she knew. If Keera had really wanted to hurt her father, she could have easily done so by now.

"That's because sometimes he's mean to you, even when you don't deserve it, and that makes you mad. It's normal to feel that way, Keera. What's important isn't how you feel but what you do with those feelings, and I've never seen you intentionally hurt anyone. Do you understand?"

Keera nodded quickly, her skull knocking against Lori's chin.

"Good. Now come on. Let's try to get some sleep. We have a busy day ahead of us tomorrow. You're going to meet the crew for the first time."

"You said they already met me."

"Yes, but you don't remember it, so for you it is the first time."

"Do you think they'll like me?"

Lori hesitated for just a second, before pasting a lie on her face. "They're going to love you, sweetie."

"That isn't twoo."

"True," Lori corrected. "And yes it is."

"No."

"Let's wait and see, shall we?"

Keera nodded and they both crawled up to the top of the bed and lay down. Keera's bed was on the other side of the room, but Richard wasn't here, so there was no point in making her sleep there tonight. Lori curled her body against Keera's and wrapped her daughter in the blankets, making sure to keep them off herself. Keera's natural body temperature was forty-one degrees Celsius. Sleeping beside her was like sleeping next to a roaring fire.

Gradually Keera's breathing slowed, and Lori let herself drift off as well.

She dreamed that Richard was sneaking up behind them with a gun to kill them in their sleep. She woke up with a muffled cry just as he shot their daughter in the head.

Terrified, Lori checked Keera to make sure that she was okay. But she was fine: no bullet holes or scorch marks anywhere, and her breathing was steady, her body still hot.

*It was just a dream,* Lori thought, lying back with a sigh.

# CHAPTER 22

Lori woke up in a fog, her body heavy and sore from carrying Keera around the night before. In addition to that, her head still felt thick and fuzzy with sleep. She'd had a rocky night even after Keera had finally calmed down and drifted off. Richard had haunted her dreams, always coming after them, trying to get at her and Keera.

Lori sat up with a grimace and kneaded her eyes with her fists in an attempt to push back the dull ache building behind them.

She couldn't leave things between her and Richard like this. Especially not now. They needed to present a united front to Captain Cross and Lieutenant Devon when they woke up. They both needed to be singing the same tune. Keera wasn't dangerous. She wasn't a threat, and she didn't need to go into cryo early.

Glancing over her shoulder, Lori noted that Keera was still fast asleep.

*Good.* She would rather talk to Richard alone. She didn't want Keera to overhear anything that would do additional damage to her relationship with her father.

Sliding quietly off the bed, Lori padded over to the door and waved it open. The metal deck was cold as ice, so she stopped to put on a pair of UNSF slippers along the way.

Cinching her nightgown tight around her waist, Lori walked out and shut the door behind her.

The gleaming metal deck curved gently up. Glowing lines of recessed lighting ran along the tops and bottoms of the bulkheads. Every couple of feet or so a safety handrail jutted from the bulkheads and ceiling. Just like any other part of the ship, The Wheel was designed to be navigated in zero-G as well as simulated gravity. Staggered doors with glowing numbers and letters on them lined the length of the corridor on both sides. Each door led to a different set of quarters. They'd chosen the largest room for themselves, *W1*.

Soon Keera would need to pick her own room. She was already at a point where that would make sense, but these fits she had been having were going to make the transition hard. Still, they'd had a breakthrough last night. Keera had finally described what was bothering her. It was just her fears about herself, partly instilled by Richard's attitude toward her.

Which was the other reason Lori needed to speak with him. He needed to know how badly he was hurting Keera. And he needed to stop, or else leave them and go into cryo by himself.

Lori spent a moment scanning the doors, trying to decide which one of them Richard might have picked last night. She tried the first door on the right on the same side as the quarters they shared as a family, thinking that Richard would probably want a forward-facing window.

It was strange to think of it that way, but since the deck settings of The Wheel were rotated with respect to the rest of the ship, *down* was actually the outer circumference of The Wheel, *up* was the inner circumference, and the windows all either faced the stern or the nose of the ship.

As the door to *W3* slid open, Lori saw a perfectly made bed and no sign of Richard. Frowning, she shut the door, and moved on to *W2* on the other side of the corridor. It slid open, and this time she saw the bedsheets rumpled, but still no sign of Richard. She walked in, "Rick? Are you here?"

No reply. She padded over to the bathroom and waved the door open. His uniform and underwear lay in a heap on top of his slippers.

Lori frowned. He'd obviously taken a shower and gotten dressed. But with what clothes? Maybe he'd found a spare uniform in one of the storage lockers. That, or he was walking around naked right now.

Heading out, she shut the door behind her and walked briskly down the corridor past the remaining rooms. Richard was probably in the mess hall eating breakfast and having a cup of coffee. Her mouth watered at the thought. Especially with the thought of coffee. She could really use a cup right now.

Coming to the end of the crew section, a sealed bulkhead appeared with the words *Mess Hall* stamped on it in thick white letters. She glanced up at the elevator doors, recessed into the ceiling. That elevator led *up* one of the four spokes to the central column of the ship.

A twinge of doubt trickled in. What if Richard had gone to speak with the crew? There were two officers up there. At least one of them would be awake and on duty at any given hour, day or night.

If Richard had gone to share his concerns about Keera, he might have convinced them to wake the captain and the rest of the crew early.

That thought lit a fuse inside Lori's brain, and she glowered darkly at the door. He'd better be in the mess hall, she thought, as she waved the doors open.

The doors rumbled open and she passed through, her eyes scanning empty tables and chairs. The ration storage bins were all sealed shut, and the food prep areas in the kitchen were clean and sparkling, just the same as they'd left them after dinner last night.

Walking in behind the serving counter, Lori ran her hands along the sparkling surfaces and checked for signs of crumbs and milk spills.

There was nothing. No coffee in the dispenser, either. Everything was clean and dry and unused. There were only a few other places on The Wheel that he could be—the control center was restricted access, so he wouldn't be there, and he wasn't a fan of exercise, so the gym was out, too. He could be in the rec room, but she knew him: he would have come here first, made coffee, and fixed himself something to eat. The fact that he hadn't done any of that could only mean one thing—

Lori turned back to face the open doors of the mess hall, her eyes drifting up and narrowing on the elevator doors in the ceiling.

He'd probably gone to speak with the crew hours ago, maybe even in the middle of the night while she was still consoling Keera.

*You coward!* she thought as she stormed out of the mess hall.

# CHAPTER 23

Lori ran back down the corridor to the nearest of the crew quarters. She waved the door to *W15* open, and then hurried over to the lockers along the wall opposite the bed. She found a spare UNSF uniform and mag boots. The uniforms were one-size fits all, and the mag boots were adjustable and padded inside so that she didn't need any additional footwear. As soon as she was dressed, Lori hurried out and back down to the elevator. Activating it with her ARCs, she waited as the doors opened up and the elevator platform dropped down on four pneumatic arms. Before it had even touched the deck, she jumped onto the platform and used her ARCs to select deck *CS17* (Central Storage, Deck 17) from the available options.

She grabbed the nearest handrail for support as the elevator platform rose up the spoke to the central column of the ship. Stars flashed past the windows in the sides of the elevator car and reciprocal windows in the sides of the spoke.

Lori looked away, glaring *up* at the doors on the far end of the elevator car. The sensation of gravity pulling her down toward The Wheel grew faint as she approached the center of rotation. Then the car jolted and *thunked* to a stop. She reached for the first in a line of folding handrails embedded in one of the two windowless sides of the elevator. They were marked with black and yellow stripes and arrows with text that read: CLIMB TO CARGO TRANSFER.

As she climbed, Lori activated the cargo transfer airlock with her ARCs, and a loud whirring sound started up somewhere above her head. She reached the top of the ladder and waited for a few seconds. A green light snapped on, and then the doors in the *ceiling* of the elevator rumbled open, revealing a boxy cargo transfer junction with more folding handrails on one side.

There were four identical junctions, one for each spoke, with adjoining corridors running between. Together they formed an independently rotating ring known as the cargo transfer airlock. Cycling that airlock meant spinning the ring up to the same exact RPM as The Wheel so that people could leave one of the elevators and enter the rest of the ship without first stopping The Wheel's rotation.

Lori climbed the rest of the way into the spacious cargo transfer junction, folding out the handrails as she went.

The sensation of gravity was lighter than ever now, maybe just a tenth of standard. She used her ARCs to stop the airlock's rotation, and it gradually slowed to a stop.

Weightlessness settled in, and Lori's stomach fluttered queasily. With nothing to give her a sense of what was up or down, her perspective changed, and she saw the deck setting the way it was primarily intended to be used: she was lying face-down on the deck. Pushing gently away from it, she tucked her legs and activated her mag boots.

The soles clamped to the deck with a ringing report, and then she set out, *thunking* along toward the set of inner doors that led to the rest of the ship.

Worry crowded in as she went: what if Keera woke up to find them both missing? How would she react? Would she go looking for them, or wait patiently for their return? Keera was a late sleeper, though, and it was still early. She could risk it. Right now the most important thing was to find Richard and stop him from waking the Captain.

* * *

The entire ship was deserted, the lights turned down to a low, power-saving golden hue. Shadows curled in every doorway and every corner. Lori's first thought was to check the bridge, but if Richard had come down here to speak to the crew in the middle of the night, he would have been tired after that and looking for a place to lay his head. She decided to check his old quarters first.

Lori reached the nearest bank of elevators and took it up to *OQ26* (Officer's Quarters, Deck 26). Richard wasn't technically an officer, but his status as ambassador gave him some of the same privileges.

The elevator accelerated quickly, easing the nauseating sensation of freefall from zero-G, but her relief was short-lived, and was accompanied by a gut-sucking inverse effect as the elevator decelerated. The contents of her stomach lurched into the back of her throat with a foul-tasting tang of acid.

Lori exited the elevator with a grimace and hurried down the corridor to Richard's quarters. She tried to wave the door open, but it resisted with an error *beep,* and the control panel beside the door glowed red. The word *locked* flashed on the panel, and Lori's eyes narrowed angrily. He was definitely here. No one on board bothered to lock their doors unless they were inside and needed privacy.

Using her ARCs to interact with the panel, Lori rang the buzzer and waited.

A few seconds later, the door swished open to reveal a dark room, and she heard Richard call out in a sleepy voice: "Come in."

The lights rose to a dim setting as she walked in, and she saw Richard just now unzipping from the bed covers. They doubled as a sleeping bag for zero-G. As soon as the bag was open, Richard drifted free.

"You found me," he said through a sigh as he used the handrails on the bed frame to maneuver his feet into a pair of waiting mag boots. He bent to adjust the straps, and then stood facing her.

Lori crossed her arms over her chest, ready for battle. "What are you doing down here?"

He shook his head, looking tired and unhappy. "I tried to sleep in the room next door, but I couldn't. I kept having these nightmares of Keera coming to get me in my sleep."

"Coming to get you?" Lori echoed incredulously. "She's just a child! And she's your daughter!"

"You and I both know she's much more than that."

"You mean less than that," Lori quipped.

"I didn't say that."

"It's how you act. Please tell me you haven't said anything to the crew."

"Not yet. I was going to, but I decided to wait to speak with the captain when he wakes up. It's just a few more hours until then, anyway."

"Did you know that your daughter is scared of you?"

Richard's brow furrowed. "She said that?"

"Yes. She thinks you're going to kill *her*."

"So it's mutual then."

"Neither of you should be feeling that way!"

"And that's somehow my fault?" Richard challenged. "I think I've done pretty damn well under the circumstances."

"Not well enough," Lori replied. "Keera told me what she was crying about."

Richard's eyebrows lifted in question, but he said nothing.

"She was crying because she thinks she's a killer, because you've made her feel that way!"

"What are you talking about?"

"I'm talking about the way you treat her, always scared, always wary and paranoid. Running away to sleep down here is just another example of that."

"Maybe she thinks she's a killer because whatever instincts she has are getting stronger. Those claws and teeth she has didn't evolve from a peaceful species. They evolved because her DNA was spliced together with some kind of alien apex predator. She could have all kinds of bloodthirsty urges that we know nothing about. She *is* a killer, Lori, whether you want to see that or not. And soon she's going to start practicing, just like any killer does."

"You're insane."

"This has gone on long enough." He rolled up his sleeves, one at a time, revealing the uneven ridges of crisscrossing scar tissue. "Look at me, Lori! We're living proof of what she is."

Lori shook her head. "Humans are apex predators, too."

"No, we were foragers. And we're omnivores, not carnivores. You *do* realize that Keera only eats meat, right? You *know* what that makes her."

"She drinks milk, too."

"Breast milk. And your breasts have a few chunks missing from them, don't they? One of these days she's going to take a real bite."

Lori spun away from him, her eyes blurring with tears of frustration—both from this conversation and from memories of the incidents that Richard was referring to. Raising Keera hadn't been easy.

She heard thunking footsteps as Richard approached, then felt his hands on her shoulders.

"We need to put her in cryo," Richard whispered gruffly. "The Union will know what to do with her when we get back."

"We'll never see her again," Lori replied, and twisted out from under his hands. "I won't let that happen."

"You don't know that they'll take her away. They might just help us to raise her in a safer, more controlled environment."

"All the while experimenting on her! Poking and prodding her like an animal!"

"There's no way to prevent it," Richard replied. "Waiting until she's older before she goes into cryo won't help. All that will do is give her more time and opportunity to hurt one of us."

Lori remembered something that Keera had said during their heart-to-heart last night: *Sometimes I want to hurt Daddy.*

She pushed the thought away, refusing to accept it. Keera was angry with her father because of his attitude toward her. She didn't know how to process his rejection, that's all.

"If we wait until she's older, she'll be more ready to deal with the way she's going to be treated on Earth," Lori said.

"I won't spend any more time with her and you shouldn't either. It's too dangerous. Speaking of which, where the hell is she?"

"I left her up on The Wheel. She was still sleeping, and I didn't want to wake her. Besides, I think it's better we have this conversation without her, don't you?"

"That's not the point—you didn't tell her where you were going?"

"No, why?"

"What if she came looking for you?"

Lori frowned. Keera didn't have her own ARCs or a Neuralink yet, but they'd taught her how to use the physical control panels in case of an emergency. Still, it was unlikely that she'd go to all the trouble of leaving The Wheel. And if she did, so what?

"What does it matter if she follows us?"

"She could bump into one of the crew and surprise them. They haven't seen how big she is yet. They won't recognize her. They could shoot her!"

Lori's eyes flared wide. He was right. Until now she'd been worried about how Keera would react. She hadn't thought about what the crew might do if they saw her. She glanced urgently at the door.

"We'd better get back to The Wheel."

Richard shook his head. "The bridge is closer. We'll go there and warn the crew first."

"Warn them about *what?*"

"Not to shoot if they see an alien walking around!"

"I'm going with you," Lori said. She was pleasantly surprised to hear him taking a paternal role with Keera. For once he was more worried about protecting her than himself.

"Fine. Let's go." Richard turned and led the way, waving the door to his quarters open as they approached.

They hurried back down the corridor to the elevators. Lori activated the call button with her ARCs and pre-selected *B27* from the available decks. The bridge was just one level up from the officers' quarters—easy to scramble to in an emergency.

Lori had never imagined she'd be scrambling there herself in order to protect her half-alien child from possible friendly fire.

# CHAPTER 24

The elevator doors slid open and Lori followed Richard out at a brisk pace. They walked down a short, curving corridor to reach the bridge. Stars sparkled on artificial viewports to their left. As they came around the bend to reach the entrance of the bridge, Richard's footsteps slowed dramatically.

"Shit! Is that..."

Lori stepped out from behind him to see what he was staring at.

The bridge doors were open. That was wrong. Standard procedure was to keep them shut and locked at all times. Lori belatedly noticed *why* the doors were open. A woman stood in the entrance, her mag boots pinned to the deck, her back arched in a limbo position. Hair drifted lazily around her head amidst shining ribbons and globules of her own blood.

Lori's hand flew to her mouth. "What happened to her?"

Richard crossed the deck, his steps slow and plodding. He stopped short of the body and began shaking his head. Lori followed him there to see what had killed the woman. Long, bloody gashes crisscrossed her uniform from her navel to her chest. Five and five. From two hands.

Lori activated name tapes on her ARCs, and the woman's name and rank glowed in bright blue letters:

*Lt. Celia Asher*

Her blue eyes were wide and staring up at the ceiling as she hung there frozen by zero-G.

Richard looked to Lori. "We have to wake the others *now*. When we confront Keera with this she might try to—"

"Daddy?"

That small, soft and husky voice sliced straight through to Lori's core. She winced, and tears sprang to her eyes. "Keera, honey? Are you in there?" She leaned around Richard to see past the snaking swirls of blood in the entrance of the bridge.

"Mommy?" Keera's voice was thick and cracking with emotion now. She came drifting into view. Not wearing any mag boots, she was floating freely.

"She's *covered* in blood..." Richard whispered.

Lori grimaced and pushed through the entryway. Ribbons and globules of blood splashed against her uniform as she did so. The blood hadn't congealed yet. It was fresh.

Keera sailed by overhead, but Lori reached up and yanked her down to the deck. Holding her at eye level, Lori searched her daughter's teary red eyes. "Keera. Did you do this?"

She shook her head quickly, and squeezed her eyes shut. "No! I found them like this."

"She's lying," Richard replied. "She's the only one who could have done—did you say *them?* Where's the other one?"

Keera broke down sobbing, and Lori glanced around quickly. Her eyes landed on another officer hunched in the captain's station in the center of the bridge. More ribbons and globules of blood sparkled around him. Lori's ARCs identified the man as *Lt. Emon Ferris*. He'd died while still strapped into the captain's chair.

Shocked and horrified to her core, Lori let go of her daughter and hurried over to check on the man. She rounded the captain's chair, checking his life signs with her ARCs. His temperature had only dropped a few degrees, but he had no pulse. It was easy to see why: his throat was missing.

Rounding on her daughter, she shook her head, flinging tears from her cheeks with the movement. "Keera, what have you *done?*"

She just sobbed harder. This was exactly like her waking nightmare from last night: a man and a woman, slashed to pieces. It hadn't just been a harmless fantasy borne of fears instilled by her father. Keera had acted on those thoughts.

# CHAPTER 25

"I didn't do it!" Keera cried through a mess of tears and snot.

"It's okay, honey. We're going to figure this out," Lori whispered, clutching Keera to her chest.

"What's to figure out?" Richard cried. "She came down here looking for us, found them instead, and killed them both!"

"Think about what you're saying, Rick. How could she do all of that? She's never been down here. She doesn't know where the bridge is. She couldn't have known they'd be here."

"I can't believe you're still defending her. There's no one else on board, Lori!" Richard jabbed a finger at Keera. She was peeking back at him with the eye that wasn't buried in Lori's chest. "She killed them. And if we don't wake the others right now, she's going to kill us, too."

"She says she didn't do it," Lori said.

"So who did?"

Lori's mind scrambled for an answer. She surprised herself by coming up with one almost instantly. "You."

Richard blinked. *"What?"*

"You were down here all night. The blood is fresh, but not that fresh. This might have happened hours ago."

"Except you found me in bed, asleep. We found Keera here, covered in blood. That evidence along—"

"I'm covered in blood, too. So are you. It's floating all over the place. And Keera wasn't down here hours ago. She was up on The Wheel asleep."

Richard sneered at that. "You can't possibly determine a time of death just by looking at the bodies. This could have happened minutes ago, right in the middle of our argument in my quarters."

Keera's sobs were growing quieter now. She sniffled, still watching her father with one eye.

"Let's check the security feeds," Lori said, and instantly regretted her own suggestion. If Keera really was guilty, then that would prove it.

Richard's eyes lit up and a cold smile graced his lips. "Good idea." He stalked over to the security station and summoned a holoscreen to life above the console. Lori walked over. Keera clung on tightly, her arms and legs wrapped around Lori's neck and waist.

"Impossible," Richard muttered.

"What?"

"Look!"

Lori stared hard at the holoscreen, blinking past tears to see the search error.

*No records found.*

Lori checked the search parameters that Richard had entered. He was looking for all on-board surveillance on this level between 0600 and now—0902, but the system hadn't found any recordings.

"That makes no sense," Lori said.

Richard just shook his head, a muscle twitching in his jaw. "It might make sense."

"How?"

"If..." The screens changed, and Lori noticed bright images flashing over Richard's eyes as he interacted with the controls via his ARCs. He glanced sideways at Keera, who was now within striking distance of him and took a quick step away from her. Keera noticed his wary behavior, and a low hiss escaped her lips.

"There it is. Look."

Lori's gaze drifted back to the screen above the console. It was a systems log. All of the surveillance data had been wiped clean twenty-six minutes ago. It was a complete data purge, authorized from...

Lori looked at the captain's station where Lieutenant Emon Ferris had died. "Why would he erase the logs?"

"Because someone was threatening to kill him if he didn't," Richard replied while glaring at Keera.

"But he died, anyway. He had to know that it wouldn't matter."

"Maybe, or maybe he was just buying himself time to do something else."

"Something like what?" Lori asked.

"It doesn't fucking matter, Lori! Look at this!" Richard spread his hands to indicate the carnage on the bridge. "Two people are dead, and the killer is wrapped around your throat! I'm surprised she hasn't ripped it out yet."

Lori scowled. "It still could have been you. The logs were erased. Keera wouldn't even know how to cover her tracks like that, but you would. And you have the clearance to do it yourself."

"She wouldn't know how to cover her tracks? She's seen the cameras. We've told her what they're for. She knows that everything on board is recorded. And besides, it wasn't just the logs that were erased. The entire security system was deactivated, too."

That just made Lori more suspicious. "And again, how would she know that she should do that, Richard? She's just a child. She's not that smart."

"What are we even arguing about?! I'm waking the others up right now." Richard stalked past her to the captain's station. His footsteps echoed strangely as he went. A second later, Lori realized that the sound was coming from extra sets of boots—approaching fast.

"Lieutenant Asher!" someone cried, and Lori turned to see Captain Cross standing in the entrance of the bridge with a group of four other officers. Several of them cursed, their eyes flying wide and hands reaching for sidearms that they weren't carrying. The captain's eyes locked with Lori's.

"Dr. Reed! What happened here?" the captain demanded. "And what the hell is that thing around your neck?"

# CHAPTER 26

Stray droplets of blood were busy crashing into all of them. A droplet snuck up Clayton's nose and he tasted the ferrous tang of it on the back of his tongue.

"It's Keera," Lori explained, indicating the creature wrapped around her neck.

"*That's* Keera?" Lieutenant Devon asked. Her bright red hair drifted around her head in glittering strands that shone copper in the overhead light strips.

"It's too big," Clayton said. "Keera's only six months old. Unless we didn't wake up when we were supposed to..." His gaze snapped to Ambassador Morgan.

"You're only a few hours early, and at the risk of stating the obvious, she's not normal, Captain," Morgan said. "She's been developing at an accelerated rate. I've been trying to tell Lori that we needed to wake you and warn you, but it's already too late."

"We don't know that she did this!" Lori snapped.

"Who else could have?" Morgan demanded.

"Maybe *you* did it so you could finally be rid of

her!"

"You're insane."

Clayton looked away from them with a frown and pushed through a glittering ribbon of Lieutenant Asher's blood to join them on the bridge. "Delta, get us some weapons."

"Yes, sir," Delta replied, following him through the open doors to stop at the weapons locker inside the entrance. Clayton waited there with him, never taking his eyes off Keera and her mother.

"What are you going to do?" Lori cried in a shrill voice, her eyes wide as Delta pulled a pair of energy rifles out of the weapons' locker. He handed one to Clayton.

"Set for stun," he said as he flicked his rifle to that setting.

"Yes, sir," Delta replied.

"It's just a precaution, Dr. Reed," Clayton explained as he started toward the captain's chair in the center of the bridge. He could already see that Lieutenant Ferris was also dead—a halo of blood was slowly spinning around his head, and he wasn't moving. "Keep that thing covered," he added, nodding to Delta.

The former Marine grunted and held his energy rifle at the ready.

Clayton rounded the captain's chair with both Delta and Lieutenant Devon to check on Lieutenant Ferris. Lieutenant Davies and Doctor Stevens remained standing outside the bridge, their expressions blank and eyes wide.

"Does anyone need medical assistance?" Dr. Stevens asked, finally finding his voice.

No one replied. Clayton saw that Lieutenant Ferris was still strapped into the captain's chair. His green eyes were staring blankly, and his black uniform was crusted with blood, the white piping stained red. There was a gaping black hole where his throat should have been. It had been ripped right out.

"Shit," Delta muttered, sparing a glance from his rifle's sights to check Ferris's wounds.

"What happened?" Lieutenant Devon asked, her tone sharp and accusing as she rounded on Keera and Lori.

Clayton added his gaze to Devon's. The human-alien hybrid buried its face in Lori's hair and cried loudly, air whistling in and out of its thin nose. He noticed the four short appendages on top of the creature's head and wondered what they were for. Two of them were turned toward him, the openings at the top cone-shaped.

"She says she didn't do it, and I believe her," Lori said.

"But she's covered in blood," Delta pointed out.

"They died recently," Doctor Stevens added from the entryway. "Maybe only an hour ago. The blood is still fresh."

"Like I said," Devon intoned. "What happened?"

"We didn't see," Lori explained.

"Did you check the security logs?" Delta asked.

"They were deleted, and the security system is deactivated," Morgan replied.

"That's convenient," Clayton muttered. He used his ARCs to check the systems log for himself. "The log shows that the security system was disabled thirty-five minutes ago, around the same time the command was issued to wake us from cryo."

"That's what he was buying time for," Lori said slowly. "To wake you up."

"Reinforcements," Delta grunted while glaring down the sights of his rifle at Keera.

Keera whimpered again. "It wasn't me!"

Clayton was taken aback by that. "She talks?"

"She's been talking for months," Lori said.

"Maybe it's time we shut her up," Delta said, hefting his rifle a little higher on his shoulder.

"Stop it!" Lori cried. "You're scaring her!" She spun away from them, and faced the nearest wall.

Clayton looked back to the captain's station with a scowl. "We'll have to conduct an autopsy. Doctor Stevens, do you think you can—"

"Keera!" Lori cried as the child jumped out of her arms.

"Get out of the way, Dr. Reed!" Delta ordered.

But Lori spread her arms to make herself an even bigger target.

The child hit the nearest bulkhead, and a shriek of rending metal filled the air. Lori stepped aside, and they saw Keera vanishing into a maintenance tunnel.

Delta squeezed off a shot, and a bright silver stun round burst from his rifle. It plinked harmlessly off the inside of the tunnel. The sound of Keera's skittering claws faded away into silence.

"Shit!" Delta muttered and dropped the rifle from his shoulder.

Lori's face crumpled and tears sprang to her eyes. They broke free and drifted glittering through the air.

Morgan scowled. "If she's so innocent, why'd she run?" he challenged.

Lori didn't reply.

"Where does that tunnel lead?" Clayton asked, his gaze skipping from Delta to Lieutenant Devon and back again.

"It goes through the whole damn ship!" Delta said. "She could pop out anywhere."

"One of us could follow her," Devon said. "She can't have gotten far."

"It's too dangerous," Clayton replied. The access grate of the tunnel had been sheared open, metal torn to pieces by the child's bare hands —just like the flesh of the two officers whose corpses were busy cooling on the bridge. Having someone crawl through those tunnels after her was a good way to get them killed.

"We'll split up and search the ship. Delta,

reactivate the damn surveillance system. We might be able to use it to track her."

"Aye, sir," Delta replied, already heading for the security station.

"And let's get the thrusters firing and gravity back! It took us fifteen minutes just to get from the damn cryo tubes to the equipment lockers."

"On it, sir," Devon replied.

# CHAPTER 27

"We're splitting into two groups!" Clayton said as Delta passed out more E14 energy rifles. "Devon, you're with Lieutenant Davies." Davies was the comms officer. He was huddled in the farthest corner of the bridge, hugging his shoulders, his shaven head gleaming in the dim light.

"Aye, sir," Devon replied.

"Delta, you and Dr. Stevens are with me."

Delta grunted again, shifting his feet impatiently.

"What about us?" Dr. Reed asked. "You're not going to hunt her down like an animal and then tell me I can't—"

"You're welcome to join us. Why don't you and the ambassador join Lieutenant Devon's team."

"Not a chance I'm going with her," Morgan replied. "I don't trust her."

Clayton swallowed a sigh. "Fine. You're with us, Morgan. But neither one of you is getting any weapons."

"I wouldn't use one anyway," Lori replied.

"Yeah, you'd sooner let it kill you."

"She's not an *it*. Her name is Keera, *Dick*."

"Enough!" Clayton thundered. "We're wasting time. We need to find her before anyone else gets hurt—Keera included. Everyone set your rifles to stun and let's move out! Devon, your team is designated Team Two for comms."

"Aye, sir," she replied.

Walking quickly now that gravity had been restored throughout the ship, they brushed past Lt. Asher in the open doors of the bridge. She was lying on her back in a pool of her own blood, bent at the knees, her feet still pinned to the deck by her mag boots.

They stormed down the corridor from the bridge, heading for the bank of elevators at the end. Clayton hit the call button from a distance with his ARCs.

The elevator doors opened just a few seconds later, and Devon started in, but he stopped her with a hand on her shoulder.

"Take the next one and head up. We'll go down. Use the ship's schematics to find all of the exits for that maintenance tunnel. Make sure you check them all."

"Understood, sir," Devon replied.

Clayton hurried into the elevator behind Delta, Richard, and Doctor Stevens.

They dropped down just one deck, and *OQ26* appeared on the display above the doors.

"First stop," Delta said as he stepped out and swept the corridor with his rifle.

Clayton nodded to Doctor Stevens and Ambassador Morgan before following Delta out. Both of them looked scared, but Doctor Stevens made a visible effort to push past it. Morgan didn't. He was the last one to leave the elevator.

Clayton frowned at that. Keera had obviously killed those two officers, but the circumstances were unknown. When they'd found her on the bridge, she'd been docile and passive, clinging to her mother's neck and crying. That didn't add up to a cold-blooded killer. Maybe she'd acted in self-defense.

And yet her own father was afraid of her, so maybe not. He ought to know by now what Keera was capable of.

"You think she killed those officers in cold blood," Clayton whispered, glancing back at Morgan as they crept down the corridor past the doors to the ship's sleeping quarters.

"Yes."

"Why?" Clayton asked.

"Because that's just what she is. She's a carnivore who likes her meat bloody and fresh. She's a killer, Captain, and I have the scars to prove it." Morgan rolled up one of his sleeves to reveal crisscrossing ridges of scar tissue running through the hairs on his arm.

"She did that?" Stevens whispered.

"And more. Lori's breasts look like they've been through a cheese grater."

Clayton and Delta traded worried glances. "We're going to have to put her in cryo for the rest of the trip," Clayton said.

"That's what I've been saying to Lori for months!"

"Should we be checking these rooms?" Stevens asked, glancing at one of the doors as they walked by.

"The maintenance tunnels don't come out in any of the officers' quarters," Delta replied.

A muffled *thump* sounded to Clayton's right. He whirled toward the sound, his rifle aiming at room number 18.

"You sure about that, Delta?"

"Positive, sir."

"Then she must have already left the tunnels," Clayton replied.

"That's *my* room," Morgan whispered, his voice trembling. "I was just in there!"

"Quiet," Delta hissed.

"What do you mean you were *just* in there?" Clayton asked.

Morgan hesitated.

"I thought you were up on The Wheel."

"I couldn't stay there with that creature any longer. I came down here last night," Morgan said.

"Before those two officers were killed," Clayton said. "That's why Lori said it could have been you."

"You saw their wounds. How could *I* have done that?"

Everyone was staring at Morgan now.

"It wasn't me," he insisted.

"The autopsy will tell us," Clayton replied. "Delta, let's get this over with."

"Aye, sir."

Clayton used his ARCs to open the door. The dim golden hues of night cycle lighting left plenty of shadows for a child Keera's size to hide within. Delta led the way in, and Clayton turned the lights up with his ARCs. The shadows fled, but there was still no sign of Keera.

Clayton's eyes found the door to the bathroom, and he triggered it from a distance as he stalked over.

But it was empty.

"She's not here," Stevens said, peering in over his shoulder.

"Let's check the lockers," Clayton replied. Leaving his rifle to dangle by the shoulder strap, he grabbed both locker handles, sucked in a breath, and said, "Cover me, Delta."

"I've got your back, sir."

Clayton pulled both lockers open and stepped back quickly, snatching his rifle up and taking aim at—

Nothing. Both of the lockers were empty except for spare uniforms and boots.

"The room's clear," Delta said, lowering his rifle. "There's no one in here."

Clayton looked to him with a frown. "Then what the hell did we just hear out in the corridor?"

# CHAPTER 28

Lori walked between Lieutenants Devon and Davies as they checked level 30. The whole deck was devoted to the Officers' mess and rec areas. The maintenance tunnels came out here, in the kitchen. Lori began walking off toward the game tables on the far side of the deck.

"Get back in line, Reed," Devon ordered.

Lori did as she was told, but her eyes narrowed at that order. Devon insisted that she stay between them because they had guns and she didn't. But Lori wasn't afraid of her own daughter. No matter how bad things looked, she knew there had to be some kind of mistake. Keera would never intentionally hurt anyone. She wouldn't have attacked those two officers. Not without provocation, at least.

And now Keera was on the run, but only because they'd threatened to put her in cryo for the rest of the trip.

The ship's lights were gradually brightening, coming out of their night cycle setting. Gleaming stainless steel surfaces snapped into focus, tables and chairs, couches and games tables, a bar... the serving counter, and the ration storage bins.

Devon led the way behind the serving counter and waved the door to the kitchen open. Lori scanned the food prep areas, sinks, appliances, cupboards, and the doors to the walk-in fridge and freezer.

Keera was small enough to hide inside the cupboards, not to mention the fridge and freezer.

Lori's heart leaped into her throat as she angled toward the freezer door.

"Any sign of her on the surveillance system?" Lieutenant Davies asked.

"None yet," Devon replied as she joined Lori by the freezer door. She stopped Lori from opening it with a shake of her head. "Let me." Devon was holding a holotab in one hand. There were three green dots on the screen projected above the base unit. Lori guessed that those dots represented each of them.

"There are cameras everywhere," Davies objected. "If Keera had left the tunnels, the system should have detected her by now."

"Not if she's smart. The system has blindspots," Devon said.

"Yeah, but how would she know where they are?"

Devon shrugged. "Maybe she's still in the tunnels." Turning to Lori, she passed the holotab to her. "Hold this."

"What is it?" Lori asked.

"Experimental tech. A life signs scanner. We're the green blips. Anyone without an *identichip* will show as red."

"Like Keera."

Devon nodded.

"Does it scan through walls?" Lori asked.

"It's supposed to, yeah, but some walls are better shielded than others—like this freezer door. Step back please, Dr. Reed."

Lori flicked a scowl at her. "She's my daughter. She's not a threat. Least of all to me."

"All the same, step back."

Lori retreated grudgingly, and Lieutenant Devon opened the freezer. A blast of icy air hit them, and clouds of condensing moisture billowed out. The freezer was dark inside, but Devon activated the tactical light below the barrel of her rifle and swept the beam around, parting the shadows. The clouds of moisture condensing around them glittered in that light.

Lori checked the scanner in her hand. "Still just three green dots."

"Let's try the fridge," Devon said, and swung the freezer door shut with a muffled thump.

They sidestepped over to it and Devon grabbed the handle. Hesitating for a second, she pulled the fridge open, and flashed her tac light around. It was mostly empty, but a few containers of half-finished rations and meals were stacked on the shelves. Those containers were labeled with the names of the deceased officers up on the bridge: Ferris and Asher.

"Nothing here, either," Devon breathed.

"Did you hear that?" Davies asked.

"Hear what?"

Devon and Lori both spun to face him. He was staring deeper into the kitchen, down to the far end of the galley where the food printers were.

He activated the tac light on his rifle, revealing a shimmering rain of dust-bunnies dancing in the air.

"The air is moving," Davies whispered.

"Yeah, because we're in here, stirring it up," Devon replied. She turned away, shaking her head. "Let's go up to the next level."

Lori began following her out, but Davies lingered. She glanced back at him; he was still standing there, staring at the far wall of the kitchen.

"Lieutenant Davies, are you coming?" she asked.

Before he could reply, the kitchen plunged into darkness.

"Shit!" Devon muttered, sweeping her light around quickly.

"Who turned out the lights?!" Davies asked. He swept his tac light around in panicky arcs. "Hello?"

"It wasn't any of us," Devon replied. "Maybe a systems malfunction? Looks like the lights are out on the whole deck."

"But we still have gravity," Lori replied.

"Which means it's not a complete power failure," Devon said. "We should be grateful for that. Let's get back to the elevators and see if they're working."

Lori nodded and started after her, heading for the mess hall. A pale silver light was emanating from there, indicating that the viewscreens were still relaying starlight from the ship's external cameras.

Lori hurried out of the kitchen.

"Davies!" Devon called, looking back into the kitchen. "Stop staring at the wall and let's go!"

Lori followed the other woman's gaze and saw that Lieutenant Davies was standing just inside the kitchen with his back turned to them, apparently frozen in place.

"Davies?" Lori asked.

A gurgle was his only reply. Then he pirouetted toward them, collapsing as he turned, like an ice skater who'd failed to stick the landing of a jump.

A dark river of blood gushed from a wide gash just below his Adam's apple.

Lori screamed.

"Shit!" Devon cried as Davies hit the deck with a sickening thud. Her rifle snapped up to her shoulder, and she peered down the sights into thin air.

Lori checked the life signs scanner. Two green dots now, but still no red.

"I don't see it!" Devon said.

"You mean *her!*" Lori's eyes blurred with tears. "Keera! We're not going to hurt you! You need to stop this! *Please.*"

One of Davies' legs kicked spasmodically, and Devon cursed again.

"I'm going in," she said. "He might still be alive. Stay here!"

But Lori followed close on her heels. They reached Davies' side and Devon dropped to one knee to turn him over. The blood gushing from his throat was down to a trickle. His eyes were dull and staring, and his lips moved slowly, but no sound came out.

"Get me something to stop the bleeding!" Devon cried.

"Like what?" Lori asked.

Devon pressed a hand to his throat. The blood bubbled out feebly beneath her fingers, then stopped. "Fucking hell!" she screamed. Devon stepped back and straightened, sweeping her rifle around in a two-handed grip with Davies' blood dripping from her left hand. Her tac light parted the shadows to reveal gleaming surfaces and appliances, but nothing else. "She has to be in here somewhere!"

Lori glanced back at the glowing screen of the scanner in her hands. Still no sign of any blips besides their own. "This thing isn't working!"

A *whoosh* of air rushed between them, raising goosebumps on the back of Lori's neck. She whirled toward it with Devon, but as Devon's tac light flashed back over the entrance of the kitchen, it revealed nothing but more dust bunnies glittering in the dark.

"Damn it, she's fast!" Devon cried. "Captain, we have contact on Level 30! And we just lost Davies. Repeat, Lieutenant Davies is KIA."

Lori's guts clenched up with those words. It was getting hard to tell herself that Keera was innocent. Davies had been killed right in front of her, and there was only one person on board who was both small enough and fast enough to have killed him so quietly and stealthily.

Lori stared at the expanding pool of blood around Davies' lifeless body. *Keera, what have you done?*

# CHAPTER 29

"She killed someone else?" Morgan asked. "I knew this was going to happen!"

Clayton ignored him, his brow tense as his mind raced in a thousand directions at once. This was getting out of hand. First Ferris and Asher, now Davies... three of his officers were dead.

"Captain," Devon breathed over the comms. It sounded like she was running. "Are the lights out on your deck?"

Clayton shook his head. "No, Lieutenant. They're out on yours?"

"They went out just before it killed Davies."

"A calculated move," Clayton decided. Keera was a lot smarter than any of them had realized.

"Are you in pursuit?"

"No, sir," Devon replied. "We didn't actually make visual contact, and there are no hits on the surveillance system."

Clayton shook his head. "That's not possible."

"Maybe the system wasn't just deactivated, sir. It might have been sabotaged."

Clayton grimaced. "We'll need to run a full diagnostic to find out."

"Want us to head up to the bridge?" Devon asked.

"No, it's too dangerous. She might anticipate you'd go there, or even just follow you. We need to get more people in on the search. Meet us on the cryo deck. We're going to wake the rest of the crew."

"Aye-aye, sir. See you soon."

"Watch your back, Lieutenant."

"You too, sir."

"Cross out."

Clayton turned in a quick circle to address the rest of his team. Delta was scanning the corridor. He had his rifle's tac light on and was shining it into the shadowy recesses of the entrances to the officers' quarters.

"Everyone on me!" Clayton said. "Delta, watch our six."

"Aye, sir."

Clayton led the way down the corridor to the elevators. His comms crackled with another update from Devon just as they were entering the elevator.

"Sir! Devon here. She took the elevator, and she's headed up. We're in pursuit."

"Check the system logs," Clayton said. "Find out where she's headed."

"I already did, sir. Cryo deck."

"What?" Clayton blinked in shock and shook his head, peripherally noticing as Delta hit the physical button for the same level—*CY44*.

"She must have overheard us talking, sir," Devon replied.

"Wait for us at the elevators."

"But sir—"

"You need backup, Lieutenant," Clayton said. "Wait at the elevators. That's an order."

"Yes, sir."

"We'll be there soon. Cross out."

Morgan caught his eye as he ended the connection. "I told you she's no ordinary child. In fact, I wouldn't be surprised if she's been pretending all this time and she's actually fully-grown. She clearly has the mental acuity of an adult. And she's already reached the same height as an adult Avari."

Clayton acknowledged that with a shallow nod. Morgan was right, but an advanced, intelligent life form going from newborn to adult in only six months wasn't just *fast* development: it was supernatural.

*Don't go losing your head, Clay,* he chided himself. Those red eyes might make her look like a demon, but she isn't invincible.

At least, he hoped she wasn't. He was almost afraid to ask Morgan if they'd ever seen her bleed.

\* \* \*

Clayton stepped out of the elevator into a wall of darkness. A flashlight swept his way, but pooled on the deck at his feet. Devon knew better than to aim her rifle at them.

"Captain," Devon greeted. "The lights are out on this deck, too."

Clayton tried re-activating the lights with his ARCs, but it didn't work. "She must have cut the power somehow," he said.

Devon nodded. "On our way out of the Officers' Mess we saw that one of the primary power conduits had been slashed open. It looked like it had been *clawed* open, sir."

Clayton's mind flashed back to the grate that had covered the opening of the maintenance tunnel on the bridge. It shouldn't have been possible for anything to tear through metal with its bare hands, but this was uncharted territory. They didn't know what they were dealing with.

Activating his rifle's tac light, Clayton traded a glance with Delta.

"Why turn out the lights?" Dr. Stevens asked.

"Because she's hunting us like the animal she is," Morgan said.

Lori glared at him. "It's because she can see better than we can in the dark, and she's trying to stay hidden. *We're* the ones hunting *her*."

"Tell that to Davies," Morgan replied. "Oh, wait—you can't, because he's dead!"

"Stay sharp everyone," Clayton said, walking by Devon and starting down the corridor to the cryo chamber. Before they'd even taken a dozen steps they found the problem with the lights. All of the power conduits in the ceiling had been torn open.

"How did she do that without electrocuting herself?" Clayton wondered aloud.

"Maybe she found the control box and turned off the power there first?"

"Maybe," Clayton agreed. He continued creeping down the hall. Dust bunnies danced through the cones of their tac lights. He swept his rifle around, checking alcoves and the entrances to the various storage and control rooms.

*Swish.*

They all froze. Just up ahead, the access door to the cryo belts was open, providing direct access to the space between the inner and outer hulls. The door slid shut after just a few seconds. Three tac lights converged, chasing the shadows away.

No sign of Keera.

"She must have just gone in," Devon whispered.

"Stay alert," Clayton added as he began inching toward the door. Adrenaline sparked in his fingertips as he flexed clammy hands around the energy rifle.

"Everyone is set to stun, right?" Lori whispered sharply.

"Can it," Clayton snapped. *They'd better be,* he thought. SpaceComm would have his head if he didn't bring Keera back alive.

They reached the access door and fanned out. Clayton took a second to steady himself before triggering the door. "Brace for contact," he breathed.

But before he could do anything, all of their tac lights flickered and died. Even the glowing interface on Clayton's ARCs vanished.

"What the—" Delta's voice cut off in a guttural scream. Clayton whirled toward the sound, perfectly blinded. He snapped off a shot anyway, guessing where their attacker might be.

A brief muzzle flash illuminated something short and crouching with jagged claws. Delta stumbled away from it, and Clayton's stun round *plinked* off the side of the corridor. A hissing snarl faded into swiftly retreating footsteps. Clayton gave chase, blindly snapping off two more stun rounds. By some miracle, one of them hit the scrambling black silhouette running ahead of him, illuminating it briefly with an electric flash of light.

Keera was the only one on the entire ship who was that short. It was her all right. But instead of those stun rods burying in her skin and shocking her into submission, they bounced off, and she raced on down the corridor. Then came a tortured scream of metal shearing. Clayton's footsteps slowed, and the tac light under his rifle flickered back on.

He found himself staring at the ruined grating of the cover to the maintenance tunnels. She'd gone back in.

A flurry of footsteps caught up to him and

more tac lights appeared bobbing over the bulkheads and deck.

Clayton noticed that Delta was bleeding, the entire left side of his uniform torn open across his ribs with three parallel gashes.

"Are you okay?" he asked.

"Just a scratch, sir. I tried to grab her, but—" He broke off in a shrug.

Clayton looked to Dr. Stevens. "Can he push on?"

"He's losing blood pretty steadily, sir. We should get him to sickbay and patch him up."

Clayton nodded absently, his eyes straying back to the shredded cover of the maintenance tunnels. "Do we have time to wake reinforcements first?"

"Not recommended, sir. He could pass out if we don't stop the bleeding soon."

Clayton swallowed a sigh. "Then let's make it fast. On me."

"What happened back there?" Devon asked as he led the way back to the elevators. "All of our lights died at the same time."

"Not just our lights, Lieutenant. All of our equipment. Anything electrical, even our ARCs."

"That might explain how she's able to tear open electrical conduits without getting shocked," Dr. Stevens said.

"But *how* can she do that?" Devon asked. She glanced at Keera's parents for the answer.

"I've never seen her do anything like that before," Lori said.

"Maybe she's been hiding her abilities," Morgan put in.

Clayton shook his head and turned to regard them as he entered the nearest elevator. "Her abilities? She's not some supernatural creature."

But the silence that answered him was proof that everyone else thought otherwise.

As the elevator dropped down to sickbay, Clayton considered it. There were handheld EMPs on board that could cause a brief electrical failure. If Keera had somehow gotten her hands on one, it would explain what had just happened.

*That has to be it,* he decided. But there was something else he hadn't mentioned to anyone: one of his stun rounds had hit Keera, and it had bounced right off. That definitely shouldn't have been possible.

# CHAPTER 30

Devon stood watching the entrance to sickbay while Dr. Stevens patched Delta up. Fortunately, the maintenance tunnels didn't come out inside of sickbay. Knowing that put Clayton at ease, but at this point, maybe it shouldn't have. What would Keera do next? For all they knew she'd gone back up to the bridge. At least access to the control stations was restricted.

"Stop squirming," Dr. Stevens said.

Delta scowled as Stevens threaded his needle for the hundredth time. He'd anesthetized the area, but it was taking a long time to stitch him up. Three gashes, each over a foot long, and wide enough that Clayton could see glistening white bone peeking through underneath.

"Can't you just spray them and be done with it?" Delta asked.

"No. They're too wide."

"It would seal them."

"And you'd end up with scars as thick as boa snakes. Now stop moving or this it going to take all day."

Clayton looked to Morgan and Lori, both standing on opposite sides of sickbay—Morgan

231

with his arms crossed over his chest, Lori looking pale and distraught. They were at odds over Keera. A mother's love was unconditional, but Morgan had always been wary of Keera.

And at this point, they all had reason to be. Clayton walked over to Devon. She glanced at him. "Sir."

"Lieutenant," he replied, acknowledging her back. Dropping his voice to a whisper, he said, "We might have a problem."

"Beside the obvious?"

"Besides that."

"What problem?" Morgan asked in a loud voice as he came over. Clayton scowled at him. Lori approached next, her eyes darting warily between them.

Clayton had been hoping to keep this between him and Devon, but now he had everyone's attention.

"I shot her," he explained.

Lori's eyes flew wide. "You what?"

"Just a stun round, but it was point blank. It hit her square between the shoulders."

"And?" Devon asked, her coppery eyebrows raised.

"It bounced off."

"What do you mean it bounced off?" Delta asked from the examination table.

Morgan snorted and shook his head. "Great."

"Maybe it wasn't a direct hit," Devon suggested. "If the stun rods hit at an angle, they wouldn't dig in."

"They could have hit bone, too," Lori pointed out. Her spine is thicker and more prominent than a human's."

Clayton nodded. "You're right. Those are all possibilities." And they made a lot more sense than the alternative. "Has she ever been hurt?" he asked, nodding to Lori.

"Yes... of course. She fell down lots of times when she was learning to walk."

"But she's never bled," Morgan said, shaking his head. "Her skin might be thicker and tougher than ours."

"Then why does it look transparent?" Lori challenged.

"Because she's a freak!"

"All right, settle down," Clayton said. "Let's all just be aware that it could take more than one round to bring her down."

"If you shoot her with more than one, you could stop her heart," Lori objected.

"It's a risk, yes," Clayton admitted.

"Captain—" Devon's ARCs were bright and flickering with imagery.

"What is it, Lieutenant?"

"We finally got a hit from the surveillance system."

"Where?"

"Level twenty-five. Walking down the corridor as we speak."

"Lock it down."

"Done. She's trapped between two bulkheads, sir."

"No maintenance tunnels in that section?" Clayton asked.

"None."

"Thank God," he breathed, his shoulders rounding as the air left his lungs and the tension left his muscles.

"What's on that level?" Lori asked.

"Escape pods," Clayton replied.

"That's it?" Morgan added.

"The auxiliary armory is there, too," Delta put in.

"Are there any other doors around her?"

"Aye, to the escape pods and the armory. I've locked them, too, but there are manual overrides on all of the doors, including the bulkheads."

"We'd better get down there before she finds a way into the armory and blows the whole ship up," Delta said.

"Lie down!" Dr. Stevens snapped. "You're going to tear open your stitches!"

"It's good enough, Doc."

"I'll be the judge of that."

"He's right," Clayton said. "Stay here with Stevens. The rest of us will go."

"Dr. Reed and the Ambassador should stay as well, sir," Devon said. "Unarmed civilians are a distraction and a liability."

"I'm not staying here," Lori said.

Clayton considered it. "Lori might be able to help, but Morgan can stay."

"Without a gun?" he asked, his voice pitching high with fear.

"Delta has one," Clayton replied as he waved the door open and started out. "Keep the door locked and you'll be fine. She can't claw her way through an inch of reinforced alloy."

Devon and Lori followed him out.

"But—" The door swished shut on Morgan's objections, and Clayton took off at a run. "Double time! We need to make sure she doesn't get away again."

"Let me speak with her before you start shooting," Lori said.

"You're assuming she wants to talk," Devon pointed out.

"We'll do everything we can to avoid a violent confrontation," Clayton reassured. What he didn't mention was that if stun rounds didn't work, they were going to have to set their rifles to kill. He wanted to take Keera alive, but he wasn't going to let anyone else die on his watch.

# CHAPTER 31

"**W**here is she now?" Clayton whispered.

All three of them stood in front of the sealed bulkhead to the section where Keera was trapped.

"Surveillance lost her, sir. I don't know. I have to check the records. Give me a few minutes."

Clayton shook his head. "We don't have a few minutes. She could be in the armory right now. Ready up."

"Ready, sir."

"Stay back, Lori," he added, glancing over his shoulder at her.

She gave no reply, her eyes wide and staring at the door.

"Power's still on," Clayton noted.

"Maybe she got tired of skulking around," Devon replied.

"Or maybe she's waiting for us to open the door before she drops the lights. Stay sharp." Clayton reached for the control panel beside the doors rather than using his ARCs to open them. That way Devon would have some warning.

As soon as he triggered the doors, he took a quick step back and snapped his rifle up.

The corridor was empty.

"Looks clear," Devon whispered.

He pointed to his eyes and then to one of the escape pod hatches. The control panel and number on the hatch were glowing red, which meant that the pod was occupied.

He led the way, walking slow to keep his mag boots from clanking on the deck.

They reached the hatch to pod 216. There was a tiny circular window in the inner hatch and a matching viewport in the rear of the pod itself. Clayton caught a glimpse of a small bony white creature curled up on one of the acceleration chairs—her snake-like ear canals poking above the headrest. Clayton's hand flashed out to the control panel, and he locked the hatch with his personal access code. Heavy locking bolts slid into place with a loud *thunk* and Keera jumped out of her chair. Bright red eyes met with his.

"What are you doing!" Lori cried.

She probably thought he was launching the pod.

"Relax. I'm just containing the threat." He got on the comms. "Delta, Cross here. Threat neutralized. We've contained her in one of the escape pods."

"Aye, sir..." Delta said through a sigh.

"We should just launch her into space," Morgan growled, his voice crowding in on the same channel.

"Who gave him a comm piece?" Clayton demanded.

"He took it from an equipment locker," Dr. Stevens replied.

"Great," Clayton muttered.

"Should we come down?" Delta asked.

"I'm not done with him," Stevens objected.

"Stay where you are," Clayton said. "She's safely contained."

"Copy, sir." Delta sounded disappointed. Maybe he'd been hoping for his pound of flesh to replace the one Keera had sliced out of him.

"We'll see you soon. Cross out."

"Now what?" Lori demanded, her eyes hard and glaring, arms crossed over her chest. "You can't leave her in there forever."

A flicker of movement and a muffled thumping sound drew Clayton's attention to the hatch. Keera was crying and smacking on her side of the windows with both palms, her voice muffled.

"We won't. Once we've woken up some of the others, we'll open the pod and stun her. Then we'll put her in cryo."

"We should just do it now and get it over with," Devon replied. "There's two of us and just one of her."

Clayton considered that. "I shot her once already and that didn't work. And Lori's right, if we shoot her with multiple stun bolts, we could kill her. We want to avoid that at all costs."

"Let me talk to her," Lori insisted. "Who's to

say that stun rounds will work on her at all? But I can get her to listen to me."

Clayton hesitated.

"Lock me in this section with her if you're that scared!"

"She could kill you," Devon said.

"She wouldn't intentionally hurt me."

"That's not what Ambassador Morgan said," Devon replied.

"He's an idiot. Trust me. I know Keera better than anyone."

Clayton chewed his lip. "We need to have her restrained."

"The armory is right here!" Lori said, turning to indicate the door. "Get me cuffs and I'll put them on her."

Clayton took a shaky breath. "Okay."

"Sir—" Devon objected with a sharp look.

"She's right, Lieutenant. This is a good plan, and it might just prevent further loss of life. Keera's included."

"Thank you," Lori said.

He nodded stiffly to her and went to the armory. After a brief search of the lockers and weapons racks inside, he found two sets of stuncuffs with smart locks. He grabbed a stun collar for good measure and then returned to Keera's escape pod. Lori and Keera were communicating through the windows with their eyes, both pressing their palms and faces to the inner and outer hatches.

"Here," Clayton said, nudging Lori's shoulder.

She turned with tear-streaked cheeks and stared at the items in his hand.

"A collar? She's not an animal, Captain!"

"She's dangerous, Lori. Even you have to admit that. I need you to cuff her hands behind her back, cuff her ankles, and put the collar on. That's the only way this is going to work. They won't deliver any shocks unless she tries to tamper with them."

"She's a child! Of course she's going to try to take them off."

"Then tell her not to."

Lori held his gaze for a long moment, glaring.

"I'm sorry, Dr. Reed. It's the only way."

She cracked a bitter smile. "Back to last names are we. I thought we were friends, Captain."

"We are. Get it done, Lori. We'll be waiting on the other side of the doors."

# CHAPTER 32

Keera fell out of the escape pod, sobbing. Lori caught her.

"Shhh, it's okay."

"I didn't do it, Mommy."

Lori nodded and smiled, kissing the top of her daughter's head. "I believe you." But she didn't. Not anymore.

"Are they going to fweeze me?"

"Yes."

Keera withdrew sharply, her eyes flashing with terror. She stumbled back a step, shaking her head. "Don't let them."

Fresh tears ran hotly down Lori's cheeks as she held out the stuncuffs. "I need you to put these on, honey. Can you please turn around for Mommy?"

Keera's eyes darted, looking for an escape.

"It's the only way, sweetheart. I promise I won't let them hurt you."

Keera's face fell and her eyes grew dull. "You don't believe me."

"Of course I do, honey."

But Keera had always been perceptive. She knew it was a lie. She turned around and something inside of Lori broke. Her eyes ran like rivers.

Lori reached for Keera's hands. They were stained red and crusted with blood, and the sleeves of her plain black jumpsuit were stiff with dried blood.

Lori cuffed Keera's hands behind her back, then did the same with her ankles, and finally, placed the collar around her neck.

"Now we can go."

Keera began rolling her shoulders and straining against the stuncuffs. An electric pop and crackle sounded and a scream tore from her lips.

"Don't do that, honey," Lori said. "Don't struggle."

"It hurts..." Keera gasped.

"Only if you struggle," Lori replied, taking her daughter by the arm and leading her toward the sealed bulkhead where Captain Cross and Lieutenant Devon were waiting. "Come with me, sweetheart."

Keera was sobbing again. "I don't want to."

Lori sent her a broken smile. "It will be okay, honey. I promise."

"You lie."

"I'll keep you safe," Lori added.

But they both knew that was also a lie. At this point, Keera's fate was out of Lori's hands. They were going to freeze her until they reached Earth, and then SpaceComm and the UNE would decide what happened to her.

A vision flashed into her head: Keera lying strapped to a table in a lab somewhere, being poked and prodded by Union doctors and scientists, screaming in pain as they tortured her in the name of science and progress.

Somehow Lori had to stop that from happening. She couldn't let them take her.

Lori bit her lower lip as she triggered the doors open to see Clayton and Devon waiting with their rifles aimed. Clayton was the first to drop his weapon.

"Hello, Keera," he said.

She just cried louder.

"Lead the way please, Dr. Reed."

Lori nodded stiffly and walked by them to the elevators. They crowded in behind her and the elevator shot up, racing back to the cryo deck.

"Stop your sniveling," Devon snapped at Keera. "It's a little late for remorse."

"Shut up," Lori said.

"Can it. Both of you," Clayton added, sending Lori a warning look, but he softened it with a grim smile.

The elevator stopped and opened into darkness. Lori led the way at a shuffling pace with the bobbing cones of light from Clayton's and Devon's tac lights chasing the shadows away to either side of her. Lori's breathing was fast and shallow. Her heart hammering against her sternum. *There has to be a way to stop this!*

Time seemed to accelerate with every step.

They walked through a congealing puddle of Delta's blood. Then came the doors to the cryo chamber. They opened with a noisy rumble.

"Over there. Nine o'clock," Clayton said, and flashed his tac light over an open pod just beside the doors.

Lori helped Keera inside. She struggled feebly and received another shock for her trouble. Gasping and sobbing, Keera buried her face into Lori's chest. "Please don't."

"I'm going to join you soon," Lori said.

Keera withdrew, looking a snotty mess. "You are?"

Lori smiled as reassuringly as she could. "Yes."

Keera knew when she was lying, and conversely, she knew that this was the truth.

"You're going to blink your eyes and you'll wake up again and we'll have arrived at Earth."

Keera's tears stopped falling. She sniffled. "What's it like?"

"It's amazing. The cities. The parks. And the food! You've never had a hamburger before, have you?"

Keera's eyes lit up and she shook her head. Lori smiled brightly at her. "You're going to love it on Earth."

Lori was afraid that Keera could tell she was lying again, but the child didn't object when Lori guided her into the open pod.

Devon came over with a syringe. The lieutenant was about to inject the sedative herself, but then thought better of it. "Why don't you do it?" she said, and handed Lori the syringe.

Lori stepped closer to Keera, and said, "This will sting just a little, okay?"

"Okay," Keera replied.

She didn't even cry as the needle went in. Her eyelids grew heavy, and a wistful smile crossed her lips. "Good night, Mommy."

Tears welled again in Lori's eyes. "Goodnight, darling," she said, stepping back as the pneumatics groaned to life and the pod cover swung shut. She waved and blew a kiss to Keera through the glass, but Keera was already asleep.

Then came a sharp hiss, and a billowing cloud of condensing moisture rippled out. Lori reached up with shaking hands to wipe her eyes.

Someone else's hand landed on her shoulder and squeezed. "I know that was hard for you," Clayton said.

"Harder for the families of the officers she murdered," Devon replied.

Clayton turned to his XO with a frown. "Yes, but I don't think she can help it, Lieutenant."

Devon snorted.

"It's just what she is," Clayton explained. "It's instinct, like a lion or a shark."

Those words sank in, taking root in Lori's mind. Richard had said the same thing about Keera on more than one occasion. Maybe they were right. Maybe it was just her nature.

A killer's nature.

# CONSEQUENCES

# CHAPTER 33

After a grisly job cleaning up on the bridge, Clayton and the others retired to their quarters on level twenty-six. Delta stayed behind, having volunteered to take the first watch.

Clayton stopped at the door to his room, and nodded to Lieutenant Devon as she walked by.

"Sleep well, sir," Devon said with a grim smile. Her red hair was down and bouncing lightly across her shoulders in the artificial gravity.

"Likewise, Lieutenant," he replied. His eyes slipped away from her to see Ambassador Morgan and Doctor Reed walking to their rooms. Separate rooms. They still weren't on the same page about their daughter. Morgan clearly thought she was a demon, but her mother remained defensive—even after everything that had happened. *That's a mother's prerogative,* he supposed. Looking away from them, he waved his door open and stepped into his quarters.

The door swished shut behind him on an automatic timer. On an impulse, he used his ARCs to lock the door. Even with Keera safely frozen in cryo, he wasn't comfortable sleeping with an open door after what had happened on the bridge.

Old, childish fears were making a steady comeback. The idea of sleeping alone in his room was fraught with ghoulish dread. He was almost tempted to look under his bunk. Clayton cracked a smile at the thought. Fear was natural after what they'd been through, but resorting to childish paranoia would be going too far.

Walking to the bathroom, Clayton removed his mag boots and socks, and then stripped out of his uniform and underwear. He took care to remove his rank insignias and Space Force emblem before tossing the uniform in the laundry chute with the rest of his clothes. The laundry room would automatically wash and press it all before sorting his clothes into a personal storage unit there. But with no crew on laundry duty, he'd have to fetch the uniform himself in the morning. Thankfully, he had plenty of spares in his locker.

He wondered if they should have woken up the rest of his watch, but the crisis was past, and they were all exhausted.

Clayton paused in front of the mirror above his compact vanity, naked and staring at himself with wide, blinking eyes, as if he didn't recognize his own face. He was still in shock. Two more officers were dead. Three along with his previous XO, Commander Keera Taylor. What was he going to tell their families?

Clayton grimaced and pushed the thought away. He'd have plenty of time to think about it on the journey home.

Turning from the mirror, he went to the shower and waved the door open. He shuffled wearily across the threshold, and his feet touched cool beads of moisture.

Clayton froze. The walls and floor of the shower stall were freckled with stray drops of water. He ran a hand across the cold metal surface between the shower jets in the walls. His fingers came away wet. Had someone been using his quarters while he'd been in cryo? Asher or Ferris, perhaps?

Too late to ask them now. Clayton triggered the door shut and used his ARCs to activate the shower on its default setting. The jets all snapped on at once, spraying him with hot water from all sides for ten long seconds. Then came the soap cycle, followed by more hot water. Tension bled from his muscles as the soapy rivulets ran down his body, taking with them what felt like months of accumulated filth. The jets turned off after thirty seconds, and then vents opened up to blast him with hot air.

In less than two minutes he was clean and dry.

Heading back through the bathroom, he stooped to pick up his mag boots, then grabbed his rank insignia and Space Force emblem from the vanity. Carrying it all over to his locker, he stowed the items inside and dressed in a plain black jumpsuit that served as his sleepwear. He shut the locker door and padded over to his bed. Time to get some sleep.

Clayton unzipped the covers and climbed into bed, not bothering to zip himself up. The engines were powered up at 1G of acceleration, perfectly simulating Earth gravity.

"Lights off," Clayton said. The overhead light strips faded to black, and then he rolled over to stare at the viewscreen beside his bed. Stars glittered brightly, imagery relayed from the ship's external cameras. He'd spent countless nights during his duty rotations on the way to Trappist-1 staring at that window, thinking about what they might discover when they arrived.

And now they knew. They'd discovered life... plants and animals, and an advanced alien species: the Avari.

They were even bringing a hybridizing alien virus and a healthy human-alien hybrid back with them.

It all seemed like a dream, or a nightmare. The mission to colonize a planet around Trappist-1 had failed miserably, but they had succeeded in making first contact. They'd accomplished one of their primary objectives. And by the time they returned to Earth, almost a hundred and eighty years would have passed. By then their first contact might actually turn out to be second or even third contact—assuming the other Forerunners had encountered life as well. But whatever they had found, Clayton was willing to bet his ship was the only one that had encountered intelligent life.

He remembered the Avari ships chasing them from Trappist-1 and buzzing them as they'd approached. And Dr. Grouse's revelation of what they'd been hunting for in his head: Earth's location.

Was it even possible to relay that kind of complex information without a common language? The Avari they'd met down in that lab hadn't been able to speak with them. Besides, for all they knew, the Avari weren't actually hostile. Their interest in Earth might be borne of sheer curiosity, and their actions around Trappist-1 might have been purely territorial. If they were looking to expand, why go to Earth? It was unlikely that they'd share the same definition of habitability.

But Keera was a perfect mix of the two species—part human, part Avari—and she would be perfectly adapted to Earth's environment.

Clayton's brow tensed up with fresh concern, but he let it go. He couldn't do anything about any of it until they returned to Earth. He allowed his milling fears to bleed away into a growing haze of sleep. His eyes shut and images swirled from the depths of his subconscious.

He dreamed of armies of children just like Keera descending on Earth in big, sloping black ships with no windows.

He saw himself standing on the front porch of the home he'd once shared with Samara. Houses and trees burned on both sides of the street, and human-alien child soldiers ran around, chasing his screaming neighbors. Bill, the old widower next door, jumped through his front window with a thunderous crash. An Avari hybrid was clinging to his back, clawing at his eyes. Bill fell down screaming, with blood gushing from his face before the monster on his back jumped off and took a bite out of his throat. It slowly turned to look at Clayton, still chewing on a grisly bit of trachea. Its mouth and lower jaw were covered in blood. A low hiss sounded, not coming from its mouth, which was still busy chewing, but from the four snake-like appendages on top of its head.

Clayton turned and ran inside the house. He yanked open the screen door and it banged noisily behind him. He slammed the old wooden door shut and activated the deadbolt with his ARCs.

A loud *thud* sounded, and the door visibly shuddered as the creature collided with it; then came a familiar scream:

"Clay! Help!"

*Samara.* His wife.

"Sam!"

He ran for the stairs, but he was moving far too slow; his entire body felt numb and useless. He hit the bottom of the carpeted stairs to the second floor.

And then Samara came staggering out of the master bedroom with blood gushing from her mouth. Her lips were moving, but no sounds other than gurgles were coming out. She went limp and tumbled from the top step.

"No!" he cried as she rolled down the stairs to greet him. He caught her in his arms near the bottom. "Sam!"

He turned her over to face him, but her neck was clearly broken, her eyes dead and staring just as they had been the night he'd had to identify her body.

Then came a low growl and a shrill whoop of blood lust.

Clayton's eyes skipped back up to the top of the stairs. An Avari hybrid stood there, its arms spread wide from its body, and blood dripping from long, curving black claws to the carpet. Its mouth was parted in a devilish grin of sharp, blood-smeared teeth, and bright red eyes glittered like a demon's.

By this point, Clayton knew he was dreaming, and that was all it took to wake up.

He blinked through a bleary haze to see a shadow crouching over him. A gleaming bundle of wires trailed from the head of his bed to a device in that monster's hand.

Clayton tried to sit up, but his muscles wouldn't respond; he tried to scream, but his lips wouldn't move.

With his heart hammering in his chest, he used his ARCs to activate the lights. As soon as they came on, the shadow faded away into thin air just as it had all those times before.

But the bundle of wires remained, and so did the device that they were connected to. Something invisible was standing beside his bed. Clayton tried to spring free of the covers—

But he was still paralyzed.

# CHAPTER 34

Clayton's eyes were the only thing he could move. They darted from the invisible *thing* beside his bed to the door and back. How had it gotten in here? He'd locked the door. And what *was* it?

It only took him a moment to answer the second question. The bundle of wires trailing to the *head* of his bed was the same as the ones they'd seen coming from a helmet on Dr. Grouse's head in that Avari lab.

Somehow an Avari had snuck aboard their ship. Clayton used his ARCs to send a text-based message to the bridge: *Contact! Invisible Avari in my quarters. Need support ASAP.*

Delta's reply appeared on his ARCs a split second later: *Copy. Backup on the way, sir.*

He knew better than to waste time with questions.

Clayton watched as the Avari standing beside his bed removed the bundle of wires from the device it was holding. The device vanished, and the wires dropped to the deck with a loud slap. Now the Avari was completely invisible, ready to ambush Delta as soon as he came in.

The bridge was just one deck away. Delta would be here soon. He had to do something fast. Clayton tried to make a fist.

Nothing. This was the longest bout of sleep paralysis he'd ever had. He thought about sending a message to Devon. She was much closer, but Delta had more specific training to deal with this. He was the chief of security for a reason. If he called Devon, she'd arrive first and probably get herself killed.

Clayton held off and tried again to make a fist. This time his fingers twitched. He could barely move them, but feeling was rushing back.

He finally managed to sit up, but his head felt heavier than usual. His hands flew up and clawed off a helmet. He tossed it aside and it bounced and skidded across the room.

Just then, the door to the room swished open. Clayton's pulse soared, singing in his ears.

"Delta! Try infrared! It's wearing some type of cloaking device!"

Softly padding footsteps answered between Clayton's own ragged breaths, but no reply came from Delta, and no sign of him appeared in the open doorway. That was when Clayton realized that the invisible alien in his room was the one who had opened the door. Somehow it had the code for the door lock.

"Show yourself!"

His eyes darted around, blinking furiously and squinting for any possible sign of the creature.

But the only sign he got was the door sliding shut.

Clayton eased slowly off his bed, wondering if he was really alone. Hearing no footsteps or scurrying of claws to answer his own movements, he hurried over to the emergency weapons locker and pulled out an E14 energy rifle. Setting the sights to infrared, he tested them on his foot. A mottled orange and red blur appeared. Sighting down the barrel, he swept the room, checking for hidden heat signatures.

Nothing but cold blue bulkheads, ceiling, and deck. He'd be out of luck if the Avari were cold-blooded, but if Keera was any indication, they'd actually have a stronger heat signature than humans.

There was a glaring flaw in his plan, however: if the Avari could block visible light, they could probably block the invisible wavelengths as well.

Clayton dropped the rifle to his hip.

And then the door slid open again. Delta appeared in full body armor with a matching energy rifle. He lowered it quickly, and Clayton noticed that Devon was standing behind him, also armored.

"Get in and shut the door. It already left," Clayton said.

Delta stepped in warily, glancing around. Devon came backing in, watching his six the whole way. Clayton waved the door shut behind them.

"If it was invisible, how do you know it was even here?" Devon asked, finally dropping her guard to look at him.

Clayton took a second to reply. He was busy changing the door code and locking it again. The bolt *thunked* into place. "We're secure," he said; then turned and pointed to the helmet he'd discarded. "I knew it was here because I woke up wearing *that*. And it wasn't invisible until I turned on the lights."

Both Delta and Devon stared at the helmet; then Devon went to pick it up. She turned it over in her hands, leaving her rifle to dangle by the shoulder strap.

"Is that...?" she trailed off.

"The same thing they put on Dr. Grouse," Clayton confirmed. "It was connected to something in the Avari's hands, some kind of portable storage device maybe."

Delta's brow furrowed above hard blue eyes. "So you think they... what—downloaded the contents of your brain?"

Clayton shook his head. "I don't know." His mind raced for answers. This wasn't the first time he'd awoken in his quarters, paralyzed, and seen a shadow skulking around. How long had that Avari been on board? Since they'd left Trappist-1? Or had it come aboard from one of those unidentified blips that he and Commander Taylor had been tracking on approach?

"She didn't kill them," Devon said slowly, still staring at the helmet.

"Who?" Delta asked.

"Keera. She didn't kill Ferris and Asher."

"We don't know that," Delta said.

"No, we don't," Clayton added, "but now we do have another suspect."

"An invisible one with an unknown agenda," Delta said. "This is not good, sir." He glanced back at the door. "We need to wake up the rest of the crew."

Clayton was already on his way to retrieve the mag boots from his locker. He pulled them out and strapped them on, then added an ear-worn comms piece in case they got separated.

"Channel one, sir," Delta said.

He set it with a thought, then straightened and nodded. "Move out, Delta." With his Space Marine background, Delta was better trained to take the lead—not to mention he was wearing a full suit of body armor.

"Yes, sir," Delta replied. He gripped his rifle with both hands, but hesitated in front of the door. He glanced back over his shoulder with one eyebrow raised. "The code, sir?"

"One sec," Clayton replied. The bolt *thunked* aside as he unlocked it. Delta waved the door open, and then they were on their way, fanning out from the room and checking both sides of the corridor.

"Left side clear," Delta said.

"Right side clear," Devon added.

Clayton checked both sides with his own sights, then shook his head. "We don't know that. Infrared probably gets blocked by the cloak too."

"We can lock down this deck," Delta suggested while glancing around warily. His posture was rigid, tense.

"You're assuming it's still here," Devon replied.

"Well, if it is, we should get out of the damn corridor. On me." Delta led the way to Lori's quarters and waved the door open. It slid aside, and they stormed in. She rose sleepily from her bunk while Clayton shut and locked the door behind them.

"Lights on," Delta said.

"What..." Lori woke with a start and sat up, rubbing the sleep from her eyes. "What's going on?"

"There's an Avari on board," Clayton explained.

Lori's eyes flew wide, then collapsed to slits. "I knew it wasn't her!"

"Let's try not to make any assumptions yet," Clayton replied.

But Lori flew out of bed and stumbled to her feet, standing with her fists clenched and shaking. "You made me put her in cryo!"

"And that was the right call at the time," Clayton said.

"It probably still is," Devon added, glancing between them. "At least she's safe."

Lori subsided and worry crawled into her eyes. "Did it ki—is anyone else..." She trailed off, not wanting to say it.

Clayton shook his head. "Not yet." He nodded to Delta. "We need a way to track it."

"We could use the surveillance system to look for elevators and bulkhead doors opening and closing for ghosts," Devon said. "Then we just have to lock the ones around it and box it in."

Clayton nodded. "Good idea. Start working that angle and let us know if the computer finds anything."

"It's probably using the maintenance tunnels," Delta said.

"Or it'll start using them now," Clayton agreed.

"Surveillance will see if cover panels are being removed or torn open," Devon pointed out.

Lori shook her head hard, blinking and squinting at them in the bright lights. "What are you talking about?" She looked to Devon. "Ghosts?"

"It's invisible," Clayton said. "Short of bumping into it, we're not going to find anything."

"*Invisible?*" Lori echoed.

"Cloaked," Clayton explained.

"What about laser sights?" Devon asked.

Clayton shook his head. "Won't work."

"We won't see the dot reflect, but we should still see where it vanishes, right?" Devon insisted.

"An EM cloak doesn't work that way," Clayton replied.

"You're talking like that's a thing," Devon objected. "It's theoretical tech."

"Well, in *theory*, electromagnetic radiation is passed seamlessly from one side of the cloak to the other. Ideally, it even does that with the wavelengths we can't see, like infrared—and definitely with the ones we can, like red laser sights."

"Yeah, that's bullshit," Delta said. "Give me a high-powered laser and we'll see how much radiation it can pass from one side to the other without burning a hole." He patted his energy rifle. "This baby should do the trick."

"You still have to know where it is to shoot it," Clayton said.

"So what's your idea?" Devon asked.

A slow smile spread on Clayton's lips. "We have training guns in the armory."

"Training guns?" Delta spluttered. "Paintballs aren't going to..." He trailed off as the penny dropped. "Oh. I gotcha, Cap. Nice."

Devon gave a sly smile. "Good thinking, sir."

"Don't congratulate me yet. We still have to get there."

"I'm coming with you," Lori said.

"No civilians," Delta said. "You're a liability."

Lori's eyes flashed. "I have weapons training."

"But no combat experience."

"Not all of you do, either!"

"He's right," Clayton said, and waved his hand to cut off the argument. "Stay in here with the door locked."

"For all you know, it's already in here with us," Lori pointed out.

Delta grimaced and made a show of looking around. "Well, joke's on us if it is, because we just told the little shit our plan."

"It doesn't understand English," Devon said.

"You mean we hope it doesn't," Delta replied.

"Let's go," Clayton said, turning back to the door.

"I'm not going to stay here!"

"You don't have a choice," Clayton replied.

"If you weren't going to take me with you, then why did you come in here?"

"To regroup," Clayton explained.

"At least now you know not to leave your room for a midnight snack," Delta added.

"Keep the door locked, Lori—and change the code," Clayton said.

"What? Why?"

"Because it knew my code, so it probably knows yours, too."

"How is that possible?"

"Probably pulled it from someone's head,"

Delta muttered.

Grabbing his rifle in a two-handed grip, Clayton opened Lori's door and stepped out into the corridor. Seeing nothing, he whispered, "On me," and set a brisk pace for the elevators. Lori's door swished shut as they left, and the locking bolt *thunked back* into place.

Delta was right. The Avari had been fishing around in Dr. Grouse's head, now Clayton's, and probably Lieutenant Asher's and Ferris's, too. If it had managed to find the security codes for doors, what else had it found?

A trickle of icy dread slithered through Clayton's gut as the answer came to him. Sick as he'd been at the time, Dr. Grouse was right: the Avari knew where Earth was.

# CHAPTER 35

"Shouldn't we warn the ambassador and Doctor Stevens?" Devon asked as they reached the elevators.

Clayton nodded. "Get them on the comms. Tell them to stay in their rooms with the doors locked. We don't have time to stop and chat."

"Yes, sir... sending message," Devon replied.

The doors of the nearest elevator parted, and Clayton stepped inside. He hesitated as Delta and Devon came in, trying to remember if the training weapons were kept in the main armory or the auxiliary one.

"Deck fifty, sir," Delta supplied, and he reached out with an armored glove to stab the button on the panel. The main armory. The button was highlighted with a red outline to indicate that it was also one of the decks with escape pods on it.

"The ambassador is calling me," Devon said as the elevator started upward.

"Better answer it," Clayton replied.

Devon made a face, then sucked in a breath and said, "Ambassador, as I said in my message, we have a situation with—oh, Dr. Reed already told you. Good. We're handling it. Just stay in your room and keep the door..." Devon trailed off, her eyes rolling as Ambassador Morgan cut her off.

"No, you can't help... yes, I realize you're supposed to handle diplomacy, but this isn't—" Another sudden pause. Clayton couldn't help smiling. "We'll let you know if we require your help. First we have to catch it. Lieutenant Devon out." She blew out a breath. "*Damn*, that man is an *ass*."

"Yes, he is." Clayton turned from her to watch the lights of passing decks flashing through the transparent windows in the top of the elevator doors. The lights strobed slower and slower as they drew near to deck fifty. "Ready up," Clayton said, and grabbed his rifle with both hands again.

The doors slid open, revealing a curving corridor with hatches to escape pods lining the outer wall.

"Taking point," Delta said. He stepped out of the elevator with his rifle up and tracking.

Clayton and Devon walked out after him, squinting through their infrared scopes to check for heat signatures.

"Clear," Delta said.

"As far as we can tell," Clayton whispered.

"Training gear is in WP06," Delta replied, gesturing with his rifle to indicate the right-hand side of the corridor. He led the way, and Clayton followed with Devon bringing up the rear.

The glowing green rings and numbers of hatches to escape pods flashed by to their left, and the full-sized doors to the armory flashed by to their right.

Clayton kept expecting something invisible to jump out and attack them as they went. For all they knew, that Avari had ridden up in the elevator with them.

Clayton cut a quick glance back the way they'd come. Devon was walking backward, keeping their six covered. She turned to look where she was going and caught his eye as she did so.

"No sign of anything yet, sir."

He nodded back. His pulse was racing, and his hands were sweating on the grip and handguard of his rifle.

"Found it," Delta said as he stopped by the door marked *WP06*. He waved it open and the lights came on automatically for them as they crowded in. Devon shut the door behind them, and Clayton waited until the locking bolt *thunked* into place. The storage room was a long aisle lined with lockers, and only wide enough for them to stand single file. Delta walked down to the end and opened one of the lockers. Clayton and Devon both followed.

Delta left his energy rifle to dangle from the strap and reached into the locker to pass out a rifle that looked almost exactly like their E-14's. Clayton took the weapon and passed it down to Devon. The main difference was that these weapons were marked *T-14* rather than *E-14*, and they were much lighter and easier to carry—with the exception of a bulky under barrel hopper full of paintballs.

"Here you are, sir," Delta said as he passed out a second rifle.

Clayton slung it across his shoulders, leaving the training weapon to dangle by his left hip, while the real one stayed within easy reach on his right.

Removing a third weapon for himself, Delta began passing out ammo belts with spare hoppers on them.

Clayton passed the first one down to Devon and then strapped on a second for himself.

"Any hits on the surveillance system?" Clayton asked, glancing back at Devon.

She shook her head. "None yet, sir."

"It could still be hanging around the bunkrooms on twenty-six," Delta pointed out as he clipped on an ammo belt for himself and shut the locker.

"Or maybe it rode up in the elevator with us," Clayton suggested.

Delta grimaced. "Or that."

Devon's eyes flared wide. That thought obviously hadn't occurred to her. "So what do we do to find it? We can't just go around spraying the ship with paint until we hit something."

Clayton took a moment to consider that. She

was right of course. He'd been counting on the ship's internal cameras to detect some kind of activity by now, but wherever the Avari had gone, it was being careful to avoid opening any doors or elevators within sight of the ship's cameras.

"We could lay a trap for it," Delta suggested.

"Except we don't know what the Avari was after," Devon said. "So we don't have any bait."

"It was after me," Clayton said. "It was in my quarters, and it put that helmet on my head for a reason."

"So..." Delta trailed off. "You want to go back to sleep and see if it returns?"

"Maybe, but it might have already extracted whatever information it was looking for," Devon pointed out.

"Assuming that it was looking for information," Delta said. "Maybe it implanted something in your head."

"That's a happy thought," Clayton replied. Turning back to Devon, he said, "I have a better idea than waiting around for it to come to us."

Devon's eyebrows shot up.

"We wake the rest of the crew. And the dogs."

Devon's brow furrowed. "Why the dogs?"

"So they can sniff it out," Delta replied.

Clayton nodded to him. "Exactly..." He trailed off, remembering how Charlie had been barking at something that only he could see during those initial tests of the Visualizers. Maybe he'd smelled a cloaked Avari skulking in the comms lab.

"Sir?" Delta prompted.

"Let's get down to cryo," Clayton said. "Delta, lead the way."

"Yes, sir." He squeezed by Clayton in the narrow aisle, their rifles clattering together, then did the same to get past Devon. "Opening door," he added, raising both of his rifles, one in each hand.

The door opened into darkness.

Delta reacted as if he'd just touched a live wire, his whole body flinching. He swept his rifles around briefly, checking for targets.

Their tac lights were still on and parting the shadows as the three of them stepped out together and scanned both sides of the curving corridor for targets.

No sign of anything.

"Let's spray some paint," Clayton said.

"You got it, sir," Delta replied.

They splattered the bulkheads with bright red paint as they swept their training rifles around for a second time. But none of those projectiles hit anything besides the sheer gunmetal grays of the corridor.

Clayton gave up with a sigh. "At least we know it's not in the immediate vicinity."

"But we know it was here," Devon replied quietly.

"You're telling me the surveillance system

didn't spot anything?" Clayton demanded.

"Nothing," Devon said. "It's set to alert me anytime a door opens anywhere on the ship. So far the only alerts I've received are from the ones we've opened."

"So it's shadowing us," Delta concluded.

"Check again, Devon," Clayton said.

Delta popped off another shot. Another red splotch appeared, this time on the deck about a dozen feet away from him.

"Thought I saw something," Delta explained.

"Devon?" Clayton prompted.

"Looks like there was something... up on level twenty-six."

Clayton's brow furrowed. They'd come from there less than fifteen minutes ago.

"What was it?"

"Dr. Reed's door, sir. Three minutes ago it opened, then shut."

"And you missed that?"

"Looks like the system went offline. Some kind of malfunction. The report just came in now as I was checking."

Clayton gritted his teeth. He'd told Lori to keep her door locked. "Get her on the comms."

"Calling..." Devon shook her head. "Everything is out on that level... lights... cameras... I've got nothing. Surveillance is also down again."

"The Avari," Delta said. "It targeted her."

\* \* \*

Lori heard the knock on her door and pulled

her knees up to her chest where she sat in the armchair by her window. She tried activating the holocomm, but the lights were out in the corridor, and she couldn't see who it was.

"Hello?" she tried. Her voice would be relayed to whoever—or whatever—was out there.

"Lori! Open the door! It's Captain Cross!"

She slowly rose from the chair, confusion swirling like smoke. He'd just been here a moment ago. What was he doing back so fast?

"Captain? What happened to the lights?"

"That thing is out here! It's hunting me! Open the door!"

Lori hesitated for just a second before triggering the door open with her ARCs. The locking bolt slid away and the door swished open. A wall of darkness lay on the other side—

And nothing else.

Lori's brow furrowed. "Captain?"

No answer. A light breeze touched her face, the air stirring.

Lori waited for a second longer. Maybe the Avari got him. Feeling suddenly stupid for opening the door, she shut and locked it once more.

She crawled deeper into her chair, tucking her knees up under her chin, her eyes darting. What if it was in here with her?

"Hello?" she tried.

No answer.

"I know you're here! I have a gun!" she said. But that was a lie. As a civilian, she didn't have clearance to access the emergency weapons locker in her room.

No answer. Lori's skin prickled with goosebumps under her plain black jumpsuit. Long seconds passed and nothing happened. She tried activating the holocomm again to transmit her voice into the corridor. "Captain, are you out there?"

More silence.

Why hadn't he just opened the door for himself? She'd changed the lock code just as he'd suggested, but he was the captain. He had the clearance to override any door or lock on the entire ship.

That realization sent adrenaline sparking through Lori's veins. Something wasn't adding up. She slowly rose from her chair. "Hello," she tried again, her voice cracking with fear.

Another breeze caressed her face, and then the lights went out inside her room.

Lori jumped with fright. She felt something cold and hard press against the side of her head. It felt like a gun.

"W-what do you want?" she asked in a shivery voice.

A low hiss sounded beside her ear, followed by a sing-song voice speaking in shrieks, more hisses, and growls. The language was completely unintelligible to her—it didn't even sound like it was made up of words.

But then words came, spoken clearly in a language that she could understand, and in Captain Cross's own voice.

# CHAPTER 36

Clayton and Devon followed Delta back to the elevators, popping off paintballs as they went to make sure they weren't walking into an invisible Avari. It looked like the intruder was up on level twenty-six, but at this point they couldn't be sure that there weren't two of them.

Clayton and Delta swept their energy rifles and tac lights around, firing paintballs into the bulkheads and deck with resounding splats.

Halfway back to the elevators they found several conduits in the ceiling torn open with severed wires spilling out.

"Looks like it clawed them open," Devon said.

"That's a long way up," Delta replied. "How did it even reach that high?"

"And not get electrocuted in the process," Devon added.

Delta answered, "Back when we were chasing Keera, she seemed to be able to interfere with electrical systems for brief periods."

"You're assuming that was Keera," Clayton whispered. "It could have been the Avari."

"I didn't think of that."

"Let's keep moving," Clayton said.

They started down the corridor again. Delta kept firing paintballs into thin air as they went.

"What about Lori's emergency locator beacon?" Clayton thought to ask.

"Offline," Devon replied.

"How is that possible?" Delta asked.

Clayton tried sending a text message to her, but an error popped up on his ARCs: *Contact offline.* "Her ARCs are down, too." Turning to Devon, he said, "What about the elevators? Are they still working on twenty-six?"

"They're powered from multiple decks, so they should be."

"Check."

Devon's eyes flickered briefly with glowing screens. "Still operational, sir."

"Good. Lock all the doors leading to them. The access chutes, too. Do that for our level as well."

"Done," Devon replied. "You think it's still down there?"

"Yes, or at least one of them is."

"One of them?" she asked.

"The lights were still working out here when we went into the armory. And they were on when we left level twenty-six, too. There's no way just one saboteur could take out conduits on both levels in such a short time. Especially not without tripping your security alerts."

Delta popped off a few more strategic paintballs as they went, scanning blindly for targets.

They reached the elevators, and Devon reactivated the doors to one of them manually so that they could leave. Clayton selected level twenty-six with his ARCs.

The elevator rocketed down for several seconds, then slowed to a stop. The inner doors opened, but the ones to the deck stayed shut since Devon had locked them. Clayton stared at the glowing number 26 blazing on the doors. The windows at the top were dark.

"Lights are still out," Delta whispered.

Clayton crowded in beside him and peered down the infrared sights of his E-14, checking the left window, then the right. "No sign of Lori's heat signature in the corridor," he said.

"Maybe she realized that we locked her in and went back to her room," Devon said.

"Or maybe her door opened because the Avari went in and killed her," Delta said.

"Let's hope not. Devon, get these doors open."

"Aye, sir."

The doors slid open and Delta pumped half a dozen paintballs off into darkness. Six splats echoed back to their ears in quick succession. The cones of Clayton's and Delta's tac lights flashed over the nearest crimson blotch as they swept the corridor for signs of movement.

"Push out," Clayton whispered.

Delta took the lead again—then froze and held up a closed fist to mean just that: *Freeze*.

He pointed with his E-14 to something beside the elevator doors. Clayton stepped out beside him and saw immediately what had caught Delta's eye. The door to the access chute beside the elevators had been torn open. The doors were mangled and blasted into the chute, charred with residues from some kind of explosives.

"Looks like our bird flew the coop," Delta whispered.

Clayton stepped to the broken doors and shined his tac light up and down the access chute, checking the ladder for signs of movement.

But there was nothing.

"Where the hell is Lori?" Clayton muttered.

"Could still be in her room," Devon said.

"Dead or alive?" Devon countered.

"Dead, if she's there," Delta said. "We should take a look."

Clayton grimaced and shook his head. "If she's dead we can't help her, and if the Avari took her as a hostage, then the best thing we can do for her is get up to cryo and wake more people to help with the search. Devon, I assume there's no sign of her on surveillance?"

"None yet... no, wait. There is something. More malfunctions. Lights, cameras, and comms are out two levels up... and they're out in one of the elevators, too."

"Clever bastard," Delta said.

"They're on their way up," Devon added.

"Check their destination," Clayton said.

"CY44."

"Cryo," Delta muttered. "Shit."

"Let's move!" Clayton said.

They hurried back into the elevator and Clayton selected *CY44* from the panel.

The inner and outer doors slid shut at the same time, and the elevator raced up.

He hoped that Lori was still alive—better a live hostage than another dead body.

*  *  *

Lori stood perfectly still in the darkness of the elevator car, with nothing but her own shallow, rasping breath to break the silence. She was completely cut off. Even the comforting glow of her ARCs was missing.

The light of passing decks strobed periodically through the elevator doors, blinding her with alternating flashes of light and darkness. Hairs stood straight up on the back of her neck, her arms covered in goosebumps beneath her jumpsuit.

The Avari was in here with her. She couldn't see it or hear it. But she knew it was there, and it had given her clear instructions:

*"Take me to the child."*

She was desperately trying to think of a way to thwart the Avari that didn't involve outright refusal to obey.

She would sacrifice herself if it came to that, but maybe there was another way. If only she could reach Captain Cross on the comms.

The elevator stopped and the doors opened onto the cryo deck. A sharp jab poked her in her lower back, pushing her forward. She stumbled slowly out into the darkened corridor. The lights were still off from when Keera had torn open the electrical conduits. If that had even been her.

"What do you want with her?" Lori asked.

No answer, just another jab in the small of her back. She would have selected a different deck just to buy herself some time, but the Avari had chosen it for her as soon as they'd entered the elevator. It seemed to already know that *CY44* was the cryo deck and that Keera was there.

That implied that this creature had been watching them. That, or it had pulled the information from the captain's head.

They came to sealed doors at the end of a short corridor. A hissing growl slithered to Lori's ears, followed by the translation in Captain Cross's voice: "*Open.*"

Lori reached for the control panel beside the doors with a shaking hand. She deliberately missed the open button twice, and received another sharp jab in her back.

More growling and hissing. A shriek. The sounds alternating low to high and back in a vaguely sing-song fashion.

Then came the translation: "*On this setting it will not kill. But it will hurt you very much.*"

Lori hit the right button and the doors rumbled open. Lights flickered on as they stepped inside. Keera's pod was still sitting there on the cryo level, right beside the door, the glass frosted blue. Keera wasn't visible through that fine patina of ice. Lori's eyes tracked over to the pod, giving it away before she caught herself and looked somewhere else.

The alien behind her jabbed her again and guttural sounds drifted to her ears.

The translation: "*Wake her.*"

"I can't," Lori lied, shaking her head.

More growls, followed by: "*You will.*"

Something sharp dug into her back. She winced but resisted.

And then it sliced her open, and a hot river of blood spilled out. Lori screamed as a blinding wave of pain lit her nerves on fire.

A low series of growls and hisses ground out. "*Wake her now. You are only alive for her sake, but this can change.*"

Lori staggered slowly toward a pod two places down from Keera's. She felt an iron hand close around her forearm, dragging her to Keera's pod.

A hiss. "*This one.*"

Lori was running out of ways to stall. "What do you want with her?" she asked again.

No reply. She stopped in front of Keera's pod, hesitating, then felt another prick as something sharp punctured her skin.

A growl. "*Wake her.*"

"What the hell?" someone asked.

Lori whirled toward the sound and relief flooded her veins as she saw Captain Cross, and Lieutenants Delta and Devon standing in the open doors of the cryo chamber, holding two rifles each.

"It's standing right next to me!" she cried.

"Paint the target!" Captain Cross shouted.

And then all three of them opened fire.

# CHAPTER 37

Crimson paint splattered Lori from head to toe—as well as something invisible standing beside her. A loud hiss accompanied each crimson splash of paint, and soon a short outline appeared.

Delta was the first to risk live fire. A bright red laser beam flashed out and hit the invisible target, dead center of one of the paint spatters, drawing a piercing shriek from the creature.

And then it appeared, wearing a glossy black helmet and a black suit with a faint fish scale pattern. Two skinny arms protruded from its chest and its legs were bent at the knee. Wicked claws and small hands were wrapped around a long, slender black weapon. Small, booted feet with claws protruding from them leapt off the deck and translucent wings spread wide from its back.

Delta opened fire again, but this time a flash of light accompanied the shot, and nothing happened.

Clayton and Devon dropped their training rifles at the same time and tracked the target as it flew up to the high ceiling of the cryo chamber. Bright red lasers flickered out of their energy rifles, stabbing the Avari repeatedly with reciprocal flashes of light.

"It's not doing anything!" Delta said.

And then the Avari fired back with a brilliant emerald laser.

Devon screamed, while both Clayton and Delta dived away to either side. He ducked and rolled, coming up and whirling around to see Devon lying on the deck with black smoke curling from her chest.

Clayton's ARCs identified her life signs as fading. Somehow, that one laser bolt had burned straight through her armor.

"Devon!"

He ran over to her, snapping off two more shots at the Avari as he went. It was still hovering over them, buzzing its wings loudly like a giant hummingbird.

The alien fired back, and a wash of heat warmed Clayton's cheek before sizzling into the deck beside his right foot. The laser left a fading, molten orange circle in the metal.

"Fall back!" Clayton cried.

Delta already had Devon under her arms and was busy dragging her out into the corridor beyond the cryo chamber.

Clayton ducked out with him, and the Avari swooped into view. Another emerald laser flashed by, dazzling their eyes.

Clayton triggered the doors shut and locked

them with his latest codes.

"She's not doing well, Cap," Delta said, crouching beside Devon.

Her eyes were wincing shut and her pulse was weak and skipping around wildly on Clayton's ARCs. "We need to get her to sickbay with Stevens," he said.

"Lori's still in there with that thing," Delta pointed out.

"We can't help her right now. It has some kind of a shield. Our shots were all bouncing off."

That triggered a memory: chasing Keera through the ship, and a stun bolt bouncing off her back. It was beginning to look like they really had been mistaken about her.

Devon's eyes cracked open and she sucked in a shuddering breath. "Kill it. I'm not going to..."

Clayton shook his head. "Get her legs, Delta. I'll take her shoulders."

"I'm already dead," Devon rasped.

"Not yet you're not," Clayton snapped. He began backing up with Devon, struggling to walk with her weight. For once zero-G would be a good thing. "I'm turning off the engines," he said.

"Good idea," Delta grunted.

But before he could do anything, Clayton felt a draft raising the hairs on the back of his neck—and then something sharp digging into his spine. He heard a hissing growl. Dropping Devon, he whirled around and pumped a laser bolt into thin air.

An abbreviated shriek sounded, followed by another Avari de-cloaking in a fish scale-patterned suit. A wisp of black smoke trickled from the middle of its glossy black helmet.

Delta dropped Devon with a curse, and pumped three more crimson laser bolts into the creature's chest before it crumpled to the deck and lay still.

"Is it..." Delta trailed off, looking pale with shock.

Clayton nodded and hurried back to grab Devon's shoulders—

Only to find her eyes staring blankly up at him. He checked her life signs with his ARCs.

No pulse.

"She's dead," Delta croaked. "Damn it!" he kicked the nearest bulkhead with his mag boot and rounded on the doors to cryo. "Let's get in there and finish it off! We killed one; we'll kill the other!"

"I shot it before it de-cloaked," Clayton said slowly. "I don't think their shields can operate at the same time as their cloaks do."

"So we concentrate our fire!"

Clayton shook his head. "It just needs to hit *us* once. We need more firepower to take it out."

The cryo chamber doors thumped as if from a fist hammering on them.

"I think it just realized I locked it in," Clayton said. "We'd better get to the armory before it finds a way out of there." He spared a pained look at Devon and then turned and started for the elevators.

"On me, Delta!"

They sprinted down the corridor to the elevators, but before they'd even made it halfway there, a deafening *boom* shook the ship and a searing wall of heat slammed into them from behind. Clayton stumbled and whirled around to see a fiery, molten ruin where the doors to the cryo chamber had been. A short, crouching black figure was picking its way through the rubble.

"Too late!" Delta cried. Two bright red lasers flicked out from his rifle to greet the Avari.

Clayton brought his weapon up and snapped off another shot, but none of those lasers did anything.

Then the Avari fired back.

This time it was with a rocket that deployed from a boxy contraption around the creature's left wrist. A gleaming silver projectile flashed past them riding a bright blue tongue of flame. It hit the elevators with a thunderous *boom*. The shockwave picked both Clayton and Delta up and threw them like dry leaves in a storm.

Clayton landed hard with the back of his skull slamming into the deck. He blacked out for a second and came to with his ears ringing. A crouching figure in a black suit ushered Lori and Keera ahead of it. Delta struggled to rise and bring his rifle to bear, looking just as dazed as Clayton felt. The Avari aimed its weapon at him. Clayton tried to scream out a warning, but his ears were ringing so hard that it was impossible to tell if any sound had escaped his lips.

Then Keera darted in front of Delta and spread her arms wide. She growled and bared her teeth at the Avari.

Clayton blinked bleary eyes, not sure he could trust what he was seeing.

The Avari shoved her aside and kicked Delta in the side of the head. He subsided, unconscious, and then the Avari's gaze swept toward Clayton.

He quickly shut his eyes, being careful not to move. He lay like that with his heart slamming in his chest, waiting for a clawed boot to connect with the side of his head, too—or worse, for a laser to burn through his chest and stop his racing heart.

He waited... and waited, but nothing happened. Counting out ten long seconds, he opened his eyes and caught a glimpse of the Avari slipping through the mangled doors to the access chute beside the elevators. It hadn't been aiming that rocket at the elevators. It had been aiming at the access chute. The Avari was leaving the cryo deck the same way that it had escaped Devon's lockdown on level twenty-six.

Clayton fumbled for his rifle, hoping to score a parting shot, but the Avari vanished before he could get a good grip.

His head spinning, eyes and airways burning with the acrid smoke rolling through the corridor from both ends, Clayton rolled onto his back and blinked hard at the ceiling.

*Where are they going?* he wondered.

The answer was clear even in his foggy, blast-rattled head. The Avari was taking Lori and Keera back to whatever ship it had used to board the *Forerunner*. If they had personal cloaking devices, their ships must have the larger version. For all they knew, Avari shuttles or fighters were clinging to the *Forerunner's* airlocks like barnacles.

Clayton tried to rise again—

And caught a glimpse of the second Avari, the one he'd been lucky enough to kill, lying just a few feet from Lieutenant Devon's body. The live Avari hadn't spared it so much as a passing glance on its way out.

Clayton struggled up to a sitting position, and the ringing in his ears retreated just enough to hear a crackling roar of flames. The elevator they'd come up on was torn open and the car inside was on fire.

"Delta!" Clayton croaked.

No answer.

He dragged himself over to the former Marine and checked the man's life signs with his ARCs. A strong, steady pulse registered.

Clayton shook him by the shoulder.

Nothing.

He tried again.

"Delta!"

A groan. He stirred and rolled over, fumbling blindly for his rifle.

"We're clear. It's gone," Clayton said.

"That little shit kicked me," he muttered.

"They're on their way out," Clayton said. "We can't let it take them. We'll never see Keera again —or Lori..." He trailed off, shaking his head. He didn't know what the Avari wanted with her, but he didn't want for her to have to find out.

Clayton pushed off the deck with a grunt. Both rifles were still slung around his neck. "Think you can get up?" he asked, reaching down with a hand.

"Yeah, why not," Delta said, taking the hand and jumping up. He stood swaying on his feet for a moment. His weapons lay at the far end of the corridor. He stumbled over to collect them.

Clayton stayed where he was, using his ARCs to check the ship's security system. Now that the Avari wasn't trying to hide, he could see it clearly on the ship's surveillance system. It was crawling *down* the access chute at a rapid rate behind Lori and Keera. Unlike the maintenance tunnels that Keera had vanished into, there were plenty of cameras inside the access chutes.

"We can still catch them," Clayton said. "Come on." He began limping over to the ruined doors of the access chute. As soon as he reached the opening, he leaned through and aimed down with his E-14. The Avari's heat signature burned brightly in his infrared scopes. It was taking up the rear, keeping Lori and Keera in its sight. Delta crowded in beside him, taking aim as well.

"Ready?" Clayton whispered.

Delta nodded.

But before they could even pull their triggers, the Avari looked up. That skinny black sidearm appeared—

Clayton ducked back from the shaft, pulling Delta away with him just as a blazing green laser burned through the space that their heads had been occupying a second ago.

"Thanks," Delta breathed, looking shaken.

Clayton watched them via security feeds on the right lens of his ARCs. They were descending the ladder past the wardroom on level 30, and still headed down.

"Now what?" Delta asked.

"The elevators are shot out on this level," Clayton answered. "We have to wait for them to clear out of the access chute or risk getting shot as we climb down." Clayton watched as the Avari and his two hostages continued down, passing level 20 and still descending.

"Where are they going?" Delta asked, his eyes bright with imagery on his ARCs. He was obviously watching the same feeds.

Finally, they stopped climbing down. The camera closest to them showed Lori opening the door to level 17.

"They're headed for The Wheel?" Delta asked.

Clayton shook his head. Level 17 gave access to The Wheel, but it also gave access to all four of the spokes leading there, each of which had its own airlock midway along its length. Those airlocks were almost never used. "I think we just found out where they docked their ship," Clayton said.

"We'll never make it down there before they can get away," Delta replied.

"No, we won't," Clayton mused. "But we could scramble to a pair of Scimitars before they launch. We'll light up the space around the airlocks." He saw the Avari leaving the access chute, and nodded to Delta. "Let's go."

"Maybe you should stay on the bridge, sir."

"One fighter isn't going to be enough to find them, Delta. We'll get the ship to wake the rest of the crew." Clayton leaned over, peering into the vertiginous depths of the access chute, double checking to make sure that it was clear.

No sign of the Avari.

"Better let me go first," Delta said. "At least I'm wearing armor."

Clayton shook his head and started down the ladder. He was about to explain the breach of protocol, but the words got stuck in his throat: body armor hadn't helped Devon.

Using his ARCs to access the cryo belts as he climbed down, he set the ship to begin waking the crew; then he mentally composed an emergency welcome message to greet them when they woke up. *Found Avari on board, invisible to the naked eye and scanners. Giving chase with Delta in Scimitar fighters. Secure the bridge and all sensitive areas. Captain Cross out.*

# CHAPTER 38

Lori shuffled through the cargo transfer air-lock with Keera. Despair and panic clutched her like a boa constrictor, making it hard to breathe. A flashback burned bright in her mind's eye: of that rocket exploding, sending Captain Cross and Delta flying; then of the Avari shoving Keera aside and kicking Delta in the head when he'd tried to get up.

Captain Cross, Lieutenant Devon, and Delta were all either unconscious or dead. Help wasn't coming this time. Besides Richard and Doctor Stevens, they were the only ones awake on the ship right now.

They reached the elevator doors, and Lori stopped, waiting for instructions.

Instead, the Avari reached out with a small hand and used one of its three fingers to stab the call button. Lori noticed that those fingers all ended in vicious black claws just like Keera's, but Keera had five fingers, not three.

The elevator doors sprang open. *"Get in,"* the Avari growled.

Lori shuffled through, pushing Keera ahead of her. She began reaching for the control panel on the other side—her ARCs were still offline thanks to whatever the Avari had done to disable them.

The diminutive alien batted her hand away from the control panel with a hiss. She couldn't see a face or expression through its helmet, but she imagined the creature was baring its teeth at her.

Lori wondered absently why the Avari was taking them to The Wheel, but at least it wasn't spinning anymore, so artificial gravity would only be pulling them in one direction.

The Avari touched one of the three buttons on the screen inside the elevator. *A01*—the airlock.

Lori blinked in shock. In hindsight it should have been obvious. It had to have boarded them with a ship of some kind. Now it had what it had come for, and it was leaving.

The elevator jerked into motion, gliding forward and swiftly picking up speed. Stars flashed past windows in the sides of the elevator.

"Where are we going?" Keera asked, her eyes big as she stared at the alien. The Avari's glossy black helmet stared back at her, inscrutable as ever.

Lori pulled Keera close and kissed the top of her bald, bony head. "It's going to be okay," she whispered.

The elevator slowed and jerked to a stop just a few seconds later, but the doors didn't open.

Lori turned to look at the circular hatch to the airlock. The Avari walked quietly over and opened it. A small vestibule appeared. The airlock.

A growl. *"Inside."* The Avari gestured with its gun.

Lori shuffled forward with Keera.

The windows in the outer airlock doors showed nothing but stars and empty space. A new fear stabbed sharply in Lori's chest. There was no ship docked on the other side. Would they have to put on pressure suits and crawl around on the outer hull to reach the Avari vessel?

The alien shoved Keera toward the hatch. She rounded on it and lashed out with her claws, raking them across the Avari's torso. Lori expected to see black Avari blood spurting out.

But Keera's claws slid right off, as if that fish-scale-patterned suit were made of glass.

*"Inside,"* the Avari growled again.

"Get in, Keera," Lori urged.

Her daughter hissed again before climbing through. Lori followed and walked straight to the outer airlock door, pressing her face to the windows and trying to find the Avari's ship.

She still couldn't see it.

"We'll need pressure suits if you want us to go out there," Lori said. Then a thought occurred to her to buy some time: maybe the Avari didn't know that there were suits stored in the airlock. "We'll have to go back to one of the storage levels to get them."

The hatch slammed shut behind them, and the Avari stalked wordlessly over to stand beside Lori.

She frowned at it. "Did you hear me?"

It touched the *Cycle Airlock* button.

Lori's eyes flew wide, and she lunged to abort the sequence, but her hand fell short.

"Hold on, Keera!" Lori said, grabbing the nearest handrail.

And then the outer doors sprang open with a blast of escaping air. An infinite sea of stars and empty space yawned on the other side, and the Avari pushed her into it. Lori lost her grip on the handrail and screamed as she fell flailing into the abyss.

# CHAPTER 39

### Five Minutes Earlier...

Clayton and Delta hurried to put on flight suits and helmets in the ready room before entering the Scimitar hangar on level five. Chatter began bubbling over Clayton's ear-worn comms —officers waking up and asking about the situation on board. He gave instructions to Dr. Stevens to go out and get everyone organized. Besides Clayton, he was the ranking officer now.

"You should stay on board, sir," Stevens objected.

"No time to argue, Stevens," he replied as he slipped his flight helmet on. "Secure the bridge and scramble the rest of the Scimitar pilots to reinforce us."

"Aye, sir."

Delta moved to open the doors to the hangar. A yawning chamber appeared with a dozen giant parallel cylinders protruding from the deck and massive conveyor belts leading to them. The Scimitar launch tubes.

Clayton and Delta ran for the tubes, racing past the conveyor belts that were used by the ship's flight crews to ferry Scimitars in and out for maintenance and repairs.

But these fighters hadn't seen any action yet, so they were all loaded up and waiting.

Clayton skidded to a stop in front of the hatch to Launch Tube 01. Delta stopped at Tube 02 and they both triggered their hatches open in the same instant. The sides of the tubes facing away from the conveyor belts slid up, toward the ceiling, revealing sleek fighters with reflective glass cockpits and gleaming black hulls. It was like the chamber of a giant rifle sliding open to expose a bullet.

Clayton waved a hand to open the mirror-plated cockpit canopy. It slid up, too, and then he climbed in. The orientation of the fighters and launch tubes made that awkward—they were facing down in the tubes, ready to launch out the back of the *Forerunner.*

Clayton straightened his legs inside the cockpit, pressing his feet flat against the pedals for the Scimitar's lateral thrusters. Pinning himself to the back of the pilot's seat, he held himself up against gravity until he buckled the four point restraint system over his chest. That done, he used his ARCs to fire up the fighter's ignition system and then shut the cockpit and launch tube.

A HUD swirled to life inside Clayton's helmet, and buttons, screens, and sliders came to life on all sides of him, glowing brightly.

He grabbed the flight stick, and the fighter

shivered as it came alive in his hand.

Pneumatics groaned as the cockpit and launch tube slid shut, sealing him in. Red lights flashed down the length of the launch tube, parting the darkness and revealing the wide, flared opening at the end. That flaring exit point made for easier re-entry.

Clayton reached down and grabbed the air tubes trailing beside his seat and connected them to either side of his helmet, sealing the openings there. Cool, fresh air began flowing into his helmet around his mouth and nose, coming from tanks behind his seat.

Delta's voice came over the comms, his deep baritone loud and clear: "All green and ready to launch when you are, sir."

Clayton did a quick pre-flight check on his main holoscreen. "All systems green. Activate launch sequence."

"Copy."

Clayton did the same, and a verbal countdown began: "Launching in five, four, three..."

A rising *hum* of energy thrummed through the Scimitar as magnetic rails inside the launch tube powered up. The entire system was like a giant cannon, and he was sitting in the projectile.

"...One—"

The doors sprang open at the end of the launch tube, and locking bolts released. Then came a violent roar that hammered Clayton into the back of his flight chair. The sides of the tube went racing past in an instant, and stars and space enveloped him. He saw Delta's fighter streaking out to port.

"Yeah-ha!" Delta whooped. "Damn, I forgot how much I missed this!"

"On my wing. We're looping back. Time to light up those airlocks."

"Copy that, Cap."

Clayton hit the left pedal, slewing the nose of his fighter around until he was facing the glowing blue engines of the *Forerunner*.

The Wheel was massive, with four thick spokes connecting it to the central column of the ship.

Clayton marked target boxes around the airlocks to either side of Spoke Three.

"You take Spokes One and Two. I'll take Three and Four."

"Roger," Delta said.

"Weapons free," Clayton said as he armed his laser cannons. Wings folded out from the sides of his fighter as the hardpoints deployed; then he pulled the trigger and a pair of bright crimson beams snapped out with loud zapping sounds. Both the visuals and sounds were simulated by the Scimitar's combat computer. Clayton fired six pairs of lasers through the empty space beside the airlocks of Spoke Three, but the beams vanished into infinity, converging on the empty target boxes before diverging again on the other side.

Delta's shots passed through empty space as well.

The *Forerunner* was drifting closer as they cruised toward it at a rate faster than its 1G of acceleration.

"Next spoke!" Clayton ordered, and marked target boxes around the airlocks of Spoke Four. He held down the trigger again, expecting his shots to vanish into empty space once more.

The Avari had probably already left. Or maybe their ship was docked with one of the airlocks on The Wheel itself.

Crimson laser beams flashed out repeatedly to either side. Then stopped abruptly. This time the beams didn't diverge on the other side of the target box. They hit something invisible dead center of it.

"Contact! Spoke Four!"

"Copy, marking target..." Delta said. A split-second later his lasers converged on the invisible target as well.

Triumph swelled in Clayton's chest. As they drifted near, he could actually see their lasers burning holes in the enemy's invisible hull. Fine white sprays of condensing air were jetting out into space.

He just hoped that Lori and Keera weren't in that part of the enemy ship.

# CHAPTER 40

Lori landed face-first on something solid. The Avari hadn't pushed her out the airlock into empty space. He'd pushed her out into his ship. Her brain had taken a second to catch up and realize that she was falling into something other than empty space.

Keera appeared crouching beside her. The girl's chalk-white face was drawn with worry, black veins standing out sharply against her skin.

"It's okay. I'm okay," Lori said, grunting as she pushed off the deck and twisted around to see where she was.

The airlock was dark, the surfaces non-reflective, metallic. Tubes and conduits ran along the walls and ceiling, much like they did aboard Union ships.

The Avari stepped into the airlock, its boots ringing loudly on the grated deck panels. Below them looked like some kind of drainage system. That was also familiar. A place for air and decon sprays to drain away or get sucked out.

The Avari paused and tapped a space beside the inner doors. A glowing screen appeared, projected over the surface. It tapped a symbol on that screen, and then the inner doors banged shut, sealing them inside. The alien turned to face them, still not removing its helmet.

Lori realized that she could breathe the air inside the ship, but maybe it couldn't. Had this Avari prepared the environment for them ahead of time, thereby making the air unsuitable for itself to breathe? Or was it wearing a helmet for other reasons?

Before she could wonder more about that, a bright flash of light blinded her, and a loud hissing sound began. She tracked the sound and her eyes landed on a molten orange hole in the ceiling of the airlock. The air inside began stirring violently around her. The Avari shrieked and ran to the doors leading to the interior of its ship. Another bright flash slashed through the air, and a wave of heat washed over Lori. A second hole opened up, and the volume of that hissing noise doubled.

That was when Lori understood what was happening: those bright flashes were lasers punching through the ship. The inner doors sprang open, revealing a long corridor with more dull gray bulkheads.

"Come on!" Lori said, and yanked Keera up with her. They ran and scrambled through the opening just as another laser punched through the ceiling of the airlock. The doors slammed shut behind them. Warning sirens started up somewhere inside the ship. Thinking this was their chance, Lori ran after the Avari, hoping to take advantage of its distraction to overpower it or take its gun. Two more flashes of light slashed through the ceiling directly ahead of her, dazzling her eyes, and she skidded to a stop.

At the end of the corridor, a set of narrow doors parted and the Avari burst through into what looked like a small cockpit.

By this point the hiss of escaping air had turned to a roar. It was whipping around them furiously, tugging her hair. Lori saw dark spots dancing before her eyes. The air was getting thin.

Another pair of lasers flashed through the hull, scalding Lori's cheek—

She sprang back, her reflexes taking over, and then fell hard on the deck.

Another laser sliced through the Avari ship, so close that it blinded her completely—

And her daughter screamed.

"Keera!"

The roar of escaping air mysteriously stopped. Lori whirled around, blinking her eyes furiously, searching for her daughter. Keera was standing a few steps back with a long, slender gun pressed to the side of her head.

A second Avari was holding that weapon, but this one was much taller than the first, and it wasn't wearing a helmet. The alien's features looked vaguely familiar as well. That familiarity registered in Lori's brain a split second later.

"David?" She couldn't believe her eyes. It was him all right, but Doctor Grouse didn't look the least bit human anymore—or sick. He looked exactly like a bigger, taller version of Keera.

He tilted his head, and his cranial stems twitched, but he didn't reply. Maybe he no longer recognized his own name.

"Don't do this," Lori pleaded, hoping to appeal to whatever humanity he might have left. "We need to get back aboard the *Forerunner* before—"

"Sit down," David growled in a flat, emotionless voice. He nodded to a long bench seat along one side of the corridor.

Lori pushed off the deck and started toward the bench on shaking legs. She heard footsteps trailing behind her as Dr. Grouse escorted Keera.

Wondering what had happened to all the holes in the hull, Lori glanced up and scanned the ceiling. But there was no sign of any damage. It had to be self-repairing. Or maybe shields were holding in the air.

Another growl sounded from David. *"Sit down."*

Something *thunked*, and Lori felt a subtle tug of acceleration as they flew away from the *Forerunner.* Somehow that acceleration didn't knock her off her feet, but even more curious was the fact that gravity continued to pull them *down* even though they were no longer sharing the uniform acceleration of the *Forerunner's* thrusters.

"Where are you taking us?" Lori asked as she sat on the bench. David pushed Keera down beside her.

"Secure yourselves," he said.

They fumbled with odd, springy restraints that were many sizes too small for Lori. She looped her arms through them, but Keera managed to buckle them over her chest.

Another thought occurred to Lori. "You were the one who killed Ferris and Asher, weren't you?"

David bared sharp white teeth at her. "They had to die. They tried to stop us."

Horror washed over her, and her jaw dropped. "Stop you from doing what?" she demanded. "Can you hear yourself?"

David wordlessly turned and walked to the opposite bulkhead. He tapped the blank gray surface, and it changed, becoming bright with stars and space: a viewscreen. A holographic keypad with alien symbols appeared to one side, and David spent a moment tapping away, then gesturing at the screen with his hands.

How did he understand Avari control systems? They'd brain-washed or programmed him somehow. That Avari hiding on board must have woken him from cryo days or weeks ago while everyone else was still asleep. Somehow Asher and Ferris had missed it, and they'd paid the ultimate price for their inattention.

David holstered his sidearm to free up his other hand.

Seeing what might be her only chance, Lori began creeping out of her restraints.

Two of David's cranial stalks turned to her, and she froze. A vicious growl erupted from him, and he whirled to face her. "Do not get up!"

Then he turned back to the screen.

"He's like me," Keera said in a small voice.

"No, honey," Lori replied. "He's not."

"Then how come I can hear him in my head?"

Lori gave her daughter a hard look. "What do you mean you can *hear* him in your head?"

"I can hear him, and if I close my eyes, I can see what he's doing."

Lori looked back to David. Were they somehow sharing a telepathic connection? By what means? Surely that wasn't possible. And yet, it would explain how Keera had predicted Ferris's and Asher's deaths the same night that they'd died. She'd imagined herself killing them, but it had actually been David's thoughts running through her head.

Lori watched what he was doing with fresh interest. Was there any remnant of Dr. Grouse left? Or was the man and colleague she'd known completely gone now?

A pair of familiar, bullet-shaped black fighters with sharply curving wings appeared on the screen. Bright red lasers were flashing from their wingtips.

Scimitar fighters. Those were the lasers she'd seen punching holes in the ceiling. Lori wasn't sure whether to be relieved or worried. She and Keera were trapped in here. If those fighters succeeded in stopping the Avari from escaping, what would that mean for them?

David tapped another sequence of symbols beside his screen, and then a group of silver projectiles leaped out toward the approaching Scimitars, riding on bright blue tongues of fire.

Missiles.

Lori's eyes flew wide as the incoming fighters broke off their attack and scattered in opposite directions. "David, what are you doing?!"

Again, he gave no reply.

Lori had been worrying about the wrong side of this engagement. The Avari obviously had some type of shielding, but Union fighters were no better than eggshells with engines strapped to them. Whoever was piloting those fighters, they needed to shoot those missiles down, and fast.

# CHAPTER 41

Clayton saw the enemy ship de-cloak, and almost instantly the sprays of condensing air escaping it vanished. In the same instant, their lasers stopped eliciting visible effects from the target.

"Shields are up," Clayton said. "Hit it with everything you've got. Target the engines."

"Torpedoes, too? We don't want to blow it up, Cap."

"Everything but torps."

"Copy. Rail guns arming."

Clayton activated the pair of rail guns in the nose of his Scimitar, all the while firing a steady stream of lasers at the aft end of the target.

Range to target was down to just 0.9 klicks. The target was artificially magnified by his Scimitar's combat computer, so he saw when it detached from the *Forerunner* and blasted away in an evasive spiral. He also saw the exact moment in which it fired off six bright silver projectiles riding blazing blue thruster tails. The missile lock alarm squawked three times in quick succession.

"Ordnance incoming!" Delta said.

"Break, break! Activate AMS!" Clayton cried as he activated his own anti-missile system. Needle-thin lasers began snapping out in rapid-fire bursts, tracking the incoming missiles. At the same time Clayton slammed the stick left to roll his fighter, then hit the pedals for the lateral thrusters in alternating patterns to execute a barrel roll. The enemy missiles tracked him easily through that maneuver, and the AMS wasn't shooting them down.

Gritting his teeth against the G-forces already pinning him to his seat, he mentally pushed the throttle up to the max and jerked the stick up at the last minute. The missiles were moving too fast to correct and screamed past him to all sides.

"AMS isn't working!" Delta said. "Those missiles must be shielded."

Clayton backed off the throttle and glanced at his sensor grid to see Delta's fighter narrowly escape the three red blips chasing it. "Flip around and hit it with the main guns," he said.

Clayton took his own advice and disengaged the main thrusters, flipping back the other way while still riding his own momentum. Now facing the missiles, he targeted the first one and then let loose with lasers and rail guns.

It took three fire-linked salvos to take the first missile out, and then he was out of time. Pushing the throttle all the way up again, he banked hard at the last possible moment and managed to lose them. Disengaging thrusters again, he flipped back and tracked the missiles for a second time. This time they were looping back faster. Their tracking systems were learning, backing off the throttle to make faster turns.

Clayton only managed to snap off one shot before it was time to evade again.

"They're adapting!" Clayton said.

Delta let out a noisy breath, blasting static through Clayton's speakers. "I just took one down. Two to go."

Clayton jacked the throttle up again, trying to buy some range, but the two blips chasing him looped around and accelerated even faster.

The missile lock alarm screamed in his ears, beeping faster and faster as the enemy ordnance drew near. He waited until the last possible second and then sent his fighter into a diving spiral.

The missiles sailed by just a few feet from his cockpit canopy. He disengaged the primary thrusters again and flipped the nose up for a parting shot. The wing-mounted lasers had an extra thirty degrees of movement, so the targeting reticle tracked up faster than the nose of the fighter. It blazed green and sang with a solid lock, and then he snapped off two fire-linked shots. Another missile exploded in a fiery burst of light.

"Got another one!" Delta crowed at the same time.

They were each down to one missile. The one

tracking Clayton's fighter came screaming back around and he executed another emergency maneuver before disengaging thrusters and taking it out.

"Three for three," Clayton said. He checked the grid and saw the final red blip wink off the screen as Delta took it out.

"Cap, you seeing what I'm seeing?"

He did. The grid was blank. Besides the two green wedges of their fighters and the giant green spear that was the *Forerunner,* there was nothing but empty blue grid squares on sensors.

"They cloaked again," Clayton said.

"Yeah," Delta replied. "Now what?"

His fighter appeared, cruising alongside Clayton's own on a bright blue tail of thrusters. Silence fell as they both considered the question.

The steady hum of air cycling through Clayton's helmet and thrusters roaring behind him filled the blank canvas in his mind. He hated to admit it, but it was over. The Avari had used that momentary distraction to perform another disappearing act, and now, short of firing lasers around randomly in the slim hope of hitting some invisible target, they were shit out of luck.

"Let's pack it in, Lieutenant," Clayton said.

"We can't just let them go."

"No choice. RTB." Clayton banked back around, heading for the distant speck that was the *Forerunner*. It had been cruising on without them at a steady 1G of acceleration this whole time.

Delta's fighter swept back into line with his, close enough that he could have seen the former Marine's face if his cockpit canopy were transparent instead of mirror-plated.

Clayton watched the fighter, admiring its smooth, sloping lines. The fight now over, Delta retracted his fighter's wings and hard points.

And then his Scimitar became limned in a fiery green light. Glowing fissures appeared, and the whole thing cracked apart in a molten wave of debris. Delta's body went tumbling free.

Anger and shock surged, leaving Clayton frozen. "Delta!" he screamed over the comms.

No reply.

Clayton sent his fighter into an evasive maneuver just before a second laser stabbed through the space he'd been flying through. He tracked that laser back to the empty space it had emerged from and brought his own guns to bear. Twin lasers flashed out repeatedly, and the rail guns in his Scimitar's nose thumped hard with glinting metal projectiles. Each one packed enough kinetic force to detonate like a missile on impact. But before the first projectile could arrive, the enemy ship re-appeared and his shots elicited bright flashes of light from its shields.

Clayton kept up a steady rain of fire, all the while juking in random directions.

Green lasers lashed the space around him, missing repeatedly. But then one scored a hit and his starboard wing evaporated.

A screaming roar filled Clayton's ears, and it took him a second to realize that it was him. He'd be damned if this alien bastard would kill him before he could avenge Delta's death.

The enemy ship took two solid hits to the engines, both of them rail gun projectiles. They exploded with brief flashes of light, and one of three engines at the back of the Avari ship went dark.

His next pair of lasers hit home as well, drawing jets of white mist as more air escaped from inside the ship.

He'd finally taken down the shields.

The Avari vessel went evasive in earnest, but Clayton didn't let up. He kept firing steadily, making sure they couldn't cloak again.

The comms crackled to life, and Clayton expected that it might be the *Forerunner*, or maybe the remainder of its Scimitar squadron come to offer support.

But it wasn't. The voice was flat and emotionless, and it was *his*.

"Cease fire immediately or the woman dies."

Shock briefly beat out all of the other emotions crowding Clayton's head. *They know our language. And my voice.* He squeezed off a final salvo before releasing the trigger.

Silence fell, and the enemy ship sailed on. Clayton kept dodging and weaving, chasing it and making himself as hard to hit as possible, but it wasn't firing on him either.

He tried sending a reply to that message on the same channel. The fact that the Avari could speak English and transmit messages was both shocking and hopeful. Now they could finally negotiate.

Clayton picked his words carefully, setting an equally hostile tone. He doubted the Avari would respond well to weakness. "Send the woman and the girl out in pressure suits or an escape pod and I'll let you go."

"There is only one of you, and we have the advantage."

*We?* Clayton wondered. He shook his head. "If you have the advantage, then why did you threaten to kill someone if I didn't stop firing on you? It won't be long before my crew sees you and trains much bigger guns than mine on your ship." Clayton spared eyes for a glance at the grid and saw green specks darting out the back of the *Forerunner*. More Scimitars. "And I have more fighters incoming."

"We'll vanish, and they'll never find us. You'll be dead long before they arrive."

"Or maybe you'll miss and I won't. I'll burn another dozen holes in your hull and this time maybe I'll hit something vital—like your reactor core, or your head."

A hissing roar of static came back over the comms. It sounded like the Avari was laughing.

"I only spared you because she begged me to.

Don't make me change my mind."

"She who?"

Alerts began chiming rapidly from sensors, and tens of red blips began peppering the grid. Sleek teardrop-shaped black vessels appeared all around the bulkier ship that he was chasing. Multiple squadrons of enemy fighters, all facing him and approaching fast.

"You have lost. Go back to your ship."

A larger vessel materialized behind those fighters, automatically magnified with everything else. It was massive. Clayton stopped maneuvering. It wasn't his piloting skill or deft maneuvers that had kept him alive. There had to be hundreds of lasers trained on his fighter right now. The Avari were deliberately sparing him.

"This isn't over," Clayton said through gritted teeth. "We'll find you."

Silence answered him.

And then static came crackling in, followed by: "Falcon Leader to Captain Cross! Please *respond.* I repeat, Falcon Leader to Captain Cross. Waggle your wings if you can hear us." The message was from one of the Scimitars racing in from the Forerunner's location.

"I'm here," Clayton said in a croaking voice. He watched the Avari ships all fade invisibly into the black of space and simultaneously drop off the grid. Only green, friendly blips remained.

A relieved sigh sent a burst of static across the channel. "What the hell, Captain! We've been hailing you for the past ten minutes!"

That broke through Clayton's shock. He hadn't received any messages over the comms. Until now, he hadn't even thought to wonder about it. The Avari must have been jamming him.

Another voice chimed in: "Hey, where did they all go?" The comms panel identified the speaker as *Falcon Two, Lt. Ike*

Clayton just shook his head. "Your guess is as good as mine, Lieutenant."

"Form up with us, Captain. Let's get you back in one piece."

"Copy that," Clayton replied, rolling his fighter and hauling back on the stick to bring the *Forerunner* into line.

That flat, inflectionless version of his voice echoed back through his thoughts as he formed up with Falcon Squadron.

*I only spared you because she begged me to.*

*She* who? he wondered again. *Keera? And if so, what is she to them that they would listen?*

Then his thoughts took a darker turn, and the dazzling emerald fire that had consumed Delta's fighter blazed bright in his mind's eye. He saw the former Marine's tumbling body... followed by Devon's dead, staring eyes, Commander Taylor's matching gaze... Lieutenants Ferris's and Asher's bloody remains.

Clayton's eyes burned and blurred with tears. What did the Avari want? Keera? Lori? Access to

Clayton's thoughts and memories?

Maybe all of the above. But whatever it was that they'd been after, they had it now.

# CHAPTER 42

Clayton lined up his fighter with the flaring, cone-shaped opening of Launch Tube 01. All twelve launch tubes sat nestled between the massive, fiery blue thrusters at the back of the *Forerunner.*

Range to the ship reached fifteen klicks, and he activated the auto-landing sequence. The autopilot did the rest from there, making micro-corrections, firing brief blasts from the maneuvering thrusters as he flew in.

Magnetic fields in the opening of the launch tube would help to line him up, guiding his fighter to the rails.

At just one klick out, a warning popped up on his nav panel. His damaged starboard wing hadn't retracted fully. The *Forerunner* had detected a small anomaly in the shape of his fighter.

Range was scrolling down fast. Just six hundred meters now.

Rather than abort the landing, Clayton summoned a nav screen to check the shape of the launch tube against the shape of his fighter. The two outlines lined up perfectly but for an offending scrap of metal that was flashing red. Half a foot wide by one foot long, a bent and curling piece of the wing. The system was designed to accept small variations in shape due to combat damage, so he overrode the warning. The offending bit would get sheared off by the launch rails.

The launch tube grew steadily larger. The other Scimitars in Falcon Squadron flew all around him in a vague star formation, the same as the pattern of the twelve launch tubes in the back of the *Forerunner*.

Then the tube swallowed his fighter. His Scimitar hit the rails, and a metallic shriek came as the offending scrap of wing got clipped off. The fighter shuddered briefly, then steadied and glided down the rails to a sudden, jerking stop at the end of the launch tube. Artificial gravity took hold, pinning him to the back of his seat.

Doors behind his fighter shut with a *thud* and air hissed in around it as the receiving end of the tube pressurized. Finally, the part of the tube under his fighter folded down, taking the Scimitar with it. He landed on the maintenance conveyor with a *thunk*, and sat there, numb and staring sightlessly out of the cockpit as the rest of Falcon Squadron folded out of their launch tubes. Pilots began climbing from their fighters, pulling helmets off to reveal short, sweat-matted hair.

Clayton's breath rasped steadily through his

helmet, loud and shallow in his ears.

He half expected to see Delta climb out of one of those fighters and flash a craggy grin.

*Denial.* That was one of the stages of grief. He knew it well. He absently brought his wrist up to his faceplate, thinking to see the comforting image of his wife's smiling face on his smart watch, but both his wrist and the watch were hidden by the sleeve of his flight suit.

Clayton shook his head to clear out the ghosts. He still had more than a thousand crew and colonists on board, all of them alive and well, and he needed to keep it together if they were going to stay that way.

He disconnected his oxygen hoses, opened his cockpit, and climbed out. Standing beside his fighter, he removed his helmet and tucked it under one arm. The Commander of Falcon Squadron caught his eye and nodded to him before walking over.

The holographic name tape glowed bright on Clayton's ARCs: *LCDR Craig Pullman*

"Captain," Pullman said, stopping in front of him and coming to attention.

Clayton acknowledged him with a nod, and Pullman stood at ease. He had a quarter-inch of red-blond hair, bright green eyes, and a baby-face that made him look a decade younger than his forty years.

"Delta was a good man," Pullman said, one corner of his mouth jerking down.

"Yes, he was," Clayton replied, his voice a ragged whisper. He cleared his throat. "Excuse me. I'm needed on the bridge." He turned and strode for the exit of the hangar with a lump in his throat and eyes burning once more. Pullman's reply came dimly back, drowned out by the thunder of blood roaring in Clayton's ears.

Then came a buzz and crackle of static, followed by Doctor Stevens' voice. "Captain, there's been a development. The Avari have de-cloaked again. We're reading one capital-class vessel."

Clayton blinked and sucked in a deep breath. Grief retreated to the background as a fresh spurt of adrenaline went sparking through his veins. He broke into a sprint, running the rest of the way to the elevators. "Ready weapons, Doc," he said.

"Aye, sir."

Flicking a glance back the way he'd come, Clayton bellowed, "Get back to your cockpits!"

Pullman hesitated for just a second before turning and repeating the order to his pilots. "You heard the captain! Scramble!"

# CHAPTER 43

"Captain on deck!"

Everyone came to attention, rotating their chairs to face him.

Doctor Stevens rose from the captain's chair and met Clayton halfway. His silver hair glowed blue in the dim lighting of the bridge. With so many other officers dead, Stevens was the most senior officer on board other than Clayton himself. "Sir, they're not responding to our hails."

That comment sounded out of place when talking about an alien starship, but the Avari had clearly proven that they'd learned enough about human comms and languages to communicate whenever they felt like it.

Clayton's gaze strayed past Stevens to the viewscreens that ran the circumference of the bridge. The enemy ship lay dead ahead, magnified to fill nearly half of the screens. Their hull was dark and non-reflecting, a dark stain on the stars with no signs of life, not even a single viewport with lights radiating out.

"Any signs of activity? Fighters launching?" Clayton asked.

"None that we can see," Stevens replied.

Clayton walked past him to the captain's chair, sat down, and buckled his restraints. "Are they giving chase?"

"Negative. They're not even facing us, sir," Stevens replied as he took his seat at the XO's station beside him.

"Try hailing them again. Open a line for me to speak."

"Aye, sir." Stevens spent a moment interacting with screens on his ARCs, his green eyes glowing blue as he interfaced with the comms.

Stevens nodded to him. "Ready to transmit, Captain."

Clayton sucked in a deep breath, but before he could say anything, the tear-drop shaped black starship on the viewscreens vanished with a bright flash of light.

"What was that!" Clayton demanded.

"I don't..." Stevens trailed off, screens flashing rapidly over his eyes.

The sensor operator replied before he could, "A sharp spike in radiation coincided with their disappearance."

"Did they cloak again?" someone else asked.

Clayton slowly shook his head. "We didn't see any radiation spikes or flashes of light to accompany them cloaking before. This was something else."

"Aye," Stevens said, turning to look at Clayton. His ARCs cleared, revealing his eyes once more. "Sensors detected gravitational waves to accompany that spike. They're still washing over us."

"Ripples in space-time," Clayton mused.

"Aye, sir."

Natural gravity waves are created by massive stellar bodies moving very quickly. They could also theoretically be created by the sudden emergence of a wormhole, or the use of some theoretical faster-than-light drive tech, such as Alcubierre warp drives. Either way, the conclusion was the same.

"I think what we just witnessed was the Avari going to FTL," Clayton said.

Silence answered him. If he was right, the implications were terrifying. The Avari were far more advanced than any of them had realized, and if they had any interest in Earth, they could be there in a fraction of the time it would take for *Forerunner One* to get home.

"What now, sir?" Stevens asked quietly.

The doors to the bridge rumbled open before Clayton could say anything, and a new voice interrupted them:

"Why was I not told that it was safe to leave my quarters?"

Clayton rotated his chair to see Ambassador Morgan striding in.

"It wasn't an intentional oversight."

Morgan stopped a few paces away with arms crossed over his chest to glare down on Clayton.

"Do you need something, Ambassador?"

"*Yes*, an update! Where is Dr. Reed? She's not in her quarters."

Clayton hesitated. The Ambassador really did have a lot of catching up to do. He dragged in a weary breath and then explained everything that had happened in as few words as he could manage.

Morgan's face had turned ashen by the time he was done. Maybe he had a heart after all.

"They took them both?"

Clayton nodded.

"Why?"

"Keera was obviously some kind of genetic experiment. I'm guessing it was a success, because they went to great lengths to recover her. For all we know, they were on board before we even arrived at Trappist-1. They might have even been the ones to impregnate Lori."

"But Stevens said I was the father!" Morgan roared.

"Maybe not the *only* father. There was obviously an alien gene donor as well."

"How did they get on board without us noticing?" Morgan asked. His tone was accusatory, as if they should have been able to see a cloaked shuttle docking with the *Forerunner*.

"Somehow, we didn't," Clayton said flatly. "Right now, figuring out *how* all of this happened is much less important than *why*. Why create an Avari-human hybrid, why extract Earth's location from Dr. Grouse's mind, why infect him with a virus, and why learn our language and comms protocols?"

Morgan's jaw dropped as those pieces clicked into place, but Stevens was the first to state the obvious: "They're going to invade Earth."

Clayton gave a stiff nod. "Yes."

# CHAPTER 44

Morgan visibly worked some moisture into his mouth. "We're a colony ship. It's our responsibility to re-populate the species. We should find another planet to colonize."

Clayton gave him a hard look. "Has running with your tail between your legs always been your go-to response?"

"Excuse me?"

"We're going to Earth, Ambassador. To warn them if we're not too late, and to reinforce their position if we are."

"You're insane. I'm in command of this mission, Captain, and I'm ordering you to—"

"Corporal!" Clayton called to the Marine Corporal standing guard beside the doors. "Escort Mr. Morgan from the bridge."

"Yes, sir!"

Morgan's face turned bright red, and he glowered darkly at Clayton as the corporal approached. "Ambassador," the Marine said. "This way please."

"I'll show myself out," Morgan snapped, and then he turned and strode away.

Clayton noticed that the rest of the bridge

crew had rotated their chairs to face them. "Eyes on your stations," he said, and they spun their chairs back around.

Stevens caught his eye and whispered, "With everything we know and suspect, going to Earth will be dangerous, sir."

"We'll head for Proxima Centauri and send a message from there, just as we were planning. Once we arrive, we'll decide whether or not to push on for Earth. If we do go, the mission will be volunteer only. Anyone who wants to stay at Proxima b and keep their heads down is welcome to do so. Fair enough?"

"Aye, sir," Stevens said. "When do we go back into cryo?" He didn't look or sound eager.

"In a few days," Clayton replied. "After the memorial for our dead, and after we've swept the ship for more Avari."

"What if they're here, but we don't find them?"

"We'll be thorough," Clayton replied.

"They're invisible," Stevens countered with one eyebrow arching up.

"If they'd wanted to kill us all, they could have easily done so by now."

"That's true... so why didn't they?"

"I don't know," Clayton admitted. "But I'm hoping it's a sign that they're not entirely hostile."

"Aye." Stevens blew out a breath. He obviously hadn't thought of that.

"Maybe studying the one we killed will give us more insight. I assume you handled the body correctly?"

"I had one of my corpsmen put it in a cryo pod in sickbay. We haven't had time for a proper analysis yet, but it'll keep."

Clayton turned his chair back to the fore and stared into the glittering wash of stars on the viewscreens. Silence fell on the bridge, and Clayton's thoughts grew loud. One thought jumped to the fore, a question: *If the Avari don't want to kill us, then what* do *they want? Slaves? More subjects for their experiments?*

This time no answers came to him. There was only one way to find out. They'd have to go back to Earth and see for themselves.

# CHAPTER 45

*Sixty-Eight Years Later...*

—2237 AD—

"Hailing Olympia Station," Lieutenant Commander Stevens announced.

Clayton nodded, steepling his hands beneath his chin as he leaned forward in the captain's chair.

Ambassador Morgan stood hovering beside them, quietly watching and listening.

They'd all awoken from cryo for the last time barely half an hour ago—right after crossing the heliopause to officially enter the Proxima Centauri System.

Proxima b was magnified on the forward screens, a dark circle with a crescent of light dawning at the far right edge. Proxima b was otherwise known as Olympia, a reference to Zeus and Greek mythology that the planet had earned thanks to its violent thunderstorms. Tidally locked to its sun, Proxima b's weather was so disastrous that landings and launches could only be safely conducted from one point on the surface: dead center of the perpetual night. There weren't even any lights visible from the colony on the surface, but that wasn't necessarily strange. Even after almost a hundred and eighty years of technological advances, it likely still made more sense to build underground. Hurricane-force winds were constantly blasting in from the scalding dessert on Olympia's day side.

A solitary silver speck gleamed bright above the day-night terminator, catching crimson rays from Proxima Centauri. Olympia Station was still there. That had to be a good sign.

"Message sent," Stevens announced.

"I assume you included the mission report that I prepared," Clayton said.

"Of course, sir."

"How long before we can expect a reply?" Ambassador Morgan asked.

"At fifty-six point two AU..." Screens flickered brightly over Stevens' eyes as he calculated on his ARCs. "It'll be almost eight hours before our signal arrives, so the soonest their reply could reach us is fifteen and a half hours."

Morgan grunted unhappily at that.

"If we're right about Earth, they might already know about the Avari," Stevens pointed out.

"Time will tell," Clayton said. He unbuckled his safety harness and stood on creaking knees, stretching out his back and neck.

And then a series of bright flashes strobed through the viewscreens, flash-blinding him.

Morgan cursed viciously.

"Report!" Clayton cried.

"Multiple contacts!" the sensor operator said.

"Incoming comms!" Stevens added. "Both audio and visual feeds!"

Clayton stood swaying beside his chair and blinking the spots from his eyes to see a massive dark gray starship directly in front of them. It was long and boxy, ridged and bristling with glittering lights and weapons platforms.

"Put them on," Clayton ordered.

The bald head and shoulders of someone in a fish scale patterned uniform appeared front and center of the main viewscreen.

Chalk-white features, black veins whorling underneath, bright red eyes, sharp facial bones, and four stalky appendages rising from its skull identified it clearly enough. But its arms didn't extend from its chest, and they weren't thin and bony like an Avari's. There was no sign of translucent wings either.

"Hello, Captain," the creature said, its voice deep and husky, but somehow familiar. "I've been waiting a long time for your arrival."

He placed the voice a second later and his jaw dropped. "Keera?"

She smiled, revealing sharply pointed white teeth. "Admiral Keera Reed. Welcome to the Kyron Federation."

Confusion swirled in Clayton's head. He grabbed his chair for support and slowly shook his head. "I don't understand. What Federation?"

"My people, the *Kyra*—the ones you call the Avari—annexed Earth. Humanity has joined a larger galactic community, Captain." He caught a glimpse of another chalky humanoid walking by behind Keera. It was too tall and human-looking to be an Avari. Another hybrid.

"How are you still so young?" Clayton asked. "It's been... almost seventy years for us."

"I'll explain everything once we come aboard. Power down your engines and stand down all weapons."

"You can't let them aboard this ship," Ambassador Morgan whispered.

Keera's head turned fractionally, and her smile faded. "Hello, Father."

"Turn the ship around," Morgan insisted.

Clayton looked to Lieutenant Commander Stevens. He was gaping at the viewscreen, his eyes wide and staring. "Power down engines, Stevens."

"Aye, sir..."

"Thank you, Captain," Keera said, inclining her head to him. "If it makes you feel better, I only asked as a courtesy. You had no other option."

"Does that sound friendly to you?" Morgan gritted out.

"Shut up, Ambassador," Clayton snapped.

"Where should we expect you, Admiral?"

An image of the *Forerunner* replaced Keera's head and shoulders. The amidships airlock was flashing in red. Her features returned a few seconds later. She was smiling again. "I have a few surprises waiting for you, Captain."

"Good ones I hope."

"The very best. See you soon."

The transmission vanished, and Keera's ship returned, front and center. Smaller wedge-shaped vessels began streaking out from it.

"What do we do, sir?" Stevens whispered.

"We go meet them at the airlock," Clayton replied.

"I'll inform the Marines."

"No. We're going to greet them unarmed."

"Are you *insane?*" Ambassador Morgan cried. "They'll kill us!"

Clayton turned to regard him. "They wouldn't need to board us for that, Ambassador. So that's obviously not their goal."

Morgan's cheeks bulged with another objection, but he swallowed it.

Clayton knew what was really behind his concerns: he'd never been very nice to his half alien daughter, and now she was all grown up, maybe with a big chip on her shoulder.

"*Admiral* Keera Reed..." Stevens muttered.

"Maybe she'll be the bigger person," Clayton said.

Morgan's face looked ashen, his jaw slack. The

ambassador's eyes darted briefly to him, then back to the alien starship on the viewscreens.

"There must be a reason why she came here to greet us personally," Clayton said.

"Revenge," Morgan rasped.

"I doubt it's anything as petty as that," Clayton replied. He nodded to the bridge doors. "Let's go."

"I'm not going."

"You're the ambassador."

"The Union is gone."

Clayton's eyes hardened. "She's your daughter."

Morgan just shook his head.

"Look at it this way. If you're right, better to fix things now with a happy reunion. She won't be any happier with you if you snub her."

Morgan made an aggravated sound in the back of his throat. "This is a mistake, Captain."

"Maybe, but as Keera pointed out, we don't have much of a choice. Stevens?" Clayton prompted.

"Sir?"

"You have the conn."

"I'm coming with you, sir," Stevens said, already unbuckling from his station.

Clayton frowned, watching the man as he stood up. "Someone needs to man the bridge."

"Ensign Reynolds can handle it."

Clayton's gaze strayed to the helm where Reynolds sat in Delta's old chair, a painful reminder that he was dead and gone. *An ensign in command of the bridge?* He was about to object further, but what difference did it make who had the conn? They couldn't run, they couldn't fight, and they'd already surrendered.

"Very well, Lieutenant Commander. Fall in. Reynolds—you have the conn."

"Aye-aye, sir."

# CHAPTER 46

Clayton stood at the amidships airlock with Doctor Stevens, Ambassador Morgan, and an entire squad of thirteen unarmed Marines in full body armor—a show of force without any force. That was Morgan's idea.

A *clunk* sounded from the airlock, followed by a loud hissing sound as the decon sprays started up. Hopefully that didn't piss off the Avari—*Kyra,* Clayton corrected himself.

The inner doors swished open, and a group of humanoids wearing familiar fish-scale armor and glossy black helmets appeared. The one standing in the center of the group removed its helmet, and Keera's face appeared. Four flexible stalks unfolded from the back of her head, their cone-shaped orifices turning to face him.

She and her entourage marched out of the airlock, coming to a stop just a few feet away. Clayton noticed that all of them were armed with sleek black rifles. Except for Keera. She wore a familiar long-barreled sidearm on her hip.

These soldiers all stood just as tall as the average human—yet more confirmation that they weren't Avari. They were probably all hybrids like Keera, which meant that they would be able to co-exist in the same environments as humans.

Assuming that there were any humans left.

Clayton put on a grim smile. "Welcome aboard, Admiral Reed."

"Thank you, Captain." Keera's gaze swept to her father, then back, and she matched Clayton's smile with a predatory version of her own.

A chill coursed down Clayton's spine as he stared into her bright red eyes. "You mentioned a Federation," he prompted.

"The Kyron Federation," Keera said.

"And humans are now members of it?"

"Yes and no. Perhaps we should go somewhere that we can speak more comfortably."

"Why?" Morgan asked in a shaky voice. "If you're just going to kill us, you may as well do it here."

She looked to him with narrowed eyes. "You've always thought the worst of me, Father. But perhaps that says more about you than it does about me, or my kind." Her gaze swept back to Clayton. "The Chimeras—others like me —" She spread her hands to indicate the soldiers surrounding her. "—are all citizens. We're free to come and go as we please. Humans and other naturally evolved species like them are not. It is the Kyra's way of unifying their empire, of giving us all a common thread to tie us together."

"So there are others," Clayton said. "Do you all look the same?"

"Of course not. But we all share common features."

Clayton's eyes skipped over the helmeted soldiers present. "None of them look different."

"They're not. They are Human Chimeras, like me. Each sub-species is different."

"Are there any humans left on Earth? Or just Chimeras?"

"Not everyone is compatible with Kyra DNA," Keera explained. "Some don't qualify for ascendance. Others die during the transformation, and some fall short to become *Dregs*."

"Ascendance," Clayton said. "You make it sound as though you're superior to us."

"We are. Physically, at least. All Chimeras are equally at home in at least two different environments—that of their native species, and that of the Kyra themselves. This means that we can serve the Kyra on their worlds and starships just as easily as we can on our own."

Clayton's Marines shuffled their feet, their armor clattering. Taking umbrage no doubt. Tell a squad of Space Marines that they're physically inferior and watch them bristle with indignation. A smile tugged at the corners of Clayton's mouth, but the gravity of the situation quickly squelched it.

"So we're not under arrest or scheduled for execution."

"No. My mother told me about you, Captain. She said that you were the one who always insisted that I be treated fairly, without any prejudice or contempt." Her eyes flicked to her father, then back. "I would like to return that favor to you now. You and your crew will not be held accountable for the two Kyra that you killed."

A sudden burst of anger flashed through Clayton's system, making it hard to think straight. *What about the officers that* they *killed? Delta, Taylor, Devon, Davies, Asher, Ferris...* He bit his tongue and smiled thinly at Keera. "That's very generous of the Kyra."

"In addition to this pardon, I have a surprise for you—" Her eyes slid to Morgan again. "And for you, Father."

Morgan paled, and Keera nodded to one of the soldiers standing in the back of her entourage. "You can take off your helmets now."

Two soldiers pressed through to the front of the group, and Clayton noticed that both of them were unarmed. They reached up to remove their helmets, and a pair of familiar faces appeared—

Lori's.

And *Samara's.*

Clayton's heart nearly stopped. He stood there for the longest second of his life, rooted to the spot, unable to believe his eyes.

"Hello, Clay," she said in a trembling whisper of a voice. Her vibrant blue eyes darted around, as if all of this was somehow just as alien to her as it was to him.

"The Kyra are good to their subjects, Captain," Keera said. "And their technology is beyond anything you can possibly imagine."

"Lori?" Morgan asked in a shaking voice.

She whispered a cutting remark under her breath, but Clayton didn't hear it over the roaring drumbeat of his own pulse. He took a quick step forward, then stopped abruptly, worried that the Chimeran soldiers might shoot him if he ran to greet Samara.

Keera nodded. "It's okay, Captain." Then to her soldiers, she said, "Stand down."

So Clayton ran, crashing into Samara, sweeping her up in his arms, and burying his face in her hair. It even smelled like her.

"How is this possible?" he sobbed. "You were dead!"

"It's okay," Samara whispered. "I'm here now."

Clayton withdrew and kissed her repeatedly. She laughed against his lips.

Keera answered his question as he withdrew, "There were many records of the deceased in your archives by the time we arrived. Samara was one of many. My mother suggested that we bring her back as our way of saying thank you."

Clayton looked his wife in the eyes—the same vibrant blue eyes that he remembered. Her cheeks were stained with tears, the same as his. She gave a shaky smile, and glanced about furtively once more.

"Is everything okay?" Clayton asked.

She nodded quickly. "I'm just overwhelmed, that's all... I only woke up yesterday, and to me it's still the 21st century."

"That must be a shock..." He looked to Keera, and she nodded.

"She's adapting very well."

"Are there others who were resurrected?"

"No. The Kyra don't believe in resurrecting the dead from their memories. Your wife is the only exception that I know of. It was not easy to get their approval."

"Thank you," Clayton said. His eyes went to Lori. "Both of you."

She nodded back.

And then it hit him. Lori didn't look a day older than when she'd left. "How *old* are you? When did the Kyra arrive?"

Lori laughed, then quickly sobered. "Almost eighty years ago. Just a month after they took Keera and me from the *Forerunner*. So to answer your question—a lot older than I like to admit."

"But you look the same..." Doctor Stevens murmured.

"Biological organisms need not age," Keera explained. "Membership in the Kyron Federation has many benefits."

"Was it voluntary?" Morgan asked.

"Was *what* voluntary?" Keera asked.

"Us joining it," Morgan said.

"Did dogs or horses voluntarily submit to domestication by their human masters?"

That reply gave Clayton pause. "So it's like that."

"Your people still have significant autonomy, and the Kyra care for their subjects far better than humans ever did for their pets—I can assure you of that."

"Good," was all Clayton could think to say. "Now what?"

"Now, we take you back to Earth. I'd let you take your ship, but we can get you there much faster."

"We'll need some time to wake the colonists and ready the crew."

"I'll give you a quarter of a cycle."

"A cycle?"

"Five hours. I assume that will be enough time?"

Clayton nodded. "It will. Thank you."

"Good." Keera nodded to him and smiled.

Clayton returned that smile. He'd been right about her. His eyes drifted to Lori.

"It's good to see you again, Captain," she said.

"Likewise," he replied.

And then Keera and the Chimeras turned and marched back into the airlock.

"We'll be waiting," Keera said, catching his eye as the airlock doors slid shut.

Ambassador Morgan blew out a breath, looking thoroughly shaken. "She didn't kill me."

"It looks like the Avari—the Kyra, I mean—might not be all bad," Clayton said.

But no one seconded his opinion.

# CHAPTER 47

**Eight hours Later...**

The Kyra lander shivered and shook violently as it sliced down through Earth's atmosphere. Samara sat beside Clayton, squeezing his hand. Several armed Chimeras were seated around them. Sweeping viewports framed the nose and sides of the cabin, making it feel bright and airy inside.

Clayton's row of seats was twelve wide, and there were at least a hundred rows just like it spread across three separate decks. Over a thousand people. All of the crew and colonists from the *Forerunner* crammed into one giant transport, and it had been one of several inside the destroyer that served as Keera's flagship.

A fluffy carpet of clouds swept up fast beneath them. The turbulence and G-forces of re-entry were somehow buffered by the ship's technology. The Kyra were so advanced that they were like gods. Everywhere Clayton looked there was something new to astound him—not the least of which, FTL drives. They'd traveled the four light years from Proxima to Earth in just under two hours. Two light years per hour. Clayton kept wanting to ask questions, but he hadn't seen either Lori or Keera again since being marched off to temporary quarters aboard her ship. And Samara didn't seem to know any more than he did.

He glanced over at her, noting the tension in her face and her rigid posture.

"Hey."

She looked at him with wide eyes.

"It's going to be okay."

She gave a shallow nod before looking away.

The transport ducked into the clouds. Gauzy curtains of moisture swept by to all sides. Dr. Stevens caught Clayton looking his way. He was sitting on the aisle seat of the same row. Stevens nodded, and Clayton smiled tightly back.

And then the clouds parted, and a futuristic city appeared beneath them. Tall, glittering towers caught the light of the sun, blinding him and everyone else. Then the lander sank below the glaring eye of the sun, and more details snapped into focus.

A collective gasp sounded from the passengers. A vast field of charred and crumbling ruins stretched out to the horizon in all directions. The ruins were overgrown and shot through with rivers of green, but a tiny freckle of civilization shone like a pearl from the center of that devastation: tall skyscrapers guarded by thick gray walls.

"What the hell happened here? Where is this?" Clayton asked.

No one ventured an answer. His eyes fell on the nearest Chimera, sitting two rows up from him. "Hey! You want to explain this? I thought the Kyra treat their subjects well."

A low hiss sounded as the Chimera turned its head. Red eyes found him and quickly narrowed. "Your people did not surrender easily." And with that, its head turned back around.

Samara had Clayton's hand in a death grip now.

He studied her. "You haven't seen this?"

"No," she breathed. "They must have killed millions!"

"Billions," a husky Chimera voice replied. This from a second Chimera sitting beside the first. It twisted around, revealing slightly more feminine features, like Keera's. Cranial stalks swiveled to face them. "Your people are still re-covering nearly a century later. The smart ones choose to ascend so that they don't have to stay in this dumpster. That's why I did it."

"You used to be human?"

The chimera nodded.

"Where are we? What is this city called?" Clayton asked again, gesturing to the viewports.

"Houston."

Shock coursed through him. The Houston he remembered had been a sprawling metropolis with over three million people living in it.

"Why haven't we rebuilt?" Samara asked.

"The ruins are populated by *Dregs*," the Chimera replied. "It is dangerous to reclaim territory outside the walls."

"Dregs?" Clayton asked.

"People who failed to ascend. The virus doesn't always work."

Clayton wanted to ask more questions, but the Chimera turned around again. Samara's nails dug into his arm, her horror radiating through that touch. They sat silently and watched as the transport hovered down to a large, flat rooftop in the middle of the high rises. The transport touched down with a gentle *thump*, followed by the sound of seat restraints clicking free and Chimeras rising to their feet.

"Everybody up!" one of them yelled. "Let's go! Let's go!"

One by one, people rose slowly and reluctantly to their feet. Some were slower than others. Clayton and Samara joined them in standing and began shuffling down their row toward the end.

Somewhere in the cabin someone was sobbing loudly.

"On your feet, *Dakka!*"

The sobbing grew louder, and Clayton turned to see a young woman sitting several rows back being dragged out of her seat and into the aisle.

"Hey!" The man sitting beside her lunged to intervene.

A bright green laser flashed out from the soldier's rifle and dropped him to the deck with a *thud.*

The woman screamed piteously and scrambled over to him. "Peter!" She began shaking him by his shoulders, but he didn't stir. "Peter!"

"He's dead!" the Chimera who'd shot him said. "Get up!" And it dragged her up by her hair. She rose to her feet with another scream, and rounded on the alien with her fists, her eyes streaming with tears.

Clayton began pushing through the crowd to reach them.

And then a second flash of light silenced the woman, too, and her body landed beside the man who'd tried to help her.

Everyone in the cabin froze. The Chimeras looked around, red eyes hard and glaring.

"The Kyra do not suffer defiance!" the one who'd shot those two said, its eyes and rifle tracking over the humans. "Learn this lesson, and learn it well, or you will not last long in the Federation. These two died, but there are fates worse than death. Remember that."

Clayton gritted his teeth and balled his fists, but Samara pulled him back into line.

No one else gave the Chimeras any trouble on the way out. The lines snaked smoothly through the ship, down to Level One, and then down the boarding ramp to see a welcome party of at least twenty more Chimeran soldiers. They took over from the ones on board.

"It's time for processing!" the leader said, his voice booming across the massive landing platform, amplified by unseen means. "You will do exactly as I say, and we will get through this without any casualties! Nod if you understand!"

Heads bobbed.

"Good! Make a line and follow me! Single file!"

People began trailing after the Chimera, and the other soldiers fanned out, keeping wary eyes on the group. A warm breeze whipped across the rooftop, but it did nothing to melt the ice in Clayton's heart.

He looked up at the cloudy sky and saw a massive shadow cruising slowly through those clouds. The nose of it poked through a few seconds later. It was another Kyra destroyer, just like Keera's flagship. Maybe the very same.

She'd lulled him into a false sense of security, blinded him with joy by bringing Samara back.

"Clay... we have to keep moving," she whispered.

"Move, *Dakka!*"

He took a deep breath to steady himself and brought his eyes down to the Chimera who'd spoken. Demonic eyes glared back and its rifle tracked slowly up. Clayton pasted a smile on his face, and started after the long, trudging line of people busy walking across the landing platform.

"What's a *Dakka?*" Clayton asked as he walked

by the Chimera who was still aiming its rifle at him.

A flash of sharp teeth appeared, black lips curving into a smile. "It's a small two-legged creature on Kyros. It lives in the sewers."

"Sewer rat," Clayton clarified. "Not so bad, then."

The alien hybrid hissed, its rifle following him as he walked by, but it didn't shoot.

"You need to be more careful," Samara whispered sharply to him once they were out of earshot.

He nodded agreeably, but in the privacy of his head, he vowed that if there were any way to resist the Kyra, he would.

The war and the invasion might be over, but the rebellion had just begun.

# GET THE SEQUEL FOR FREE

*The story continues with...*

**Occupied Earth (Book 1)**

*Now Available!*

**Get it From Amazon**

**( https://geni.us/occupiedearth )**

**OR Get a FREE digital copy** if you post an honest review of this book ( http://smarturl.it/encounterreview ) on Amazon and send it to me here. ( http://files.jaspertscott.com/freeoccupiedearth.htm )

Thank you in advance for your feedback!

# KEEP IN TOUCH

**SUBSCRIBE to my Mailing List**
and get two FREE Books!

http://files.jaspertscott.com/mailinglist.html

**Follow me on Bookbub:**

https://www.bookbub.com/
authors/jasper-t-scott

**Follow me on Amazon:**

https://www.amazon.com/Jasper-
T-Scott/e/B00B7A2CT4

**Look me up on Facebook:**

Jasper T. Scott

**Check out my website:**

www.JasperTscott.com

**Or send me an e-mail:**

JasperTscott@gmail.com

# OTHER BOOKS BY JASPER SCOTT

*Suggested reading order*

## Ascenscion Wars

First Encounter (Book 1)
Occupied Earth (Book 2)
Fractured Earth (Book 3)
*Coming June 2020*

## Scott Standalones
*No sequels, no cliffhangers*
*Under Darkness*
Into the Unknown
In Time for Revenge

## Rogue Star

Rogue Star: Frozen Earth
Rogue Star (Book 2): New Worlds

## Broken Worlds

Broken Worlds: The Awakening (Book 1)
Broken Worlds: The Revenants (Book 2)
Broken Worlds: Civil War (Book 3)

## New Frontiers Series (Loosely-tied, Standalone

## **Prequels to Dark Space)**

Excelsior (Book 1)
Mindscape (Book 2)
Exodus (Book 3)

## **Dark Space Series**

Dark Space
Dark Space 2: The Invisible War
Dark Space 3: Origin
Dark Space 4: Revenge
Dark Space 5: Avilon
Dark Space 6: Armageddon

## **Dark Space Universe Series (Standalone Follow-up Trilogy to Dark Space)**

Dark Space Universe (Book 1)
Dark Space Universe: The Enemy Within (Book 2)
Dark Space Universe: The Last Stand (Book 3)

# ABOUT THE AUTHOR

Jasper Scott is a USA Today best-selling author of more than 20 sci-fi novels. With over a million books sold, Jasper's work has been translated into various languages and published around the world. Join the author's mailing list to get two FREE books: https://files.jaspertscott.com/mailinglist.html

Jasper writes fast-paced stories with unexpected twists and flawed characters. He was born and raised in Canada by South African parents, with a British cultural heritage on his mother's side and German on his father's, to which he has added Latin culture with his wonderful wife. He now lives in an exotic locale with his wife, their two kids, and two Chihuahuas.

Made in the USA
Las Vegas, NV
10 December 2022

61754436R00208